Book Offer

Thank you for purchasing this book!

Pick up a FREE download of my novella, Winter's Kiss, when you join my newsletter.

www.katerinasimms.com

Sapphires AND SECRETS

HARLOW SERIES BOOK ONE

KATERINA SIMMS

One

THEN

From: Emilia Bonacci
  To: Emilia Bonacci
  Subject: So excited!

Dear Emilia,

I know it's strange writing emails to myself, but the most amazing thing happened today, and I know I'll want to remember this day forever.

I met a boy…

"The house is over ninety years old and needs some fixin', but it stands strong as ever and could be worse."

Emilia Bonacci stood before the rag-tag rural cottage and wrapped her arms around her ribcage, the unfamiliar older man speaking from her left. His faded delivery van stood parked just behind her, her faded red Pinto next to that. All she really knew of him was his name, Frank Cooper, and that he and his wife owned the grocery store in town.

The cottage's ancient, banged-up exterior pulled at the tension surrounding her heart. So much for agreeing to rent a place sight-unseen, but what choice did she have?

Despite the bad omen, the Minnesotan countryside, with its sprawling gold-green and sun-drenched hills, offered redemption. But even that redemption wasn't so clear-cut.

No. Unlike any normal person, the quaint spring scene didn't lend her total comfort. The added solitude here offered equal parts privacy with the potential for her uninterrupted and violent death.

That's only if he finds me. He might not find me.

She squeezed her eyes shut and sucked in a breath. No one in Harlow knew her story. She had to control her fear, or this man beside her would guess something was wrong.

She opened her eyes and looked for a positive. The cottage's timber walls housed sizable windows with cornflower-blue shutters. Perfect. Simple. Sweet. Small panes of glass sat between those shutters, a grid of squares, some stained in a mix of joyful jewel tones. The wheat and grass plains as a sparkling spring backdrop didn't hurt.

She cleared her throat, her voice rusty from days of having nothing but her own company. "I can work with this."

A lie. She'd rarely held a hammer, much less repaired a house. At 5'4" with an oft-reported "prim" demeanor, she couldn't blame Frank for his dubious sidelong stare.

Still, her heart danced with a glint of excitement for the first time since leaving Los Angeles. Maybe her new life wouldn't be so bad. Living in an apartment had never suited her, and the cottage reminded her of the rickety house she'd grown up in long before her family's "good fortune" ruined everything.

"I wouldn't go fallin' in love just yet." Frank trudged up the tapered dirt path, his heavy work boots crunching gravel. "The last tenants didn't treat her good, so the inside's not so great."

Her stomach sank. Love or not, she'd already paid her rental deposit and invested too much into staying in Harlow. This cottage was her only option.

She padded behind Frank, not inclined to make waves, like the good little woman she'd been raised to be. Being invisible could be a literal lifesaver.

A cool gust swept over the hill, pushing dark brown curls from her eyes. The sun beat on her cheekbones just a fraction too strong, and the cottage in its ramshackle state added to the discomfort. This was the second last place in the world she wanted to sleep tonight, and she would have loved to mumble a peeved, "Fuck my life," but even swearing wasn't in her MO.

So, double "fuck my life."

In reality, all she did was groan under her breath and make her way up the veranda steps, where Frank held the front door open and allowed her in first. An eyeful of a rough-and-tumble hallway greeted her, and dust particles caught the light ahead while white powdery debris coated worn floorboards. Meanwhile, the wall's yellowed plaster bore a gray tinge that made her poker-straight spine slump.

"Ya, I figure they didn't know how to unblock a chimney." Frank's voice had her turning toward him, the man rubbing the back of his neck, his lips pinched on one side. "Smoke marks on damn near everything. I fixed the blockage, but the place still needs a good clean."

She snapped her shoulders back again and lightened her expression. "There's a fireplace?"

The apartment hadn't had one of those. Besides, Frank here didn't need to feel any worse about this place than he already seemed to.

"Right this way." He led her through a door to the right, into a cozy living room—messy but still inviting. "So, I saw from the I.D. you supplied that you're from LA. What made you choose little ol' Harlow?"

She made a show of inspecting the room, of running her fingertips over the dark wood mantle, her fingers collecting gray, chalky residue —all an attempt to distract herself, and Frank, with her room-gazing. First thing, she would open some windows and let some fresh air in. Well, after she found the bathroom and did something about her dusty fingers.

Does this house even have running water?

My pale pink and white wardrobe wouldn't do so well in a place like this.

Oh, shut it! None of this will change the fact there wasn't enough time to take all the money I needed or cover my tracks all that well.

She dropped her hand to her side. Sticking to the truth would mean less chance of getting caught in lies. Maybe she could take advantage of these new people knowing stuff about her. Besides, she had her burner phone and would use nothing but cash to get by, and Harlow itself seemed safe enough…

"I just looked at a map and liked the name Harlow." She gave Frank what she hoped was a playful, casual shrug. Oh, she hated lying. "And I figured, 'Why not?'"

Why not, indeed. Minnesota was the home of *Prince*, a musical genius who'd been her happy place for as long as she could remember. That was a positive, right?

Why, oh why, did all the good artists die young?

Then there was Betty White, or at least her character, Rose Nylund from the 90s sitcom, The Golden Girls. Emilia had grown up watching the reruns, and Rose was downright adorable with her outlandish stories about St. Olaf, Minnesota.

That said, Emilia's first and only love had once lived here too. He'd insisted Minnesota had its charms. The relationship had ended in a literal bloody mess, though she couldn't exactly hold that disaster against the state.

Fargo. Yes, that had Minnesota written all over it too. She'd always liked Fargo. The detective lady in that movie seemed nice. Maybe she'd meet more nice people like that here, minus Fargo's murders and extortion, of course. With all she'd been through, she really did need more "nice" and less "murder and extortion."

She blinked up at Frank, with his pale blue eyes and weathered, narrow face, who seemed to take the dragging silence as his cue to instigate a guided tour. There weren't that many rooms, but he skipped all the glossy talk in favor of pointing out what needed repair. For such a small place, the list grew and grew, and his blunt honesty added weight to her already burdened shoulders.

The last room was the kitchen, and it turned out to be the worst. Lopsided cabinets barely clung to life on the right wall, the puke-green color somehow competing with the garish, chipped laminate counters in an outdated shade of blinding tangerine.

The whole scene screamed desperation, as in, only a desperate person would choose to live here. Someone with limited funds and nowhere else to go. Someone like her. Desperate and broke. Lucky for Frank.

Though, lucky for her too, maybe. At least, Anthony would never *ever* expect to find her here. In a remote town, and a house so... so one rung above dilapidated. All because in nine years of marriage, he didn't know her well enough to understand that, unlike him, her happiness didn't rely on lavish surroundings. He'd probably already scoured her credit card bills for charges to the Hotel Bel-Air.

Or maybe he's already in jail?

Even that wishful thought didn't stop her from glancing over her shoulder since defeat and trauma did not fade so easily. Maybe never. Besides, even if Anthony was locked up, she couldn't be confident he wouldn't send someone else to find her.

Frank returned to rubbing his neck. "You should know, I've called in a favor with a friend. He'll swing by and start work on this kitchen right away. Maureen and I, we don't expect you to go knockin' things together yourself, and now that we have a renter, we consider the upgrade an investment."

Her first instinct was to jump up and down out of pure gratitude, but then a different, more sobering thought crept in. The fewer people who saw her, the better, so maybe she was best to try to throw this helpful man off.

She tore her gaze from Frank, certain he already read her impending lie. "I can handle this all on my own. I'm quite handy, you know. And the mess, it will keep me busy while I figure out what to do with myself in this town."

Her face heated, and her limbs lost strength. Again, lying didn't come easy, and the list of things she *could* do—mopping, scrubbing, maybe painting—didn't compare to the much longer list of things she *couldn't* manage. Ripping out non-functional cabinets, for one...

Frank swatted his hand in a dismissive gesture. "We'll hear none of that now. People round these parts like to help just about anyone who needs it, and lady, you need it. Call it 'Minnesota nice' if you wanna, but Harlow folk love to poke around in each other's business, especially new people, so you best get used to the locals invitin' themselves over."

Her mouth fell open, and she readied to insist on privacy, but her words seized at the crunch of tires outside. The louder-than-normal engine noises indicated a larger vehicle; one parked close to the back door attached to the kitchen.

She startled at the slam of a car door, her gaze hitting Frank, his brow now etched in deep quizzical lines.

Had Anthony found her so soon? He did own an SUV.

She wanted to move but couldn't. The thud of boots over the back veranda made the old boards creak, and her heart thundered so hard it seemed to reverberate against her ribs, triggering a heavy wave of nausea. At the same time, her skin stung all over as if her baby pink sleeves were made of sandpaper and not luxury cotton.

A large silhouette crossed the kitchen window. Frank turned toward the back door, his hand reaching for the handle.

She cleared her throat, but Frank didn't seem to hear. "I. Umm. Need to go."

He cracked the door open, giving her a glimpse of the fly screen just behind. She mumbled something about washing her hands in the bathroom and spun away.

"Emilia?"

Whoever the male voice belonged to, she hadn't seen him, but he'd seen her. Or maybe her slow escape wasn't so much to blame as her being thoughtless enough to speak. Either way, this man recognized her, and she didn't know how.

An eerie silence filled the room, daring her to turn and look at him.

An ancient memory trickled in like water through a crack in a stone, and a bigger part of her didn't need to turn to know who this was.

Not Anthony. No. Someone even more unlikely.

And though she should have been relieved, with all her heart, she still wanted to escape.

Two

EMILIA SQUEEZED HER EYES SHUT, still too boneless with shock to move. The energy around her shifted, and her body wobbled back and forth, threatening to introduce her to the floor.

She sucked in a breath and vowed to treat this moment like ripping off a plaster, unpleasant but necessary. While her back remained to the room, she ached for an ability to teleport out of this nerve-shredding situation.

I could run again. I've already done that once this week.

No, she really couldn't, no matter how much she wanted to. She'd exhausted her funds running that first time. The least she could do now was dig out her courage and face her uninvited guest. She'd spent years faking pleasantness and could do it again.

She forced her eyes open and turned from the ugly olive-green wall ahead, shuffling her feet slowly beneath her. Harsh morning light poured from the open back door and stung her eyes; that light caused her to squint. All she could make out of her visitor was the silhouette of a long torso and strong-looking calves, a pair of weighty work boots, and…

The tradesman.

No, he's more than that. So much more.

He'd only said one word. Her name. It sailed upon his warm, rumbling tone and still somehow ricocheted within her brain, refusing to leave.

He took a small sidestep, the sun no longer obscuring her view. That view ripped at her heart and brought about a genuine pain. One that flowed from her chest and into her back, before a sharp shockwave shot through her muscles and burrowed that pain into her bones.

Oh yes, she recognized him. And recognition had her fearing her heart might fall out altogether and land with a bloody splat on the already disgusting wood floor.

Useless blasted heart. When have you done me any good?

Certainly *never* when it came to this man.

His pale green eyes, so familiar—as if ten years hadn't passed— they darkened to a deep chartreuse, his full lips tightening into a perfect frown. The ex who'd once lived in Minnesota. He *still* lived in Minnesota. Or at least, he'd moved back. Why?

Her pain intensified, prodding the idea that maybe she already knew why. His conflicted glower burned holes through her, seeming to confirm her theory; and still, nothing stopped his name from falling from her lips. "Blaine?"

Blaine. Despite the hard tug at her heart, it felt good to say his name. Maybe because she'd been forbidden from speaking it for over a decade. But saying his name, even just thinking it, should have been the last thing she wanted.

He was the beginning and end of her teenage rebellion. Nothing less than the end of her freedom as an adult... before her adulthood had even started.

Maybe I'm seeing ghosts. No. Not ghosts. Demons! Ghosts or demons would be better than this.

Not that there'd ever been anything bad about him. No, the complete opposite. Though his presence now proved once again that hell had, and still did, exist.

"Emilia."

Her name fell from his mouth, another full and unwavering statement, like he didn't need to bother posing her identity as a question. Like whatever glance he'd had of her earlier provided enough proof.

Like he'd never forgotten.

Of course not. He's etched on my soul forever, and maybe I'm etched on his...

That thought alone stole her next breath from her lungs. So, she did the one thing most likely to spare her from collapsing. *She ran.* Literally ran. Though not in a true straight line, which meant she cracked a shoulder into the vomit-colored door frame, the thing exacting revenge for her earlier thoughts on its ugliness.

Pain shot through her shoulder and down her back, but none of that mattered. She kept running until she reached the bathroom Frank had shown her minutes before.

She snapped the locks shut and sank to the cold tile floor in an attempt to catch her breath.

"You are to stay away from that Irish boy. I won't hear the name 'Blaine' in this house ever again. Do you understand?"

Her head ached from a rush of adrenaline, her father's voice haunting her.

His thick Italian accent rang in her ears as if he'd spoken those words just yesterday. Stupid girl. She should have listened. Should have played by the rules and played her part. The great Vittorio Bonacci had designs for her life, and far be it from her to stray from that plan.

Still, even as she'd done as her dad decreed, time and a wedding hadn't faded anything. Blaine Callaghan remained the old flame she couldn't extinguish.

Her tiny bathroom lights blinked, almost like they protested at having to do their job, but that blinking gave enough distraction to snap her from her tailspin of thoughts.

She couldn't stay curled on the floor forever. Besides, she'd caused enough of a scene already. Frank waited for her in the kitchen, and she had a new reputation to build. Coming across as flighty and irrational wouldn't do.

She gathered the energy to hook her hand to the bathroom counter and pull herself up. Her earlier vow to forget the past lay in tatters, but that didn't mean she had to fall apart. At least, not outwardly, anyway.

The mirror above the sink revealed a pitiful reflection, one that made her tummy churn anew. She'd been living in her car for the last few days, so she shouldn't have expected much. But her high bun lay in a frazzled mess, and loose curls stuck to her clammy forehead. Her left cheek was smeared in black dust from the fireplace. Worst still, the front of her light-colored outfit had somehow collected wayward soot, and she straight-up looked like a maimed creature from a C-grade zombie movie.

She took a steadying breath, pushed aside her overwhelming desire to cower on the floor again, and turned the tap on so she could run her shaking fingers beneath the cold flow.

She'd go out there and face the two men, and she'd do it with the confidence befitting a normal twenty-eight-year-old woman. One who hadn't hightailed it minutes earlier. One stronger than the scared shadow of a woman who'd left LA.

Her entire life thus far was a blur of numb acceptance that the men around her could dictate her destiny. *Again, stupid girl.* Maybe she'd had no other choice, but she couldn't afford to be that girl any longer.

She splashed handfuls of cold water over her face, removing the black marks while willing her nerves to settle. No towels hung in here yet, so she ran her sleeve over her wet skin, the classless gesture so far from her days as a big-city socialite.

Next, she lifted her posture and tidied her hair; anything to avoid looking like a woman who'd just flipped her lid. She'd make something out of this sucky situation. *She had to.* The cottage was *hers*. *Her* sanctuary. *Her* new beginning. Decrepit as this place was, she wouldn't let yet another man keep her from the independence she so desperately wanted.

Uncertainty nipped at her heels, and still, she pried the bathroom door open a crack and waited for a beat, sussing out the hallway before marching onward to the kitchen, where a giant metal box sat on the floor. The lid lay open, a bunch of workman's thingies visible inside.

Thingies? Tools, Scatterbrain, they're called tools…

Yes. Right. Tools!

Blaine's back was to her, his arms outstretched while he measured the overhead cabinets. He hadn't noticed her in the room, or if he did, he ignored her. And bless her soul, an effervescent tingling spread through her torso, the ease with which he worked and carried himself taking instant effect.

His distinct masculine form, the khaki work shirt pulled over well-defined shoulders—the stretched fit highlighting a steady interplay of taut muscles beneath light fabric. This was as close to a religious experience as she'd had since... Well, since the last time she'd seen him more than a decade ago. And the fact that he did still affect her didn't bode well.

He'd been nineteen back then—still gorgeous, with a heart of gold —but now he had to be closer to thirty-one. It should have been impossible for Blaine Callaghan to get more attractive, but his broader build and steadier stance took him to full-scale Adonis status. Just being in the same room as him made her knees want to liquefy beneath her.

A sudden jolt of shame rocketed up her spine. She'd only just left her awful marriage. Admiring another man's bulging biceps felt wrong. Not that Anthony had any bulging biceps to admire.

Maybe the view would be good for her. Might help her move on. She didn't owe Anthony anything, after all.

Good idea, Genius. Move on? Maybe one day, but not with this guy. It's not like the last encounter with Blaine didn't end in disaster or anything...

The grind of someone clearing their throat snapped her attention away from admiring "the view." *Frank.* Oh right, Frank was here! He'd tucked himself in the farthest corner, which made him downright invisible compared to "the view."

The older man raised a brow, suggesting he'd caught every second of her sightseeing. "Seems you two know each other, then?"

Blaine slowly lowered his arms and turned, his gaze training on her like he, too, wanted an explanation. She refused to offer him one. The past was strictly off-limits.

"I wouldn't go that far." She nodded at the cabinets. "So, what's the verdict?"

A muscle on Blaine's jaw ticked, and he narrowed his eyes as if to say, *Are you really going to pretend we're strangers?*

She skittered her gaze from his because, yes, yes she was. Maybe her lie annoyed him, but it was a lie she would tell either way, even though a part of her wanted to mouth the words, "I'm sorry. I'm so, so sorry."

"Frank already let me know what he needs." Blaine's easy rumble washed over her and set her heart to flutter as if she was the only one unsettled with this surprise reunion. "I'll take these measurements back to the workshop and put something together over the next couple of weeks."

She turned to Frank and offered a sweet smile, hoping he'd be her salvation. "Seems I'm lucky to have Frank and Maureen as landlords."

"Yeah, they're good people." Blaine's voice dragged her gaze back to his steely stare and the muscle in his jaw still twitching away. His rigidity made no secret of questioning whether *she* was "good people."

To be fair, the way things had ended, she didn't blame him.

But what really turned her insides to water was how the color of his eyes retained the same ocean-green flecked with gold. Even though the years had turned his expression more reflective and soul-baring, a tight wariness indicated he had zero patience for her need to save face or her submissive compliance. A submissive compliance that had hurt them in more ways than one.

Where once he'd looked at her with wide and hopeful wonder, now, hard lines and a clenched jaw took over. She let her vision fall to the scuffed floor, the swirling, honeyed pattern on the wood a weak distraction from the heat engulfing her face. If only she'd been stronger back then.

She lifted her chin and gestured at the house. "Seems I have my work cut out for me here."

He glided his attention over her dirt-stained sweater. "Seems you've made a solid start."

More heat rushed to her face, and she questioned the presence of a barely noticeable smirk tugging the corners of his mouth. That smirk softened the hard planes of his face, and that softness, the subtle yet somehow unescapable welcome, clenched a tight fist around her heart, hinting that maybe a mutual spark still existed.

Her treacherous lips wobbled, but she clamped her teeth over her lower lip, holding back the rebellious glint of joy. Given the moment's uncertainty, given the past, given the show she'd made of denying they had one, joy had no place here.

As if he'd heard her thoughts on joy, Blaine's gaze trekked down to her right hand; a frown taking over before his stare slammed into hers.

Sharp iciness grew throughout her body, and she was quick to tug her sleeve over her hand. Not quick enough. He'd seen the scrapes on her knuckles, knuckles already blue with bruises. Her hands still ached every time she clenched her fingers.

At least Blaine didn't question those bruises out loud, though she would need to find a way to keep him at a distance. Maybe she'd call Frank later and ask if he could warn her next time Blaine would be over. She'd find a way to stay out of the cottage, and then she wouldn't have to see him. Or maybe there was someone else in town who could take over the job…

Frank stepped toward her, a set of keys hanging from his fingers. "These belong to you now."

He dropped the keys into her palm, and she frowned down at the silver, jagged edges. A symbol of her new home, even though she didn't even have a bed yet.

"Thanks." She lifted her gaze and scanned the room. No table. Or chairs. Or even a couch in her dusty living room. "Could you recommend a furniture shop around here?"

"Oh ya, that's easy." Frank gave a choked and bumpy kind of laugh before reaching out and giving Blaine a solid but friendly clap on the back. "He's not just the best carpenter in Harlow, but his shop is also the *only* place to get any furniture around these parts."

Blaine's pickup rocked as he made his way down the long and uneven dirt road. His heart pounded, and his attention darted all over the place. Had he really just seen Emilia Bonacci? In Harlow? Had he really been roped into working on her house?

Holy shit!

Of all the screwed up, messed up, fucked up things life could throw at him, this was the cruelest of all.

Just like everyone else in these parts, he whizzed past a speed limit sign, though perhaps with added vigor today. His foot pressed extra heavy to the gas, and his fingers squeezed around the steering wheel until his knuckles turned white. Maybe she'd come to town to find him? No. That wasn't right. Not with the frenzied way she'd run from the kitchen the second she'd spotted him. Wide-eyed panic wasn't the reaction of a woman looking to reconnect.

The muscles in his chest pulled, and he struggled for his next breath. At one point in his life, this exact scenario would have been all his wildest dreams come true. But he wasn't a nineteen-year-old kid anymore, and he knew enough to understand Emilia Bonacci was nothing but bad news.

Her father owned a lucrative jewelry empire, and she was the princess he kept locked in the highest tower of his self-made castle. Untouchable. Priceless. A possession. Not that Blaine personally saw her as a possession. She'd been sweet and fun, and everything he thought he wanted.

Shut up. Just shut up. Don't even think about any of the good stuff.

No. He wouldn't hurt himself with the nicer memories. Not anymore. Not again. Better to focus on how she didn't belong in a small town like Harlow, so why was she here? Why a dingy old cottage on the outskirts of town?

He dragged a hand over the rough stubble on his cheek, the muscles on his forehead strained and hinting at the start of a headache. He'd been exiled from LA, and those closest to her were to blame. They'd reduced him to seeing his family just a couple of times a year. And even then, only when his family could come down to see *him.*

He had reasons on top of reasons to stay away from Emilia. Maybe Frank would understand if he stepped back from working on her house…

The speed gauge caught his eye, and he eased his foot off the gas.

As unnerving as her reappearance had been, he couldn't deny the fear in her eyes. Though his better judgment told him not to care, he did. *Damn it.*

The people of Harlow had looked after him when his own family couldn't. This community *was* his family. And since trouble liked to follow Miss Bonacci, he wanted to make sure everyone in this town stayed safe.

It's not just that. I want to know she's safe too.

Damn it, again. He'd changed. He'd built a decent life away from her circus. Besides, her father had been right all along. Blaine and Emilia were a bad fit. He was nothing more than an average nobody, somehow lucky enough to have been important to her for a brief moment in time. Well, lucky and then unlucky…

He guided his truck down the quiet main street, its aging buildings still shining with original beauty. He parked before his shop, "Oak Tree Furniture," its classic concrete flourishes accenting the giant polished windows, the evidence of his years of hard work on display. Handcrafted dining tables, ornate cherry wood cabinets, bookshelves he'd designed and made with his own two hands—a testament to what he'd done with his life in the years he *hadn't* been with Emilia.

And still, in all those years, he'd been haunted by the memory of her dark curls encircling his fingers as he played with them, the song in her laugh, and the glint in her deep brown eyes. Though the shadows under her eyes today made him think she probably didn't laugh all that often anymore, and maybe that wasn't entirely her fault.

He leaned back in his seat and pressed his palms to his eyes, groaning at the vision of her in that kitchen. The wild, chaotic curls. Her dirt-stained sweater. Her crossed arms and the slight blush to her cheeks. She hadn't been comfortable in her disheveled state, and still, she was the most beautiful mess he'd ever seen.

Three

From: Emilia Bonacci
To: Emilia Bonacci
Subject: Even more excited!

Hey,

Remember that boy I wrote about? The one who bought a pink sapphire butterfly bracelet for his sister's sixteenth? Of course, you do. Well, he came back!

I don't think he knows I used my own money to pay for the difference on that bracelet. I think he figured I wrangled a store discount or something, which is perfect. I don't want him feeling bad about how much that thing cost. Besides, how was he to know my dad's store is way pricier than the average jewelry chain? Anyway, the boy's name is Blaine, and he must have been super happy about that discount because he came in bearing a blueberry bagel and hot chocolate just for me. How sweet, right? I couldn't believe it. I totally just wanted to faint from excitement. He's so cute.

. . .

It's a good thing he waited a week to come back to the store too. You know, since I only work on Saturdays. Must be fate, right? Ha! Anyway, I took an early lunch break with him. Bethany wasn't too happy about that, but hey, I'm the boss's daughter. What's she gonna do? Fire me?

Blaine's nineteen, just a couple of years older than me. He said he wants to see me again, and I can't wait. He seems so sweet, so I was cool with swapping numbers. I'm totally not going to tell him that Bonacci Jewels belongs to my dad. Not right away, anyway. I don't want to scare Blaine. Better he thinks I'm a shop girl or something. Honestly, I like it better that way. I want someone to get to know me for who I am.

I know I'm getting way ahead of myself here, but this is me writing to me, so why not? Maybe one day I can let Blaine and Dad meet. Dad would have to see that Blaine is a big improvement on Anthony. God, I can't believe anyone thinks we should be together. Puke! Anthony is a total leech. Why can't anyone else see that?

I don't like Anthony, never have, and I already really like Blaine. Well, what I know of him so far. I want to see where this goes. Maybe If things work out with him, I won't have to worry about Anthony OR the Stuccos ever again.

Emilia awoke to an eerie symphony of creaky old walls and leaves scuttling across the ground outside, the morning sun already bright through her bedroom's thin, white curtain. *A bedroom without a bed.*

The hairs along her neck prickled. Not a new sensation since being on high alert had become her natural state. For a city girl totally unaccustomed to quiet, there was an irony in how these tranquil country sounds set her on edge.

Maybe Harlow hadn't been the best place to stop.

Too late now. *Far* too late.

On top of all the fear, her body ached from a night spent sleeping on the floor, nothing to support her but the solitary blanket and pillow she'd taken from LA. Still, she couldn't spend one more night curled up and exposed in her car, so she'd decided to tidy this room before any other and slept on a blanket-covered floor.

She sat and rubbed her pained shoulder, twisting to stretch out any stiffness in her back, all while her mind drifted to the documents she'd faxed her father almost immediately after her escape. The documents proving she'd been right all along.

She'd left a copy of those same papers for Anthony to find. He'd be fuming, belligerent, probably more so than if she'd simply left.

She had guilt, but not enough to undo what she'd started.

A heavy knock on her front door startled her. She hugged her pillow and hoped that if she stayed quiet, maybe the person outside would go away. The pounding didn't stop, and now a female voice accompanied the knocking, the words too distorted to decipher.

Emilia pried herself from her makeshift bed and yelled, "Just a minute."

Not a bright move for a woman meant to be on the run. Then again, the voice outside didn't belong to Anthony, so maybe she'd be safe.

The mirror inside her near-empty wardrobe door showed pillow marks crisscrossed over her face, concave lines that exacerbated the dark circles under her eyes. She wrinkled her nose at her haphazard image. The people of this town had a knack for catching her looking a mess.

Her white cotton robe lay folded on a shelf, and she pulled it out, covering the underwear she'd slept in since she'd forgotten to pack pajamas.

The breeze from her hurried stride to the door blew tangled curls across her nose. She shook the tickling strands away, unbolting the front door and using the time to consider that if she was lucky, her deranged appearance might scare her visitor away. Or at least shame them into thinking they'd woken her.

"Oh, hey there! Welcome to Harlow."

She jolted at the overly enthusiastic woman outside her wire screen, ice-blonde hair and light-blue eyes sparkling over a beaming smile. The woman was maybe a few years younger than Emilia and clung to a wicker basket with a blue-checkered tea towel covering the top. She extended the basket now, like some kind of religious offering.

"I saw from Blaine's notes at the workshop that Frank and Maureen had a new renter, so of course I had to swing by and meet you." The woman bounced where she stood, her sunny yellow dress brighter than the spring day behind her. "I figured I'd also save you the trouble of making breakfast."

The woman's smile shook just a little, and Emilia felt her eyelids flare, her mouth wavering open and closed a few times with no semblance of sound escaping.

Who was this woman, and how did she know Blaine?

What normal person just invited themselves over for breakfast? Especially with someone they'd never even met? The skin over her cheekbones tightened, and she shelved a desire to school this woman on stranger danger.

"I don't have any coffee." She kept her voice flat and gave a sorry-you-wasted-your-time sort of shrug. "I don't even have a kettle."

Despite all expectations, the woman's eyes twinkled all the same, and she dug around in the basket. "Oh, that's okay. I bought a flask. I even have cups. I cornered Frank, and he said something about you arriving with next to nothing."

Emilia's heart seemed to shrink, her muscles coiling with the implications that these townsfolk already gossiped about her. Perhaps she would have been better off disappearing within the throng of a busy city.

The woman's hand materialized from the basket, and she indeed waved a silver flask in the air, the contents making a muffled sloshing sound.

Emilia buried a scowl. She hated rude people and didn't want to be one, but she wasn't all that certain someone in her predicament should be making her presence known.

"I don't have a table. Or chairs. Or a couch. Or a fridge. All I have is electricity and running water." She stepped back, wrapping her fingers around the door's edge, ready to close it. "Maybe some other time…"

Or never. Never sounds good too.

The blonde's already pale skin turned ashen, and her lips parted. Guilt swelled Emilia's throat, that guilt acknowledging this woman had put considerable effort into this introduction.

"But you have a veranda with a giant old porch swing. It's lovely out today. We can eat out here. I don't mind. *Please?*" She fluttered her long, mascara-coated lashes and gestured to the veranda around her, before smashing her palm to her forehead. "Oh my. I'm so sorry. No wonder you're reluctant to meet with me. I haven't even introduced myself. Ally. My name's Ally Egan, and I work for Blaine. I'm the next best person aside from him to help you with sourcing all the stuff you'll need to settle down here in Harlow."

Emilia stared ahead, her mind blank while she searched for another excuse to turn Ally away. Only, the strain in her body eased suddenly, and she figured that maybe she shouldn't.

If what Ally said was true, then maybe Emilia could do with the help. Besides, this girl seemed about as desperate for an introduction as Emilia was to avoid one. Rather than becoming known as the town recluse, maybe she would stand out less if she tried to blend in.

Before she had time to overthink this, she reached out and unlatched the screen door, careful to use her left hand so this woman wouldn't see the scrapes and bruises on her right. In stark contrast to her cool approach, the younger woman gave a high squeal and bounced on her heels, backing away to let Emilia pass.

Ally took a seat on the dove gray porch swing and unloaded a blue plastic bowl of bright red strawberries onto the long seat. "I picked these this morning. They're from Mom and Dad's garden, and you're going to absolutely love them."

Emilia sat on the swing's far end, one hand resting on her chest and clutching her robe's lapels closed. "Ah. Thanks?"

What was she even doing? Sitting out here in next to nothing, clearly. Catching the cold morning air with a woman she'd only just met.

Next came a plate piled high with oven-fresh biscuits, steam rising from their warm, golden dough. Ally's gaze lifted to meet Emilia's. "Mom made these from her own special recipe. She said to say hi, by the way."

Emilia surveyed the basket's assortment of jellies and a bowl of fluffy, whipped cream. A million times more appealing than the convenience store hot dogs and half-stale bread she'd survived on up until now.

"You went to all this effort for me?" She settled deeper into the seat and allowed an elbow to dig into the armrest. Maybe if Ally wasn't fussed about this encounter, she shouldn't be, either. Besides, she glanced at the empty fields in all directions. With no one nearby to spot her, maybe she was safe enough...

Ally's focus held to the flask she worked to unscrew. "You betcha, though I have to admit, my motives are a little selfish. The last few years have seen most people my age move outta town for work or college. Harlow lacks young blood, and well, when I heard you'd moved in..." She gave a crooked smile. "I tried to ask Blaine about you, but he just grunted something inaudible. So, I found Frank and Maureen as they were closing up the general store, and they filled me in. Anyway, I thought maybe you'd be someone interesting to know."

The dark, rich scent of fresh coffee had a small smile pulling on Emilia's face. A few seconds passed before Ally's words about getting to know her filtered through.

"I'm really glad you visited, but I don't know how long I'll be staying in town." She reached for the coffee Ally extended, hoping to drop the topic now.

"Still, it'd be nice just to have some company." Ally's grin twisted at the corner, her gaze falling to her coffee cup. "Even if just for a while. I don't expect you to entertain me or anything."

Emilia paused, her first taste of blessed coffee a mere inch from her lips. She had zero plans to make new friends but still hadn't decided which tactic would serve her best—getting to know Harlow's residents or remaining as mysterious as possible.

Well, too late for mystery now. Not with what Frank said about locals inviting themselves in, a claim Ally here had already proved true.

Then again, at least this way people might notice if I go missing. If Anthony...

No. She couldn't go there. At least, not in front of Ally. Emilia needed to get into the habit of forgetting him, of moving on with her life. Maybe she could find some sort of middle ground with Ally, like being polite but a little distant, while not being blacklisted as the local pariah. It would be a cruel move to let this woman think they could be fast and forever buddies.

Besides, it's time I worked on my rusty social skills. I'm not Anthony's quiet little woman anymore.

She braced herself with a sip of coffee and let that memory slide. "Okay look, please don't say anything, but I don't think Blaine likes me all that much. So maybe you're right, maybe you are the one to help me set up house."

Ally's eyes widened, and she gave an open-mouthed smile. "Oh my, really? Anyone who knows me, knows I love art and design. I even have a growing business selling my handmade plant pots over at Aggie's nursery. If you show me around the cottage, I'm sure I'll have a bunch of ideas."

Emilia held up a hand, warning Ally to slow down. "It's a disaster in there, and I haven't had a chance to make much of a dent on the mess, so I'm not subjecting poor innocents to the place just yet. Besides, I'm not looking for anything too complicated, so maybe I can let you know my budget, and you can help me figure out what I can afford?"

All her money was cash, notes rolled up and hidden inside a few pairs of shoes since she'd wanted to avoid Anthony tracing any bank transactions. She hadn't taken a whole lot of money, but she could afford to buy a few things.

"Ya sure, I heard things got weird between you and Blaine yesterday, so does that make this a covert decorating mission?" Ally's leaned-in whisper seemed to ignore the fact that there were about a thousand acres between them and the next person. "Don't worry about him, okay? He's a prickly one occasionally, but you get to love him once you know him."

Emilia opened her mouth ready to defend Blaine, but then the line about knowing him and loving him hit her square in the chest. She *had* known him and, because of that, had loved him. And she'd ruined their lives in doing so.

She pressed her lips together and said nothing. Maybe it was best that only Frank knew of their past. Blaine didn't deserve the local gossip and questions, and she wanted a clean slate too.

Ally clapped her hands in a super-energized display of excitement. "Will we be slipping secret furniture orders past him? Cause that would be so much fun and would serve him right for being rude to a town newbie."

Emilia gave a tight smile, still unable to produce any words, which Ally seemed to take as a "yes" since she proceeded to talk again. "Oh, I know. I'm going to Maynard's Tavern tonight. You should come with. We can swap ideas, and I can introduce you to the locals."

Somehow this woman flipped from buying covert furniture to introducing Emilia to the whole town. Emilia blinked a bunch and ground out some sounds, her frozen state hard to escape. She'd planned on *maybe* getting to know each person one at a time and never imagined a mass meeting involving booze and potential run-ins with the love of her life.

Ally threw a sideways glance, her lips coated in a happy shade of cherry-red lip gloss. Everything about her exuded youthful exhilaration, something Emilia had lost the day she'd been pried from Blaine's side.

"Okay, sure." Her skin prickled, not all that certain where those words came from.

Maybe she just wanted an escape from thinking about *him*. Besides, what was the point of escaping if she didn't at least try to enjoy her freedom?

Four

OH GOD, I shouldn't be here.

Emilia clutched her open car door, the parking lot of Maynard's Tavern disproportionately quiet despite the number of other cars in the area. Her Pinto cast a pitiful image beside her, the vehicle's faded red paint and spots of rust failing any attempt at prestige or even any semblance of being an average car.

At this point though, she should have been thankful for the Pinto, and appearance shouldn't have mattered. This car had gotten her out of LA. It had saved her sanity and her life. Saved her from ever having to relive her final night with Anthony ever again. *Hopefully.* She'd paid for it in cash the morning of her escape, from a used car lot a few blocks from the apartment. She even handed over more than she should have on the proviso she could take the Pinto straight away.

There'd been a method to her madness too. No one in her elite circle would think to look for her in a run-down and worthless heap. By all accounts, her somewhat impromptu plan had worked.

A huge neon sign flashed bright, vying for her attention. She cringed at the glaring colors atop the small-town bar, a heckling chant playing over in her head. *I don't belong here. I really don't belong here.*

She had nothing in common with these people. No shared life experience. Maynard's looked like a typical country establishment. Stools and tables scattered all over a wrap-around porch, and people sat with drinks half-finished, laughing in waves of boisterous conversation.

They seemed so light. So well adjusted. Everything seemed so simple.

A clammy sweat broke out on her forehead at the prospect of walking through those doors, and a queasy churning took over her tummy. She'd made a promise to Ally and herself. As much as she wished it, she couldn't keep living in the same controlled bubble. Heck, that bubble had well and truly burst already. She would have to learn to be normal. To blend in with society. To survive.

She nudged her car door closed using her hip, then shuffled toward the veranda's edge. A group of five men flanked the venue doors, huddled together at a high table. She averted her gaze and gave them space. But despite her attempt to hide, the group fell silent, all eyes turning to her.

I should go.

She peered down at her clingy, cream-colored dress, a ruffle around the low collar breaking up the whole figure-hugging look. It had been her one indulgent purchase amongst all the cleaning products and non-perishable food she'd bought during her trip to town early that afternoon. That and the white lace gloves she'd found at a secondhand shop.

She tugged at the cuff of those gloves now.

To anyone else here, they probably looked like a quirky fashion statement. To her, they were a shield between these people and the truth hidden beneath the white lace.

She kept her chin low but turned her gaze up to the men, all in flannel shirts and bootcut denim. In her former life, what she wore was considered casual, but it seemed here she'd somehow overshot "casual" by about ten miles.

"Now, aren't you the prettiest woman ever to set foot in Harlow?" Maynard's doors swung open and closed behind Ally, and she breezed past the men, hooking her arm through Emilia's like they'd been close friends their entire lives. "Jack, honey, close your mouth before you swallow a fly."

Emilia's face burned, and she tried hard not to stare as the man she presumed to be Jack snapped his mouth shut. The rest of the group returned to drinking their beers, a few indecipherable mumbles passing between them.

Meanwhile, Ally walked behind Emilia, taking her by the shoulders and guiding her through Maynard's doors. "Don't worry about that lot. They're just a bit clueless when it comes to a pretty face." She stopped her pushing once they got to the bar and pointed at Emilia's outfit. "Oh, fer cute! I tried that one on last week. What with your lovely warm skin tone, the white suits you a whole lot more."

Emilia blinked in silence for a few beats, the bar's clash of chatter and rock music somewhat overstimulating. "Ahh… thank you and, umm, thanks for saving me just then."

For someone who'd felt out of place her whole life, she should have been used to the emotion. In fact, the only time she hadn't felt out of place was those brief few months when she'd been with…

No. Nope. Don't do it. Don't think of him.

Besides, Ally here did a fine job of putting her at ease, so she would not wallow in self-pity tonight.

Ally took a seat on one of the high bar stools and patted the stool beside her. "Come on. Let's get a drink, and then we'll get to meeting people."

Emilia sat just as a bartender strolled over. Ally ordered on both their behalf's, not giving Emilia a chance to say what she wanted. As a person who rarely drank, she would have been content with simple soda water, white wine at most; but when an oversized beer landed in front of her, she balked at how she'd ever finish it.

Over the next couple of hours, curious locals took turns wandering over, each stopping to chat. During this time, she learned all about the "Minnesotan Goodbye," which really just described a ritual of saying goodbye about twenty times, in countless different ways, before anyone actually moved on. All this while she struggled to keep track of names, roles, and relationships, though Ally carried the conversation so naturally that Emilia barely noticed she hadn't said much. Maybe no one else did, either.

During a quiet break, Ally nudged her gently in the ribs with an elbow. "You're sure getting a lot of attention. You know, I could set you up with someone here if you're interested. You're single, right?"

"I... ahh." In all her rush and panic to leave LA, she hadn't given this part of her story much thought. "I mean, I guess you could say I'm separated."

One thing she had found time for in her days before arriving in Harlow was a call to her lawyer to start divorce proceedings. It had felt so good to finally say those words, to put in motion the end of a marriage that never should have happened in the first place.

"Well then"—Ally held up her glass in a kind of toasting gesture—"here's to new beginnings."

Emilia raised her glass in a rare moment of unabashed agreement, only to scrunch her face at the next sip of bitter beer, still not used to the taste, the scent something akin to foot odor. Why did she keep torturing herself with this drink? Did she want to maintain the pretense she was just like everyone here? Clearly, she wasn't. Then again, she'd never been out in the world alone, so she couldn't even say *who* she was.

"Got your eye on any men in Harlow, then?" Ally raised a brow, the cheeky glint in her eye suggesting she very much wanted the answer to be *yes*.

Emilia shuddered and gave a dramatic shake of her head. "That's the last thing I need."

"Shame. We could've been each other's wing lady. Besides, being the newbie and all, you would make a killing with this lot. Well"—Ally tipped her head to a point over her shoulder—"everyone except that guy."

Emilia turned so she could see who Ally gestured to, only for her line of sight to slam right into Blaine. He sat at a far-off table, his stare burning holes through her—so intense a wave of heat struck her body—until the sounds of chatter and clinking glasses overwhelmed her senses once more.

She swung back around to Ally but failed to string any words together.

Ally shrugged. "He's usually pretty nice, I swear." She grabbed Emilia's hand and tugged, pulling her off her barstool. "Come on, it's time you two made up."

"No!" Emilia's voice half-stuck in her throat and not much more than a broken, choked sound came out.

If Ally heard the protest, she didn't let on, the woman not breaking stride as she marched across the space, dragging Emilia with her.

Lucky for Ally, Emilia had been raised as a strict Roman Catholic. And even though she no longer considered herself religious, swearing was something she just didn't do. Even the word "hell" was about as evil as "fuck," but right now the wild panic running through her made her want to yell, *Just fucking stop!*

She tugged in the opposite direction, desperate to break free, but Ally overpowered her by several extra inches and pounds, weaving through the maze of tables with ease.

"You two live in the same small town." Ally called behind her, almost steering Emilia into the back of someone's chair. Somehow, she found it in her to just be thankful she didn't fall flat on her face. "There's no room for enemies in Harlow. Not without making things awkward for everyone else."

Emilia scowled at Ally's back. She'd had a lifetime of making room for other people's feelings and not her own. "What about this being awkward for me?"

Or Blaine...

Ally kept pulling, as if she either didn't, or refused, to hear. "Besides, now I'll have an excuse to chat with Wayne."

Emilia didn't know who Wayne was; she'd glimpsed a couple of other guys seated at Blaine's table, so maybe he was one of those.

Her ankle tangled with a chair leg, and she hissed at the pain. "What happened to our covert furniture moving mission?"

"*Pfft.*" Ally swatted at the air and resumed the journey. "I'm not giving up on the hilarity of watching Blaine try to figure out what happened to his stuff, but you know how that saying goes"—she turned and winked over her shoulder—"make love, not war."

Emilia stopped again, those words a cold shock to her system. She tugged at Ally's hand, forcing her to stop too.

Emilia had learned the hard way, love on its own couldn't overcome everything. She'd learned that lesson with Blaine. And her heart had broken every day since.

His footprints were trekked across her soul, footprints that fostered a hope that good people still existed. Perhaps in some small way, he'd contributed to her finally leaving LA. Because of him, she'd never forgotten what true love felt like. Not even a soul-crushing marriage could obscure that memory.

Except her and Blaine's love had done more than just foster hope, it had started a war.

"Listen, Ally." She raised her voice, vying for attention. Desperate not to reopen old wounds. Desperate not to speak with Blaine again. "I don't—"

"Oh. Hiya, Blaine." Ally's overly bright and confident tone snapped Emilia out of her reverie. "Weren't you going to say hello to Emilia?"

Emilia tugged her hand from Ally's. *Traitor.* She had no doubt the woman meant well, but heck, she lacked the ability to read a room. Emilia focused on the three men in front of her, her stance stiff and aching, while Ally gave a small cheeky wave to a guy with floppy nutmeg hair and brown eyes, presumably Wayne.

Blaine's glare burned like wildfire. Her chest constricted as if that fire licked at her heart. She wanted to look away, but even when Blaine seethed, he held her captive.

"Nice gloves." His stare dropped to her hands again, hands she rushed to tuck behind her back.

The upward flick of his gaze to hers acknowledged what they both knew. Her past. Her current situation. The gloves. All of it was a lie. And because of that lie, her insides twisted with shame. And because of *him*, guilt had her wanting to disappear.

But she didn't need to disappear. He spared her the pain of his stare now and took a long swig of his beer, before slamming the bottle down with a thud. She flinched at the sound. No one spoke as he rose from his chair, all six foot of him so much taller than her meager 5'4" frame.

His severe green glower held her for one more long moment, and the hard set of his jaw made her insides sink. The fact was, she understood his dislike for her, agreed she deserved it, but no amount of understanding stopped her from hating this part of her past. That her mere presence could grate on a man who'd loved her without question. A man who'd loved her, now a man scorned.

Maybe it was just her imagination, but even as he glared at her, the strain across his cheeks dropped by the slightest degree. His focus dipped to her hand again. Well, a hand now hidden behind her back. And then his eyes narrowed once more, this time less angry and more as though he was trying to figure something out.

Her breath bottled within her chest. If he was confused, then she was doubly so.

As if to read her thoughts, and as if to deny her any answers, he shook his head and pulled back, soon stalking away in determined footsteps and out the bar's exit.

Does he hate me so much he'd abandon a night with his friends? Did I hurt him so badly?

Come to think of it. Yes, I did.

Ally blew out a loud sigh. "*Oofdah*. Now that was different."

Wayne shrugged, too busy peeling the label off his beer bottle to look at Ally. "He's hardly spoken all night. He just stared at the bar, holding that prickly look he gets sometimes."

Ally turned her head to the bar, a wrinkle forming between her brows. Her line of sight leveled up to a tall and attractive blonde woman, her long, flaxen locks glinting in the light, as she wiped down the counter. "I bet he's having problems with Sarah again."

Goosebumps rose over Emilia's skin, and she worked hard to hide her frown, the thought striking her that maybe she hadn't been the cause of Blaine's misery after all.

Sarah looked around the same age as her but moved with a precision, and speed, and most notably a purpose Emilia simply didn't have. The woman paused and peered up, her stare colliding with Emilia's as though she'd sensed the attention.

A sinking feeling forced Emilia to turn away, to hold back her anguish, to hold back her next inappropriate question. A question she couldn't hold back at all.

"Who's Sarah?"

$\mathcal{F}ive$

BLAINE ARRIVED at Oak Tree Furniture an hour earlier than usual, remnants of a bad night's sleep scraping like gritty sand behind his eyes. He'd learned to compensate for Ally, his all-too-easygoing shop assistant with a tendency to delay the store's opening after a night out. Not only would he be the one to pay the price for her tardiness, but she'd made a new friend last night. The worse friend she could have picked in the whole of America. But unfortunately for him, Ally had a way with customers he couldn't easily replace.

The OPEN sign still clinked against the glass front door behind him as he strolled across the spacious showroom switching on lights, his head pounding and muscles stiff.

Within seconds of Emilia entering the tavern last night, his world had shifted to only seeing and thinking of her. Damn that woman and whatever unnatural hold she had over him. An involuntary electric current had run over his skin, her body-hugging dress drawing his attention to her soft, rounded curves. The light fabric glowed against her deep-golden skin tone. And even under Maynard's dingy lights, she'd been a radiant vision too beautiful to miss.

Miss? I don't miss her. At least... shit... I shouldn't!

And what about her glove-covered hands? The ones she'd hidden the second he'd mentioned them. Her abraded knuckles weren't the only thing she was hiding, and he knew from first-hand experience, whatever she felt the need to hide was bound to be something very wrong.

He rounded a corner and entered his light-filled workshop, where he picked up a few pieces of untreated pine from along the sidewall and slapped them onto his workbench. The loud *thwack* helped break the silence and gave him a momentary place to put his anger.

He'd focus on work. His small contribution to keeping this town alive, so much more important than his hang-ups over being just one face amidst a sea of hot-blooded men at Maynard's admiring Emilia Bonacci.

Oh, fer crying out loud. The sear of unwanted jealousy spread hot tendrils through every one of his veins. He laid his hands flat to the bench top and squeezed his eyes shut, sucking in a few tight breaths. There'd been a time when she would have spotted him in a crowd. A time when no one else mattered. Her face would have lit up. She would have run into his arms and…

Shut up. Those days are over, knucklehead. Move on. She has.

Right. And regardless of his issues, he'd worked too damn hard to rebuild his life. Other people relied on him now. He'd promised Frank he'd fix Emilia's kitchen—a promise he so desperately wanted to renege on, if only being true to his word didn't mean so much to him.

He also had out-of-town orders flying at him left, right, and center. And if things went to plan, he'd be able to hire more staff, which meant maybe more young people would stick it out in this town over trying to make it in a bigger city, just like he had at one point.

And then there was someone else who relied on him, far more important than the rest. The doorbell rang, and he dropped his ruminating long enough to venture out to see who had entered.

He leaned against his workroom door and waited while Ally traipsed by. "You're an hour late."

Even though he loved Ally like his own little sister. Even though he loved running a business. Sometimes this woman made him question whether he actually did want to work with other people.

"Good grief, it's always quiet this time of day." She fluttered her long lashes, her unconvincing show of innocence, and shrugged. "Anyhoo, what's your problem?"

He strode after her to the backroom while she hung her coat on a hook. "You're not the one who makes the rules around here. You know there's stuff to do even if there are no customers."

Darn, the walls echoed his voice back to him. He sounded like a nagging father.

"Geez, Louise." She strolled past, her shoulder brushing his, her twisting-teasing, sing-song tone setting his blood to boil. "There's no need to take your bad mood out on me. Besides, your deepening lack of charm means you need me here more than ever, dontcha know?"

"Lack of charm?" His earlier headache intensified, and he stomped after her again. "There's not a person in this town I don't get along with."

He pressed his jaw shut, realizing the lie the moment it slipped from his mouth.

There was *one* person.

"Really?" She rose a brow, and he couldn't even argue back. For once in her life, Ally Egan was right. "You were all sorts of disgruntled yesterday, even before your whole toddler tantrum at Maynard's, whatever the hell that was about. If you keep this attitude up, you'll scare away the customers."

Just as he'd been worried about sounding like her dad, here was Ally, sounding like his mom. He wanted to laugh; instead, he settled on standing in front of her while she slipped behind the counter. "And I'm supposed to believe you're genuinely concerned about how my mood affects business?"

"No, not really." She tilted her face down to a pile of receipts in her hand. "But maybe I could help you if you'd just let me know what's got you so worked up."

Besides having to watch one man after another ogle Emilia's tiny hemline, while resisting the urge to punch each and every one of them out… Or worse, the urge to whisk the woman away altogether, so he could figure out how to entangle himself in her life once more?

Stupid. Moronic. Foolish. Thoughts like that will only unravel my life all over again.

"I'm not worked up." The lie tasted bitter on his tongue, but he half-blamed Ally.

If she'd just minded her own business and left him alone last night, then he wouldn't have had to watch Emilia's smile turn to dust the moment she'd spotted him. And all that after he'd watched her offer a beaming grin to every other person who'd approached her.

But not him. No. Her face had paled, and she'd dug her heels into the ground, begging Ally to stay at the bar so she wouldn't have to talk with him.

Ally blinked up, her lips pursed like she held back a smile. "My guess is you've got lady troubles."

He forced back an angry growl, his muscles tense from having to control his true aggravation. "That's is none of your business, and this conversation is over."

"Ooh. Well now, so you *do* have lady troubles." She unleashed her famous mega-watt smile, leaning into the counter as she spoke. "And your personal problems *are* my business when you're being all snippy, and I have to work with you. Plus, you were rude to my new friend, who also just happens to be new to this town. And you're all about keeping people in this town, ya? You mightta at least *tried* to make Emilia feel welcome."

The mention of his life's mission, paired with Emilia's name, along with the myriad ways her presence in town messed with his existence, brought a strain to his heart.

Just over ten years ago, he'd been an idiot teenager whose biggest worry was which party to go to or which beach to visit. He'd grown up in Harlow, but LA, with its endless opportunities, had been perfect for him. He'd had plans to live out his dreams of being a craftsman in a big city. He'd wanted a big and glossy showroom and his work to fill the homes of anybody who was anybody.

All that had changed the day he'd met Emilia.

He turned his back and worked on storming away, a dull ache taking up space in his chest. "I'm sure Emilia will recover just fine."

And probably better than he had.

"Oh my!" Ally's words crossed the store, and she soon chased close behind, like a small dog nipping at his heels. "You like her, dontcha?"

He stopped in his tracks but didn't turn. "Get back to work."

A high-pitched giggle cut through the air. "I knew it. I *knew* it. If you play your cards right… Oh. Oh no. But what about—"

He spun around and started marching toward her, angry heat engulfing his torso. Ally's expression fell, eyes wide, her abrupt silence making it clear she didn't want to finish her sentence.

"You said something to Emilia, didn't you?"

Ally held up both hands, professing innocence. But it wasn't enough to reassure him. "This isn't one of your schoolyard games, Ally. What did you say?"

"I didn't say anything. It's all fine, only…" She took two steps back and used the counter as a barrier between them.

He growled, aware he was a jerk for scaring her but needing to know what kind of damage she'd done. "Only?"

"You won't get angrier than you already are, will you?" She looked down and fidgeted with her papers.

"I'll try not to."

She nodded, though her face lost all color. "After you stormed off last night, we were all wondering what your problem was. I figured… Well… I might have mentioned Sarah."

He slammed an open palm onto the glass countertop, and an electrified jolt tore through his arm while the whole counter shook. Ally startled, and again, guilt twisted at his gut.

He'd scared her. He hated himself for that. Regretted his reaction immediately. But goddammit, did she always have to leave a trail of destruction in her wake?

He leaned forward, digging his fingers into the counter, so he had somewhere to release the strain that was eating at him. "Tell me exactly what you said."

He waited as her gaze darted around the room, and she bit her lower lip, stalling for time. She didn't know a thing about the complexities of his situation with Sarah, and his not-so-trusty shop assistant here would one-hundred percent say something that would get someone hurt.

Sarah deserved more than being the focus of local gossip, especially when that gossip occurred within the walls of the very establishment her family owned. Maynard's Tavern.

"I didn't say much." Ally shifted in her spot, her voice small. "Just that you were acting weird, and maybe Sarah was the reason. At first, Emilia asked for more information, but I made an excuse about needing to use the bathroom, and she seemed to get the hint after that. I mean, you're my boss and all, and I figured I should probably watch what I say, right?"

She gave a weak smile, which dropped as quickly as it appeared.

The tension he only now noticed in his shoulders slipped, and he lowered his chin, zeroing in on what she'd just said. "Emilia asked about Sarah?"

Ally pressed her hand over her heart, the strain on her face all but gone, like she'd pick up on his shift in mood. "Yes, but I didn't say much. I swear."

He nodded and tapped his knuckle to the counter again to distract from her seeing any sign of his satisfaction, before he doubled back toward his workshop.

"What did I do?" Ally called out behind him. "Blaine, what just happened?"

He gave her no answer, his mind tangling with the possibility that Harlow's newest resident wasn't above a little jealousy. Then there was the war of emotions clashing within him. Not only that, Emilia knew at least something of Sarah. In no time at all, she'd know even more. That's how Harlow worked. If anyone was going to tell Emilia about Sarah, then he wanted that person to be him.

Whichever way he looked at this, something had to change, and he had decisions to make, conversations to have, confessions to give. With Sarah. Maybe Emilia too. And he would have to do all of this sooner rather than later.

Six

EMILIA HELD a hand above her brow and squinted against the sun above the expansive nursery yard ahead. A ten-foot wire fence edged the perimeter, while a small cottage-type building stood to one side. The rest of the lot sprawled with seemingly endless rows of potted plants and trees. Maureen's directions to Aggie's Nursery had been spot-on.

"Well, hello, Miss." A woman who looked to be in her eighties trudged over, waving her wrinkled hand, her clothes consisting of loose, beige slacks and a gray-knitted sweater. Her hair was a long, white braid that tumbled over one shoulder. "You look like a woman on a mission."

"Oh, I am." Emilia smiled and shuffled a little closer, her gaze catching on the small pieces of dried straw mulch tangled on the older woman's sweater sleeves, no doubt a hazard of working at a nursery. "I take it you're Aggie McKey?"

"You betcha, child." Aggie's giant grin grew, and she turned toward the open wire gate, gesturing for Emilia to follow. "Now, come tell me how I can help today."

"Wasps. I have lots and lots of wasps." Emilia shuddered and prayed the woman could help. She'd already had to chase three of the bright yellow beasts from her kitchen this morning. "Maureen said to come here and ask if you had any advice. Otherwise, she and Frank will have to call in pest control, which could take a while."

Aggie put her hands on her hips and scowled at the sky. "Hmm… I guess that depends. Have you found where they're coming from?"

"The ground, there's a hole just past my back veranda."

Aggie threw a knowing wink before waving over a teenager busy potting plants on the yard's farthest edge. The boy trudged over, his chin tilted so low Emilia struggled to see his face beyond a mop of strawberry blond hair.

"Get the lovely lady some wasp dust from the stock pallets, will ya?" The boy continued to stare at the ground while Aggie spoke. "I'd get it myself, but they're buried right at the bottom of the stack, and there's no chance I'll reach."

The boy failed to move, and the silence grew thick and heavy as he switched his gaze between the two women. Aggie not-so-subtly cleared her throat, startling the boy, whose eyelids flared, before he skittered away.

The remnants of the boy's odd delayed reaction lingered in the air, and Aggie narrowed her blue-green eyes at Emilia, inspecting her anew. "Oh, I get it now. You're the new girl who's taken on Maureen and Frank's old place."

Something about the way she said it, as a fact rather than a question, left an uncomfortable heat burning through Emilia's cheeks. "I arrived earlier this week."

"Yes. Everyone's talkin' about some new thing just moved in from LA. The way that kid's been talking, you'd think Marilyn Monroe herself had been reborn and taken up residence in our little old town. If memory serves me right, your name's Emilia, ya?"

"Talking?" Emilia glanced over her shoulder and locked gazes with the boy. He averted his focus elsewhere, quickly dashing behind a metal shelf. She couldn't imagine that kid talking, much less prattling, so she turned back to Aggie. "I don't understand."

Aggie rolled her eyes. "You wouldn't. Beauty and youth are wasted on the young. Now, lemme just scoot right past and you follow me, okay?"

Emilia frowned, uncertain where they were headed since they were meant to be waiting for wasp dust. Despite Aggie's shrunken frame, the old woman moved quickly, and Emilia had to hurry to keep up.

"Ya know, I've been in Harlow my whole life." Aggie's papery hand moved to a stack of wire shopping baskets before she pulled one from the very top. "I remember when Frank and Maureen's cottage belonged to someone else, long before they ever owned it. I know just what'll suit that place."

She guided them down a tree-lined row, grabbing a red potted flower on her way through and placing it into the basket. It was the kind of flower often found in window boxes, though Emilia had no idea what the flower was called.

"So, what brings a city slicker like you to Harlow?" Aggie stopped and gave her a full stare.

Emilia shrugged. "I guess I just wanted a fresh start."

Aggie gave a slow and knowing nod as though she heard far more in Emilia's few words than what she'd actually spoken.

"City life got difficult for you?" She narrowed her eyes, and Emilia's heart beat faster for it. This woman and her unabashed stare seemed to look close enough to guess the small details that had forced Emilia's exit. Then Aggie's face relaxed, and the feeling of being interrogated faded. "It's fine. You don't need to worry about me. There's always a story of why a person drops everything for a place like this. You wouldn't be the first."

Emilia's gaze trekked over to the red brick building attached to the nursery, where a large ginger cat sunned itself on the inside of a window. Her mind slowed at the cozy image, falling back to that day in her kitchen when Blaine had described Maureen and Frank as "good people," before implying she wasn't…

Well, at least Aggie seemed to like her, and she wasn't the only one. There'd been Ally and a whole bunch of people at Maynard's, though it was weird that so many could be so trusting of a stranger. Meanwhile, she tied herself in knots second-guessing everyone and everything, including and especially her own family.

Aggie's ocean-blue eyes softened, and she patted Emilia's arm. "I hope Harlow has what you're looking for, dear."

Once again, she got the sense this woman saw into her soul. Still, she settled on expressing no more than a simple, "Thank you."

Aggie's eyes lit up, and her papery skin crinkled with her smile. "Hey, ya know we've got a boy in town who lived in LA for a while. Maybe you know him?"

Emilia released a shaky laugh, following as Aggie recommenced walking. "I've been here for a week. I doubt it."

Aggie tilted her head to one side and gave another narrow-eyed I'm-rummaging-through-your-soul sort of gaze. "He's about your age. I figured you mightta bumped into him in the big city back when he lived there some ten years ago. His family has a long history in these parts, and his dad used to run round this very nursery hangin' off my trees and ripping out branches. His rascal boy did the same before they all moved West."

Emilia's stomach churned, but she played dumb, nonetheless, staring off into space and scrunching her face as if to think. "Amazing how time flies, isn't it?"

Aggie laughed, then threw a few seed packets into the basket. "Darn right. His name's Blaine. Sure ya don't know him?"

Emilia shivered at his name and wished Aggie would just let up already. Then again, without stubbornness, Emilia might never have made it out of LA, so maybe she could appreciate the attribute.

Still, the silence dragged out long enough that Aggie swatted the air. "Ah, never mind. Los Angeles is a big city, and he came back to us here in Harlow so long ago. It doesn't matter much anymore, now does it?"

Judging by her own turbulent emotions and Blaine's storming off last night, Emilia doubted his leaving LA "didn't matter" to him anymore. Not that she was about to admit anything to that effect to Aggie.

Aggie brushed remnants of soil from her hands, a hint of sorrow weighing on her expression. "I doubt many round here remember, but he returned to Harlow a different young man. Young men and broken hearts, dontcha know? Took some time to get himself back together." She released a soft sigh and nodded down to the basket. "Anyhoo, how's about we take this lot to the table on my front veranda, and I can bag this all up for you there."

She forced an unaffected smile and allowed Aggie to lead the way, all while trying to forget what being forced out of LA must have done to Blaine. Not that trying to forget had ever worked for her. She'd known all too well he'd wanted a big life in the big city, and because of her, he'd lost that dream.

She got to the veranda table and laughed down at the basket filled with garden things, eager to return to the blissful isolation of home. "You know, I only came here for wasp dust, and I don't know the first thing about gardening. I'll probably just end up killing all these plants."

"Now dear, that's where I come in. You have any questions, you just call, okay?" A light chuckle broke from Aggie's lips, and she tapped a finger to the side of her forehead. "And trust me, I'm doing you a favor. Before you know it, you'll find yourself a little too idle in that cottage alone, and that's when people round these parts get in trouble. The way I see it, the best way to get through tough times is to have something or someone else to look after. You can't go wrong with a few plants here and there."

Emilia gave Aggie a side stare, suspicious of what she meant since they hadn't exactly discussed Emilia's "tough times."

Perhaps her troubles were written all over her, and this woman had been around long enough to spot a person's hardships. Though what kind of "trouble" Aggie anticipated Emilia could get into, while living alone in a tiny cottage, was anyone's guess.

But just like a bumbling dolt, Emilia opened her mouth and answered her own question. "You know, I think I might have met Blaine. Would he be the man Frank has working on my kitchen?"

"You betcha, that's him." Aggie gave a quick smile, pushing a plant into a small plastic carry bag, the wasp dust left waiting on the table. "Now, all this is kinda spendy, so I won't charge you for the plants. Just the seeds and the dust. Call it a housewarming gift."

"Wow. Thank you." And because Emilia *was* a bumbling dolt incapable of letting things go, she spoke again, "Ally mentioned a woman named Sarah. Sounds like Blaine doesn't have a broken heart anymore."

She offered a hopeful smile and tried hard not to groan at the lengths she'd cross to cover her guilt. Maybe he wasn't brokenhearted anymore, but he sure was still pissed at her. And despite his unmissable irritation, she didn't want him to be anything other than happy.

Aggie shot forward a pointed stare, one that reached down her face, holding her lips pursed and capturing the silence a fraction too long, like maybe she saw through Emilia's charade. "It's common knowledge that Sarah is Blaine's fiancée. Other than that, it's not my place to talk on other people's private business."

The older woman snapped an arm out, extending the shopping bag with plants, seeds, and wasp dust inside. "But if I had to say anything, it'd be to remember my warning about not getting into trouble."

Seven

A ROLLING DARKNESS took over outside as Emilia retired to her bedroom, still missing a bed. On a positive note, a second-hand fridge had been delivered, thanks to Ally, and furniture would be snuck into the cottage tomorrow at a time Blaine was scheduled to be out of the shop.

Emilia's entire afternoon had been tied up with cleaning and cottage repairs, then she'd ventured to her front yard to put the plants Aggie had given her into the ground. To be honest, she didn't hold much hope for their survival, but Aggie had been right about her needing more to fill her time. Her current funds would run out, eventually. She'd need to find a job, but for now plants would do.

Her feet ached from the day's work, so she lowered herself to the floor with a groan and lay down on the minimal softness of her solitary blanket.

Oh, how the rich have fallen.

She chuckled to herself, still struggling to think of herself as wealthy since she'd grown up far from it. Her dad's choices over the years might have been hard to understand, but there'd been no doubt he'd beaten the odds. He'd risen above the limitations of a dirt-poor migrant and built an empire. And while he'd exceeded in providing for her materially, in other areas… Well, all she could say was that money hadn't kept her safe, loved, or happy.

Maybe their rundown home with no heating or cooling wasn't so bad after all. Nor the carefully portioned meals or clothing worn until too thin to function. Because sure as anything, money hadn't made life any simpler.

How ironic that she lay alone now, so little to her name, her current circumstance originating from her father's insistence he knew best. She stretched out and grabbed the cell phone on the floor beside her, the one she'd bought after throwing her old phone away so no one would easily track her through it.

She dialed her father's number, hoping by now he'd had enough time to cool off.

"Hello, Vittorio Bonacci."

Her stomach churned at the husky fatigue in his voice. "Dad?"

"Emilia?" His tone lifted with a hint of concern, but overall, he held his usual stubborn rigidity. "Say something."

"Dad, I…" She paused, about to apologize for all the upheaval, only to realize she'd done nothing wrong. "I wanted to let you know I'm okay."

Dads were supposed to care if their runaway children were okay, right? Only, her dad's expression of concern had been to coerce her into marrying Anthony, so maybe she could be excused for not being so sure.

What a predicament. She'd never changed her last name to Stucco because she'd never felt like part of that family, but could she say her feelings on being a Bonacci were in any way different?

Her dad let out a sigh; whether relief or exasperation, she couldn't tell. "Well, at least there's that."

She blew out a breath. While he could have been happier to hear from her, at least he wasn't yelling. And if it weren't for their history together—her mother's death, and the undeniable toll it had extracted from them both—she probably wouldn't have understood his lack of compassion when it came to relationships and love. She probably wouldn't have called him now. Because as much as she'd worked to shut this man out, the little girl in her still pined for her daddy.

A long silence stretched, and it was her dad who spoke first.

"I got your fax. I'm taking care of everything, Em." His tone dropped, like maybe these last days allowed resignation to settle in, his plans for her life in tatters. Well, one look at Blaine shone a spotlight on her tattered plans too, so maybe now she and her dad were somewhere close to even.

"Things are a big mess right now, aren't they?" She swallowed at the hitch in her voice, hoping her father didn't hear.

A loud sigh crossed through the phone, but he didn't reply for the longest time. Personal affairs aside, she'd done the right thing by Bonacci Jewelry. If she'd kept her mouth shut, Anthony would have bankrupted the entire company. Hundreds of employees would have lost their jobs.

She sat up and, like a child, hugged her knees to her chest. Even with all her reasons for leaving, a lifetime in an old-fashioned Italian community still messed with her head.

Any little girl in that environment learned there was no place in the world for women who left their husbands. Fraud. Adultery. Any kind of abuse… these were not reasons for divorce. There was *no* reason for divorce. Through love *and* hate, Italian families stuck together. What she'd done was less forgivable than murder.

"Em, I can see why you felt the need to do what you did. Anthony was always hot-headed, and I thought marriage would settle him down. But the other Stuccos are understanding people. If you're ready to come home, we might be able to salvage this."

She scowled at the apricot wall ahead of her, surprised and not surprised. This argument was not a new one. Her dad still held the same archaic attitudes he'd been raised with, but a piece of her somehow always hoped he'd put her ahead of tradition.

"Salvage what exactly, Dad?"

"Salvage our family honor."

She sat taller, rubbing the flat of her palm over her forehead. "Our honor? Did you see *everything* I sent you? Not just the fraud stuff, but the—"

Her dad cleared his throat. "I know what you sent me. This isn't just about our honor, Em, but the Stuccos too. Without them, there would be no Bonacci Jewelry. You know it. I know it. We owe them. So while I've reported Anthony to the police because I have a legal obligation to our investors, I expect you to return from whatever spa retreat you're sulking in. Once the legalities settle, we'll sort things out between you and Anthony."

She pulled her hand from her forehead and clenched it into a tight fist, her next words spoken through gritted teeth. "I've repaid your debt to the Stuccos a million times over, Dad. They got ten years of my life." Her eyes began to sting, but she refused to cry. Being in Harlow. Seeing Blaine. Hearing from Aggie that he was engaged. Emilia's family had taken so much more than just years. "I'm not coming back."

"Em, we've talked about this. Your marriage is much bigger than just you and Anthony. *Listen* to me." Her father's emphasis on the word "listen" had a slight bend to it and sounded like pleading, but she knew her dad well enough to know that Vittorio Bonacci never pleaded. "He can't work for us ever again, I know that. His access to the family fund will be cut off, but he'll never pull a stunt like this again. We'll make him play nice. We'll give him no choice. You won't be the first couple to figure something like this out. Don't you understand? Emilia, this time you will hold all the power. In time, everyone else will forget that you left and anything ever happened."

Her body drew tight, and she squeezed her eyes against the pain radiating through her head. Her dad didn't get it. She didn't want power. She didn't want to figure things out. She just wanted freedom. A chance to live without a bunch of men dictating her every move. No husband. No riches. No gossipy community.

"Dad." She sucked in a gulp of air, her breath shaking as she tried hard to keep her tone even. "What about *my* honor? You know everything now. You know what he did. The money. The cheating. What honor is there for *me* in going back?"

"Em, you're being melodramatic." Her dad's words were short and stabbing. "Not every marriage has to be perfect."

Yes, because in her culture, only physical death was an acceptable excuse to exit a marriage. But she'd been emotionally dead in her marriage for years. Didn't that count? Or would she have found more "honor" in waiting until that emotional death led to her actual death?

She pulled her hand away from her face and gazed at the half-healed bruises on her knuckles, a distinct sickness overrunning her tummy at how those bruises had occurred.

There'd been one thing to push her from her gilded cage. Anthony's broken promise. His final mistake in a lifetime of misdeeds. She couldn't tell her dad what had happened. They simply didn't have that sort of relationship. Chances were, he wouldn't understand, anyway. That fact alone made her want to strike out at him just as she had her husband.

"You're right, Dad. Not every marriage has to be perfect." Her voice came out much smaller than she intended. "But yours and Mamma's came pretty close."

And as jaded as I should be, a piece of me wants that too.

Yet another thing she couldn't say to her father.

"Emilia." Her father's voice matched hers in volume, like any mention of her mother winded him. "Don't talk about her. Please."

"You loved her. She loved you too." A mass of tension took up space inside her chest and made breathing harder.

"Real love…" Her dad paused, almost as if he didn't want to finish speaking. "It's… Sometimes it's easier not to have."

Silence grew between them, providing room for the reminder that her father hadn't always been so heartless, nor had he cared so much about appearances. Only since her mother's death. Perhaps her dad figured a marriage of convenience would spare her a different kind of heartbreak. The kind he'd already experienced.

How wrong he'd been.

"I guess you succeeded, then." Her shoulders rounded, and her posture sagged with the admission. "Anthony never once told me he loved me. In fact, I'm certain he never did."

And now she mourned the years trapped in her loveless marriage, while other young women had the freedom to go out and date or attempt relationships that might turn into genuine love… like the relationship she'd had and lost.

A deep pain swelled within her heart, and she shook her head, trying to move the conversation forward without having to stop to think about what that pain meant. "Anyway, the money Anthony stole, do you think we'll get any of it back?"

"I'm not sure yet." Her father let out another heavy sigh. "It was good that you informed me before Anthony. The police were able to freeze his accounts, and he won't be touching any of what's left."

She cringed, imagining Anthony's reaction, glad she was miles away while all this played out.

What made Anthony's theft so hard to believe, was that the Stuccos weren't exactly poor. Sure, the Stuccos had money, and maybe the Bonaccis had accumulated more, but Anthony was still the oldest male child set to inherit the bulk of his family's fortune. Then again, Anthony was one of those people where too much was never enough.

She lifted her chin and tried not to release a maniacal laugh. So much of this story was downright outlandish. "I take it since I sent those documents to you in the morning, Anthony was arrested at the office?"

"About that—" Her father's tone drew out slow and strained. "We stopped the remaining money from being moved, but Anthony was gone by the time police went looking for him. No one knows where he is."

Her body went numb, and her chest stung from her lack of breathing. "I... I don't understand. Did he get away? How did he get away?"

She began to shake, and she struggled to hold on to her phone.

"The police have footage of him entering and leaving your apartment building before they got to him. Maybe he went in to check on you and decided to run when he figured out you'd left. The detectives say he's likely too busy saving his skin to cause anyone any problems."

She let out a sudden and loud laugh, her mind on the edge of cracking. Her father might have described Anthony as a "hothead", but he hadn't seen firsthand how true that description could be.

Anthony *hated* losing. Even with small things, like if she distracted attention away from him at a party, or if she didn't measure up to his standards in behavior or looks. There was no telling what he would do now that she'd monumentally unraveled his life. Though one thing was certain. He wouldn't just let this go. And he *would* be looking for her.

"Em, I have to go." Her father's voice cut through her silent despair. "Think about what I proposed. Anthony will eventually calm down and show up. When he does, I will talk to him. We will fix this. Just try to understand what you're letting go of here."

She buried her face in the palm of her hand, fighting an urge to growl, or scream, or even just argue back. Arguing had never gotten her anywhere, but maybe rebellion would.

She'd called to reconnect with her father, to maybe salvage something of her life back home. But clearly, none of that would happen. Just as she'd feared, she was as alone as ever; though so far, her solitude in Harlow did her far more good than all the company that had surrounded her in LA.

"Goodbye, Dad." She took a deep breath, one that shook on the exhale, and ended the call.

Her father hadn't offered any kind of support or protection. Not that she'd expected he would; otherwise, she wouldn't be hiding in Harlow. Perhaps it was time to let go of this relationship too.

She slumped back and lay on the floor, blinking away tears and swallowing the thick tension clogging her throat. Somewhere out there, Anthony roamed free while she couldn't. Not really, anyway. All she could do was lie in her unfurnished bedroom, hoping that the law would catch him before he got to her.

And what if he does find me first?

No one would be around to hear her screams, not here alone in this cottage, and anyone associated with her would be at risk.

Dark spots flashed before her eyes, and her throat turned dry and scratchy. He would want his revenge. He would go for broke. Only her pain and subservience would do. Maybe even her life.

More than ever, her life revolved around looking over her shoulder and waiting for an end to her brief freedom. What stupidity had made her think she could escape?

She did have one choice though. A choice on how she would spend her potential last days. She could pass her time just as she had in LA, living in fear and trying to stay alive... Or she could take hold of these first and last gasps of freedom and run with what she'd started.

Eight

From: Emilia Bonacci
  To: Emilia Bonacci
  Subject: What next?

I know it's been months since I wrote, I've been busy with school stuff, and work, and seeing Blaine every single chance I get. Until this week, things have been great, and I'm writing again because I need to get out how I'm feeling. More than that, I just want to know everything will be okay.

My father wants me to stop seeing Blaine. Dad came home from work about a week ago really angry. He'd somehow heard Blaine and I were dating, and he really lost his cool when I told him we'd been seeing each other for five months now. And I get it, I do. Maybe I should have said something earlier, and my dad feels like I wasn't being honest—that I was hiding things from him. And honestly, it's true, I was and I did.

. . .

I don't really know why I did that. I guess on some level, I knew he wouldn't be happy about the news. Seriously though, he's never happy about anything, ever. Or at least over these last few years. What with everything that happened with Mom, I understand why he is the way he is. But I'm still here, and I still need him. I want him to just be happy that I'm happy. Is that too much to ask?

Anyway, him being happy was NOT what happened. He was really pissed and insisted that if I'm keeping secrets, there must be something bad about Blaine. Dad said he knew who Blaine was, he wasn't part of our community, and didn't belong. Somehow my dad got it in his head that Blaine's only interested in my money. I really didn't think all that money and reputation stuff mattered to Dad. Apparently, it does. Like, a lot.

I tried to explain that Blaine's never asked me for a single thing, that he uses what little money he makes from his apprenticeship to pay when we go out. Honestly, it's so sweet that he insists, even though my allowance more than covers the cost of our dates. Anyway, my dad didn't want to hear any of that, and he demanded I end it with Blaine.

God, just hearing those words, having to entertain that stupid demand broke my heart, and I ran out of the house pretty quick. My dad didn't stop calling my phone the whole time I was gone, but I switched it off and ran to Blaine's house. I was so upset, he drove me to the quiet cliffs not far from his house, and we talked and talked until I started to feel better. It was beautiful. The cliffs and the ocean stretching out made me feel like there's this big world out there, and maybe Blaine and I will find a place away from all the silly rules my dad wants me to live by. Somewhere we can be together.

. . .

And it wasn't just the cliffs, it was spending time with Blaine, knowing I wasn't alone, that he doesn't want to lose me, either. He's always gone out of his way to protect me and be there for me, even when he hasn't had to. I felt so loved and needed. I haven't had that in so long. He's just everything that's good in my word. The best thing in my life, you know?

We were sitting in his car on that clifftop, no one else around, when the sky got dark, and we started kissing. Things just kind of happened. We were careful, but things happened. I don't regret that Blaine was my first, not one bit. Nothing anyone says or does now can change what we shared. I love him, and I want him to be my only. I really do, more than anything I've ever wanted, besides getting my mom back. And Blaine and I made a promise that we'll make this work, so because of that promise, I went on a mission to find out how Dad learned about me dating Blaine.

At first, I thought someone at the store must have betrayed me, trying to score professional points by telling my dad that Blaine was picking me up sometimes. I asked all the ladies at the store, only for Rosa to tell me that Anthony had come in looking for me some weeks ago, claiming I was meant to be meeting him for a date. Except, I'd already left with Blaine.

Honestly, what is Anthony's deal? Truth is, he sent me a text a while back asking me to go out with him after my shift. I didn't even respond. I don't know how much more obvious I can make it that I'm not interested. Who even takes no reply as a "yes" and turns up anyway? The fact I'd already left means he must have arrived late to "pick me up." What a Prince Charming, right? Kind of hilarious and infuriating all in one.

Anyway, I'm not talking to Anthony now, but I found out through friends that he saw Blaine and me sitting in the mall's parking lot talking. He recognized Blaine from his school basketball team. Apparently, they'd played against each other years ago. So, it's obvious Anthony is the one who ratted me out to my dad.

I'm glad I wrote this email. It's given me a bit more hope. I'll get my dad to see that Blaine and I should be together. Or I'll run away. Or something. But I won't be without Blaine. I just won't.

———————

The time had just passed midday when Blaine stopped his truck behind the beat-up Pinto in Emilia's driveway. His afternoon job had been rescheduled, so he'd come here, and now scowled at the vehicle's faded red paint, the rust-mobile not at all fitting with the cashed-up woman he'd known her to be. Yet another thing that simply didn't fit with her reemergence.

A moment passed before he jumped from his vehicle and onto the dry beige path below. A few yards away, Oak Tree Furniture's large delivery truck lingered with its back doors wide open. He'd watched the thing *whoosh* past him on his way over. Something dubious was afoot.

He grabbed his toolbox and marched past the truck, peering inside at a few of his pieces not yet unloaded. *Ally.* This had to be Ally's work. He needed to hurry inside before Wayne and Jacob came out to ruin his ambush.

He headed toward the back of the cottage, stopping to glance through an open window at the side. The boys had a boxed-up bed frame balanced on a lifter trolley. Wayne pushed while Jacob guided him. They maneuvered the trolley down Emilia's narrow corridor, disappearing out of earshot before the woman herself stepped into view.

Blaine ducked away and continued toward the back of her house, trying but failing to remove the new image of her in a snug white t-shirt and burnt-orange pleated shorts.

He stopped at her back door, the hardwood inner door open, while the mesh screen remained closed due to the spring at the top. No doubt if he tugged on the handle, the thing would come open, but he chose to wait. Despite living in a close-knit community, unlike some in this town, he drew the line at letting himself into other people's homes.

Laughter and footsteps echoed down her hall. He rolled his shoulders back and raised a brow, awaiting his big reveal. Emilia came out in front of the boys, a wide smile dimpling her cheeks as she peered over her shoulder at Wayne. She turned her head and her gaze caught his, a petrified scream breaking from her lips.

He swore under his breath and dropped his toolbox to the ground. He'd aimed for surprise, not sheer terror. Now she stumbled back, her balance faltering as she slammed into Wayne behind her.

"Oh, God." Her voice wobbled, even as Wayne hoisted her back to surer footing. She pressed the flat of her palm to her chest, hunching over through panted breaths. "For a second there I thought—"

Tension clamped at her jaw, and she didn't finish the sentence, her expression drawing into a frown.

He glared at her through narrowed eyes, forcing his attention to stay far from her bruised hand.

For a second there, she'd thought... *What?*

He had every intention of piecing together all the bits about this woman that didn't make sense, but for now, he settled on leaning down and picking up his toolbox. "You know, you don't have to sneak around to buy furniture from my shop."

She padded over and opened the screen door for him, chest still heaving under a slew of heavy breaths. "I thought it'd be easier if I stayed out of your way."

Once again, he forced his gaze higher, but for a whole other reason. He lowered his toolbox to her ancient counter and stepped out of Wayne and Jacob's way, their hands cupped over their mouths in a clear attempt to hold back laughter. "That's a noble plan, but you didn't think I'd recognize my own stuff sitting here in your house?"

The boys disappeared outside, leaving him alone with Emilia while she switched her gaze from side to side like she tried to locate an answer to his question. This time, he was the one restraining a laugh, though unlike Wayne and Jacob, his prior negative experiences with this woman bolstered his attempt.

She let out a sigh and leaned against the far wall, probably because her table and chairs hadn't been wheeled in yet, so sitting wasn't an option. "Honestly, you've been so short with me, I only thought about how to get the furniture here without having to talk to you."

She lifted her hands in a resigned gesture, only for silence to take over.

He hadn't shown her much warmth during that first meeting, and then he'd stormed off at Maynard's. Given his general frostiness, he understood her reticence now, but understanding didn't stop the burning in his stomach. That hot and familiar sense of rejection.

She huffed out a breath, one strong enough to push a loose curl winding down the side of her face. "Look, I'm sorry about the covert shopping, okay? Wasn't someone supposed to tell me you'd be turning up today?"

"Frank and Maureen own this house, and they're paying for my services." He turned his back to her, getting his tools out so he could hurry up and finish this last job for the day. "They knew, so take it up with them."

Wayne and Jacob came back in wheeling Emilia's new mattress. She followed them down the hall, allowing him to get on with smashing out the overhead cupboards; where he found relief in the long minutes lacking in unease, coupled with the exertion of swinging a sledgehammer. If he were lucky, he'd get through today without having to speak another word to her.

Though it took the boys some time to assemble the bed frame and set up the mattress, the time alone wasn't nearly long enough before the trio's voices traveled down the corridor, and everyone returned to the kitchen. Once again Wayne and Jacob ventured off to the truck, and Emilia stayed in the kitchen somewhere behind him. Maybe it was all in his head, but he could feel her eyes burning into his back.

"Blaine?"

He wrenched a loose cupboard door off with his gloved hands and contemplated not answering. But all too soon, the sound of her speaking his name worked its magic ability to pull him back to her every time.

He spun around quickly, hoping the speed in his movement would portray some kind of annoyance, even though despite all expectations, he wasn't so annoyed at having to talk to her again. "Yep, what is it?"

Her chin was lowered, her sweet brown stare upturned and focused on him, churning his stomach anew. "I know seeing me at Maynard's upset you. I can see how my presence would stir unwanted feelings. I guess I'm just saying I don't want things to stay weird between us."

His jaw clutched of its own volition, the absurdity of her request taking instant effect. He'd spent ten years wondering what had happened to her. Of course, it was weird seeing her again.

"Why are you here?" The question fell from his lips more abruptly than intended.

He swore her hands began to shake a little before she crossed her arms over her chest and tucked her hands under her armpits. "I'd rather not say."

Right. Well if her goal had been to avoid things being awkward, she'd just shot a big fucking hole through that idea. He shook his head and turned back to his work.

He hadn't expected to ask about her reason for being in town so soon, much less at all. He didn't want to give the impression he cared, but he'd be lying if he said her safety didn't concern him. She lived alone in this house. And then there was the safety of Harlow as a whole. Bad things tended to follow Emilia, and the bruises on her knuckles hinted that was still true.

The boys returned from the truck, Jacob pushing a teal couch on the trolley while Wayne followed lugging a small, four-seater table in his arms. Blaine would have a talk with him about better protecting his back, but for now, he was just hopeful Emilia might go away again.

Except, she didn't go anywhere.

She just pointed Jacob down the hall and told him to put the couch anywhere in the living room to the left, then turned back to Blaine. "I didn't know you lived in this town, otherwise I would have chosen anywhere else in America. Trust me."

Her unrepentant and hissed remark crossed the space, all while Wayne positioned the table in the background. Blaine picked up his hammer, unwilling to engage in this conversation, much less in front of his employee, even if she had attempted to lower her voice. The sooner he got this job done, the better.

"Blaine?"

God, what did she want now?

His life was complicated enough. No doubt hers was too. Why couldn't she just leave this alone?

"Blaine?"

Her voice rang out. Taut. Insistent. Like she wouldn't let him get on with his work until he talked to her.

Fine.

He turned, acknowledging her. "I wasn't upset with you at Maynard's, okay? Not everything is about you."

Those were two big fucking lies, but he would give her nothing more. He glanced over to Wayne, his not-so-subtle or truthful warning for why he shut her out. She followed his line of sight before her dark gaze widened in seeming remembrance of her need to hide any history with him.

"Fine." She marched toward him and grabbed his hand, tugging him forward.

If not for pure shock, he would have locked his knees and planted his feet. He would have refused to move. But his hurried steps swept him wherever she guided, his pulse thundering, while her soft, slender palm burned against the roughness of his.

He peered down at her pale pink nails, a wall of heat blooming in his chest right about where his heart would have been. Their first physical contact in ten years and nothing about his reaction made any sense.

By the time he looked up, they were halfway across her house and in her tiny bathroom. She turned the lock, setting off a sharp panic within him before she whizzed past.

"What are you doing?" He stepped as far from her as he could.

She leaned with her back to the sink, her darting gaze suggesting her heavy breaths had more to do with mutually raging emotions than any exertion from racing into this room. "I don't know. I don't know what I'm doing. But we can't keep living in this town without talking."

Everything happened so fast, and if he wasn't imagining things, a whole decade-old heat still lived between them. And just like ten years ago, he towered over her, his size taking up too much space in this cramped room, which only brought them closer.

Whatever her plans were in here, he needed to get out.

"I'm sorry." Her voice came out small.

"That's the second time you've apologized today." He pinned her with an unwavering stare. "What are you sorry for this time?"

"I don't know." She gave a tight laugh but looked away. "Maybe for ruining your perfect life. Twice."

He parted his lips, about to reply, but really, he didn't know what to say to that. Had his life been perfect back then or even now?

"Look." She flicked her gaze back up to him, the beautiful depth of her eyes stalling his heart for a beat. "We're bound to keep bumping into each other, so we need to come up with a way to co-exist without things being so awkward."

He scoffed and shook his head at the ridiculousness of that idea. "We have a hell of a lot to talk about, Emilia. We could be here all night."

God, even that, the mention of being with her the entire night, deepened the thumping in his chest.

He looked her up and down, not wanting to make her feel like a piece of meat to be ogled, but not wanting her to get too comfortable around him, either. "And the not-so-funny thing about all that is, I don't want to waste another breath talking about the past with you."

Having not realized how true that statement was, his shoulders eased. The past hurt. The past also kept him from reality. The reality of what he felt here, of what he owed those close to him, and the emotions he perhaps had no place exploring. But fucking hell, he'd missed her.

Her fingers curled taut over the sink's edge, her knuckles bent and jutting. "Fine with me. I don't want to talk about the past, either. Let's just figure out what to do while I'm living in Harlow."

Whatever levity he might have had dimmed. *While?* So, her stay in Harlow might not be permanent.

Deciding to use the tight space against her, he leaned forward, hating her ability to leave him tied up on the inside when his reaction to her should have been simple. He should have hated her. Should have wanted to be anywhere but here. But now, he wasn't so sure. And given the aching need stealing at his breaths, the limited space worked against him too.

"So, what's your plan? We smile coyly at each other when we pass in the street, the only ones who know we've seen each other naked?" He schooled his face with a taunting smirk, a voice inside yelling at him to ease up. This wasn't him. He didn't want to hurt her. But another part wanted just that. "Or do we pretend we're just a couple of friendly townsfolk who barely know each other? Or maybe I should come over every week, and we can braid each other's hair…"

Her cheeks reddened along with the whites of her eyes, bringing his attention to the dark shadows underneath. Miss Bonacci wasn't getting enough sleep. *Why?*

"That's not what I meant." Her words came out a hoarse whisper before her chin tilted down, and she stared at the floor.

His regret grew in the silence. Sure, he'd been hard on her, but the horrendous truth was, they couldn't live in the same town *without* things being weird.

And unlike her, he didn't want to pretend their hellish history didn't exist.

She pushed off the counter and moved toward him. "Let's just forget this. I should let you get back to work."

A dull ache rose in his chest, the force of her impending exit hitting him with another horrendous truth. Emilia still dominated his thoughts. She still stirred his emotions. He still wanted to know her.

Or maybe I just plain want her.

Right. Which was why he stepped in her way and watched as her eyelids flared in beautiful surprise. He had no intention of letting her leave.

Nine

"No, wait. You're right." Blaine paused to swallow at the thickness coating his throat, unsure of what he wanted to say here, only that there'd been this gaping, unacknowledged hollow in his chest for the last ten years. With Emilia around, that hollow didn't seem so bad. "I'm being a jerk."

She eased back, still staring up at him, the slow release of muscles across her face hinting at hope amidst uncertainty. "Yes, you are."

A fragile smile grew on her lips, and she maintained eye contact.

Weakness ran through his body, and his own smile shuddered to life. *Damn. After all these years…*

After he'd just lectured himself about not wanting to talk to her. About hating her. He *did* want answers and *didn't* want yet another of their interactions to end in bitterness.

She jutted her chin forward as if to gesture to the world outside the bathroom. "You're amazing at what you do."

Her compliment sent a shower of tingles over his skin, the hairs along his arms rising. Right about now, Wayne and Jacob would be finished unloading furniture, which meant he'd soon be alone in this house, in this tiny room, with *her*.

"I've been a carpenter for a long time now." Added to that, he'd be a bald-faced liar if he said he wasn't a little happy that a few pieces of him would be with her in this house.

"I remember." Her shoulders finally relaxed. "I'm proud of you. You did it, Blaine."

That's right. He'd been an apprentice when they'd dated, and this was the first time she'd made a genuine and positive reference to their past.

A sincere glow lit her eyes. If she'd meant to avoid any awkward moments, she'd failed miserably. He felt like a gawky teenager standing before the most gorgeous girl at school, waiting for her to notice him. Except, she *had* noticed him!

He dipped his chin and rubbed the back of his neck, not sure where to go next. "So. Umm. How are you finding Harlow?"

The glow from her eyes extended to the rest of her face, and in turn, an instant warmth surrounded his heart. This was the first unabashed smile she'd worn in his presence and because of something *he'd* said. He'd missed that smile. A smile that held gratitude at his lame attempt at casual conversation.

"Actually, I love Harlow." She stood taller and shoved at her curls, exposing the sweet roundness of her face. A feature he'd always loved. "Everyone's been so helpful, and I enjoy having a place of my own. I'm hoping to get out and see more of the town."

He clenched his jaw and held back an offer to show her around. Just making easy chatter here seemed like pushing his luck. Maybe he could be completely wild and aim for eliciting a laugh. "So, has anyone offered to bring over a hotdish yet?"

Her eyelids widened, and she jerked back a little. "A what?"

He pressed a knuckle to his lips and chuckled through his explanation. "If you're lucky, it's just a casserole made with various frozen and canned vegetables. But I gotta warn you, many people around here like to add lutefisk and cream of mushroom soup into that mix."

"Oh, no." She shook her head slowly. "Lutefisk? As in, that jelly-like fish stuff that's been re-cooked a bunch of times or something?"

"Broiled or baked, that's the one." His muscles relaxed at her theatrical grimace, followed by her crack of laughter—the reaction he'd hoped for and one that encouraged him to continue the exchange. "And has anyone told you, you're supposed to refuse pretty much everything you're offered *at least* three times before accepting?"

"Seriously?" She shifted forward, a good sign of rapt attention. "I thought that was just a weird thing Italians did. How many people have I offended in the short time I've been here?"

"Probably a lot." He shrugged and then laughed when she clapped her hands over her eyes and groaned. "No. It's fine. You're a blatant out-of-towner. Most people will recover easy enough."

She lowered her hands in a slow and cautious motion, her gaze sweeping over him and stopping at his chest while a defined silence drew out. What he'd do just to crawl into her mind and get a glimpse of what she thought. Having her eyes directed his way sent a surge of electricity through his veins. If things were different, he would step closer. Wouldn't allow for any space between them.

Her attention flicked up, snagging on his. The rapid flutter of her lashes and her sudden slack expression brought strain into his body.

"Is everything okay?" The question broke free of him, lighting the knowledge of just how much he'd wanted to ask that. Just how much more lived in his seemingly simple question.

Are you okay being alone in this town?

Do you need help?

Are you safe?

Her shoulders slumped, and she tore her focus off him. "Blaine, you of all people shouldn't worry about me."

He winced at her quick dismissal, having only just gotten her to relax. "What if I want to worry about you?"

Her lips parted just a little, like he'd blindsided her. And so just to drive home his point, he did something he'd feared doing earlier. He took a step closer. Made it clear that despite his reservations, he would lower his defenses if that's what it took to break through a few of hers.

But the change in proximity made his fingers ache to reach out and touch her.

"Don't." She sucked in a shuddering breath, like the command hurt her about as much as it did him. "Please."

His thoughts flashed to what he knew about her. The violent

circumstances that had exiled him to Harlow. The years of wondering what had happened.

"It's your family again, isn't it?" His voice rose, but she didn't reply, wouldn't even look at him. "Emilia, are you in danger?"

His heart clamored, and his mind fumbled with every worst-case scenario. All while her eyes dulled with a hard edge, her skin turning ashen. "I'm fine, Blaine. Just… Everything's fine."

A terse laugh tore through his throat. She'd always been a terrible liar, and right now, that lying only made a fool of them both. What wasn't she saying? What were the consequences if she did speak up?

He prowled closer, his motivation more to do with intimidating her into talking than trying to touch her. If she didn't speak, he couldn't help. "Tell me."

Her gaze shot back, hot and hostile, though the rest of her body pressed deeper into the counter. "Leave it alone, Blaine."

"Tell me what's happened." He shifted closer, his voice a low growl, all while she squeezed her lips into a defiant line.

Well, he could do defiant too. He took his final step and closed the space, bringing his body within less than an inch of hers. She cut the silence with a sharp intake of air, warmth radiating off her body and onto his in a luxurious wave.

She felt that wave too. From him. Her shaken reaction said as much. And like him, she felt more than just warmth. She felt the charge pinging between them.

Fuck.

Even as he sought to get the information he needed to help her, he had to wrap his fingers into tight fists to keep from taking her in his arms. From lifting her onto the sink and letting nature run its course.

Hell. What was that about?

He crushed the desire as quickly as it started. This wasn't the time to get horny over some woman he hadn't seen for an entire decade.

She's not just 'some woman' though, is she?

Right. Even that admission scrubbed at him like extra coarse sandpaper over cheap pine, which made staying away from her even more critical. She needed his help without him lusting over her. He needed to find out what trouble she was in to satisfy the dumbass need to throw himself at anything posing a threat to this woman.

Shit. I really am pathetic.

Her gaze ignited from wide-eyed confusion to twisted anger, and she brought her palms to his chest, attempting and failing to push him away.

She shoved again, her delicate build working against her.

"Look around you." He held firm, even though her expression darkened further. "Who else are you going to talk to?"

"I don't want to talk." More pushing, and her words shot out in a slap of loud defense. She used her balled-up fists now to beat at his chest. "Stop. Move out of my way."

"No." He grabbed her wrists. "And being angry doesn't give you the right to hit me."

"You're the one not letting me leave." She swung her captured wrists side to side but wasn't strong enough to break free. "I said, *move.*"

"I heard you." He lifted his voice to meet hers. "First, tell me what's happened."

This time she gave no reply. Well, unless a solid kick to his shin counted as no reply. Instant pain coursed through his leg, and his eyes stung from the sharp agony. He did his best not to grunt, or swear, or double over, half-expecting to see a visible dent in his leg the moment he looked down.

With her point made, he moved back, though the sheen across her forehead might have left anyone thinking she was the one who'd been attacked. Thank goodness, he'd heard Wayne and Jacob leave some time ago. Otherwise, there'd be all kinds of strange chatter at the shop tomorrow.

Shit! He replayed what had just happened. There'd been her refusing to talk, him moving in closer, her telling him to back up, and him not complying. Then she'd snapped. Understandable, yes, but her physical lashing out was still disproportionate, and he'd never in their time together given her a reason to feel threatened.

His gaze dropped instinctively to her hand and stopped at the still-healing graze over her knuckle. His stomach sank. "Is that how that happened?"

Her attention dropped to her hand before her stare shot back up, her expression wide-eyed and motionless.

In an instant, he forgot his throbbing shin, and once more, she tucked her injured hand behind her back as if her injury were a source of shame.

Something inside him broke, a chasm opening within him like a hot knife dragging over soft butter. They'd spent years apart, and already he knew this outburst wasn't normal for her. Something had happened to sweet-natured Emilia. Something or *someone* had changed her.

Her brow crinkled at the center, and prickly energy flowed from her. "What is it with you guys and not listening to the word 'NO'?"

That sharp sensation in him collapsed, the chasm deepening, one layer of understanding after another.

Her eyes glistened, but no tears fell. All she did was sag against the sink's edge, attention falling to the ground while she shook her head.

"Emilia." He curled his hands at his side, forcing himself not to move and especially not to touch her. "I'm sorry. I'm so sorry."

She glanced up, her cheekbones bunching into a scowl. "About which part?"

God, he was so confused; somehow his brain conjured all possibilities while unable, or unwilling, to decipher all the new information flooding in.

A familiar, dull ache squeezed at his ribcage, pressure coming at him from all angles. His memories of her past. The horrible people who'd surrounded her. People who'd never stopped for a second to think about what she wanted.

They'd gone so far as to resort to violence, forcing him out, because he didn't measure up to the plans drawn up for her life. But surely this, this scared and wounded woman, wasn't what they'd wanted either.

Or was it?

He'd hoped she'd figured out a way to shake them off, but maybe she hadn't.

Guilt burrowed down into his bones. Maybe he should have done more to save her. But what? He'd been little more than a kid himself.

So, he reached up now to the thick, jagged scar at the base of his neck and offered what closeness he could. He ran his fingers over the scar, waiting until her attention found him again. "I know a little about your problems, Emilia. You don't have to do this alone."

Dark pools opened in the center of her eyes. She remembered the scar and how he'd gotten it. She wasn't the only one carrying battle wounds here.

"I keep forgetting." Her face paled, and this time, a tear did roll down her cheek. "I'm the one who should still be apologizing."

The afternoon sun shone strong through the window behind her, light catching the edges of her hair, those incandescent beams igniting a halo of deep chocolate and auburn tones. The years had refined her beauty, while remnants of her youth lived on in her soft, angelic features. Those features doomed him now as fiercely as they had ten years ago.

The gentle and compassionate Emilia he'd known was back. The one he'd loved into literal ruin. The reminder of that love hurt about as much as it made his heart sing.

He shook his head, wanting to absorb her pain. "It happened a long time ago, and you're not the one who should be apologizing."

She blinked. Another tear fell, one that she swiped at. And then a broken laugh pushed past her lips. "I can't do this."

She surged forward, brushing past him on her way to the door.

"Emilia." He spun around to follow her.

She held a hand up, signaling for him to leave her alone. "If you have to get work done here, then do it, but we really should stop hurting each other."

A sickening feeling seized him, and still, he stayed where he stood and respected her wishes. God knew, not enough people had.

He wanted to tell himself to let her go, that he could move on from her again. But none of that was true. With this single interaction, he'd handed over his power to her once more and gotten sucked back into wanting to be there for her. That truth was agonizing. And so was the truth that Emilia remained the only woman he'd never been able to escape. He knew that now more than ever.

Yes, he had work to do, but some things were more important than work. Things like maintaining his sanity and reducing the cracks forming around his heart.

Right now, the gaping silence in this bathroom was more than he could bear. It screamed for him to go. *Now*. Or completely lose his wits and the life he'd worked so hard to scrape together.

Ten

EMILIA SLAMMED the front door behind her and fled from her house. She had to get out. Had to escape Blaine and every dark memory and yearning he pried from her. Her running didn't just come from how close he'd been, either. His perceptiveness posed a huge problem too.

That man could open his mouth and say things she would never utter to another person. Unlike him, she wasn't from a small town, a place where everyone got into each other's business and asked all the personal questions. In her world, anything worth a damn went unsaid.

She raced down her veranda steps, her head bowed and the heel of her hand pressed to the hot damp of her cheek. She hadn't even cried the day she'd left Anthony. The day she'd left her entire life behind. But this… *this* she cried over.

"Hiya, hope I'm not interrupting—"

She stopped dead in her tracks, and her gaze slammed into Aggie trudging down the path, an enthused grin on her face as she waved a plastic spray bottle filled with a dark green solution in the air. "I saw you made a start on the garden and thought I'd bring—" Her smile dropped, and she lifted her wrinkled fingers to her lips. "Oh dear, are you okay?"

Emilia opened her mouth to say everything was fine. Everything would *be* fine. If she could only leave for a walk to clear her head. But the loud crash of her backdoor cut her off, the crunch of footfall over gravel soon growing louder.

Blaine marched out from the side of her house, his scowl pinned ahead and freezing her out. Aggie tried to utter a "Hiya," to him too, but he stayed on mission, barreling past, white-hot resentment etched in every hard line of his face.

Aggie shuffled closer to Emilia, her cheeks pale and head shaking. "What on earth?"

An invisible force squeezed Emilia's heart. She didn't know how to answer that question, much less want to. Poor Aggie already had one emotional person charge past her without reason, and as much as Emilia wanted to, she wouldn't be the second.

She swiped at the remnants of cold tears and gave the older woman a wobbly smile, but no matter how much she tried to conjure words, nothing came.

"Oh, child." Aggie scrambled forward and put her arms around Emilia's hunched shoulders. Meanwhile, Blaine's truck roared to life. "How about you take a seat on that lovely porch swing of yours? I'll go inside and make us some tea."

Emilia allowed Aggie to coax her toward the veranda swing while Blaine's truck sped away, leaving her momentarily alone with the strong afternoon sun and a lingering cloud of road dust ahead.

She'd woken this morning with a simple plan—get her furniture delivered and spend the afternoon alone in her garden. Now, she didn't even want to be near her house, much less in the same state as Blaine Callaghan.

A rush of memories hit her square in the gut, causing her to hunch with real-world pain. The scene in her bathroom. He'd stepped closer and brought with him that paralyzing hot rush of need. There'd been her hesitation. Her fear. What giving in to her need had cost and would cost again. The past was a crushing predictor of what could happen. Then there was the bitter memory of a time she'd been free to reach for him, to pull him into her without reservation.

I'm free, but not free.

He's not free, either.

That stupid, inane moment. Her first bit of genuine intimacy in years. Her first taste of someone's genuine concern. And that person was Blaine. That moment now sat like a branding iron pressed to her palm. As quick as she'd been to get away, the damage was done. The feel of his heat was enough to spark something in her heart.

She groaned, her reaction everything ridiculous. Anthony might have been a classically attractive guy, but their relationship had always lacked connection. Maybe because few people took well to being controlled, and that's exactly what he'd done to her, year in, year out, day after day. *But Blaine.* Holy hell. *Blaine.* He pulled emotions from her that were something else entirely. Something untamed and frightening.

She slumped forward and pitched her elbows on her knees before resting her head in her hands. She didn't want to think of what any of this meant. All she wanted was the peace she'd sought when she'd first escaped.

But the encounter replayed in her mind, over and over again.

In light of her conversation with her dad last night, she wanted to cave and let Blaine look after her. Oh, but she'd let others take the reins in her life before. That hadn't turned out well at all.

She couldn't tell him everything. Couldn't fall into the safety of his arms or allow his gentle coaxing to cloud her better judgment. Even if he was the embodiment of everything she craved but lacked in her life. One overriding thought stopped her. She'd lost him before and wouldn't cause him any damage once again. Not now that she knew what her family was capable of. Not now that she knew about Sarah.

Her chest jolted over a shuddering sob she worked hard to hold within, and she pressed her hand to the base of her throat. "Hold it together. Just let him go. You've done it before."

The whispered chant didn't help. All she could think about was how she'd spent ten years as Anthony's shadow, never really getting much of what she wanted, a husk of the woman she could have been. So much time and opportunity had gone to waste. She wanted to rage, to seek revenge, when logic now called her to focus on the boring but necessary task of surviving.

"Let him go." She commanded herself on a hard whisper, closing her eyes in search of relief. She had a chance to build some semblance of her own life. That was something. *Everything*. Right now.

"Hush, now."

She jolted at the sound of Aggie's gentle voice, then snapped her attention to her right and the woman extending a cup of steaming tea. "Tea makes everything better. Drink."

Emilia did as she was told and took her first sip, the hot liquid uncoiling a small portion of her tension. If she kept sipping, if the tea came in a bucket or a trough, maybe then her problems might disappear.

She huffed out a small laugh and lowered the cup.

"You see?" Aggie maintained her smile. "It works, doesn't it?"

Emilia returned a weak nod. "Thank you."

Aggie swatted the air and sat down on the swing beside Emilia. "*Pfft*. It's just hot water and leaves, the best placebo in the world. Now, get it off your chest, tell me what that boy's done to upset you."

Her pulse quickened, and she sat bolt upright. "Oh God, no. It's not him. Blaine and I, we—"

What to say? How much to say? She lifted the cup to her lips and frowned over the rim before sipping again. She wanted so much to keep everything to herself, but more than that, she couldn't remember the last time she'd had a real chance to talk about her problems.

Aggie took Emilia's hand and patted the back, the old woman's brows lifting with seeming concern. Emilia's shoulders sank. Maybe she'd get some relief from talking to someone who'd been alive nearly three times longer than her.

"Blaine and I knew each other. I mean, before I came to Harlow." Her voice came out ragged and weak, but Aggie's smile stayed soft and encouraging, and she nodded for Emilia to continue. "At the nursery, when you mentioned him coming to Harlow because of a girl —I'm that girl."

Aggie drew back, her fingers tightening around Emilia's hand. "Oh ya, that explains a lot."

Emilia turned her attention to the picturesque scene ahead, the green and wide landscape and the light twitter of small birds. A tranquil scene that didn't at all match the story she had to tell. A story no one outside her family knew.

"Blaine and I dated for a little over six months, back when I was seventeen and he, nineteen. My dad didn't approve. Blaine wasn't Italian, and his family didn't have money or social standing. He didn't have plans to climb any corporate ladders. As you know, he just wanted to make beautiful furniture. So like typical teenagers, despite my dad's disapproval, we kept seeing each other, anyway. But there was another man my father wanted me to consider, someone 'more appropriate,' someone whose family had done a lot for mine. Anthony."

An incredulous laugh burst from Aggie's lips. "That sounds like a fair trade, 'Help us and we'll give you our daughter.'"

Emilia laughed, too, even as the pain in her heart returned. "Well, yeah, when you put it like that, it's ridiculous, right? But the pressure's usually a lot more subtle, and life can get difficult if family obligations aren't met. You'd be surprised how common these agreements are, even if the expectations aren't stated in any obvious way."

"Oh no, that's not right. What about what you wanted?" Aggie shook her head, her gaze drifting out to the field opposite Emilia's front yard. "And Blaine. He never said much, but that boy returned to Harlow aimless and heartbroken." She turned back to Emilia, pupils wide. "He loved you, Emilia. He loved you so much."

Emilia winced against the truth in those words. No longer able to drink, she merely peered down at her cup and the umber liquid inside. "If my father hadn't interfered, we'd probably still be together."

Though she didn't look, Aggie's fingers continued to caress the back of her hand, the comfort in that touch implying support, almost like her own mother returned to her.

"It all fell apart the day I came home to find Anthony and my father plotting to send me interstate."

Eleven

"My dad didn't like my rebellion with Blaine, and Anthony didn't like anyone toying with something he assumed was his. The plan was to break Blaine and I up, send me away to distant relatives until I 'got over' Blaine, and matured a little. Then I could come back to LA and marry Anthony."

And here Emilia sat, a good decade later, overwrought and dabbing at her tears. Clearly, the whole "getting over Blaine" thing had been a spectacular fail. Her heart still wanted him, even though that was the last thing either of them needed.

"Oh no, you poor dear." Aggie's voice lifted in pitch, though it trembled with what sounded like genuine emotion. "Is that why Blaine returned here? You married someone else?"

"No. First, I ran away. The very same night I learned of their plan."

A chill ran over her body, and she shivered against the discomfort.

She must have run two miles in heavy rain to get to Blaine's house that night, and when she arrived, he'd tried to talk her out of leaving. He'd mentioned family friends who lived far away, that if she'd just give him time, maybe they could take off together and build a life there.

Oh, the irony. He'd meant for them to be together in Harlow all along.

She flicked her gaze back to Aggie and swallowed hard, the difficulty of relaying her story causing the muscles in her throat to bunch. "The hour was so late, and he wanted a day to say goodbye to his parents and his little sister, while I wanted to leave that very minute. I had no idea when my father would send me away and didn't want to risk never seeing Blaine again. So, he agreed and bundled me up into his old Jeep."

She squeezed her eyes shut, the memory overwhelming, her hand beginning to shake beneath Aggie's. "I thought we were free, that we'd hit the road and spend the rest of our lives together. But Blaine's car only rolled forward a few yards on the driveway before he was forced to brake. A flashy black sports car blocked our exit at the end of the drive, and Anthony and some gargantuan-sized friend launched out of the car toward us. Blaine got out and tried to reason with the other guy, the guy headed for my door. Only Blaine ended up getting slammed against my window, the glass exploding all over me. I had a second to register that shock before a strong hand yanked me from the Jeep."

Aggie gasped, her mouth falling open. "But how did Anthony know you'd be there?"

"My father noticed me missing, so he called Anthony, who took it upon himself to find me. It wouldn't have been hard to guess where I'd go, and he picked up some help on his way to fetch me."

"Oh no, child. I'm so sorry." Aggie patted Emilia's hand again. "You must have felt so alone."

"Maybe it would have been easier if it *had* been just me, but it wasn't." She took a deep breath, forcing new air into her lungs. Aggie's flowery perfume at least offered a token of sensory distraction. "I always was a piece of property to Anthony. And my father, in all his grief-addled stubbornness over my mom's death, confirmed he felt the same. Anthony laughed when his friend threw me into the back of his car. There'd been no love or concern in his tone when he called out, 'Be careful with her, that's my future wife.'

"He could've driven away there and then, could have been happy to leave with his prize, me. But he wasn't. He went back to Blaine, already injured and on the ground from the impact with the car window, and laid into him with a series of hard kicks to the stomach. At one point, he pulled a small pocket knife. I started to scream, I guess loud enough to penetrate the car I was in because a light came on inside Blaine's house. Anthony stopped with the assault then and bolted, but not before burying that knife into the top of Blaine's shoulder."

Aggie reeled back and released a loud hiss, as though she'd witnessed the whole bloody event herself.

There'd been Blaine's gut-wrenching scream as the knife went in, his face contorted, and his bloodied fingers clutched over his shoulder around the knife. His parents rushed out of the front door, but he'd pinned a desperate look her way, just in time for the car to pull away.

And she never saw him again.

Never learned what had happened.

Never even knew the extent of his injuries.

Until today. The scar at the very base of his neck…

Her stomach knotted now while she failed to shut down her drowning sorrow.

"Oh." Aggie sat silent for a while, her eyes glistening. "And you had to stick it out with Anthony in the end?"

Emilia nodded, remembering how she'd clawed at the car's tinted glass, her fingers also bloodied from the earlier exploding window. She'd wanted so badly to let Blaine know she saw him, that she didn't want to leave. "I tried to find out about Blaine, but no one would talk to me, not even his family. And I get it, they were scared. Just like my dad, they'd drawn a line through our relationship. Then I got sent away, and so I gave up. On everything."

There'd been no proper goodbye. Just violence and tears. Of course, she'd given up. In her mind, if she couldn't have Blaine, then what difference was Anthony? The misery of an unwanted marriage matched the misery she already felt. But even with that distraught thinking, she'd had no idea just how much bleaker life could get.

"Good grief, so you married that scumbag?" Aggie's harsh tone mirrored the abrasiveness of Emilia's thoughts.

The older woman sank back into the swing and blew out a hard breath that denoted disbelief. Emilia eyed the field ahead, too ashamed to face Aggie. "I married Anthony not long after my eighteenth birthday, and I'm still married to him. There isn't a day I don't regret it."

"Oh, honey, dontcha know?" Aggie's voice cracked. "You were so young and without any experience or help to make it on your own. Those would have been hard years for anyone."

Emilia shifted toward Aggie, determined to toughen up and meet her gaze. "You have to understand, what you saw of Blaine today. His anger… it's not his fault."

One corner of Aggie's lip quirked. "Let me guess, Blaine came here with plans to revisit the past?"

"Not exactly." Emilia smiled, Aggie's innate cheekiness contagious. "But the past seems set on revisiting us all the same."

Aggie pushed the teacup forward and jutted her chin out for Emilia to take a sip. "Judging by the way he stormed off, that boy still cares for you a great deal, Miss Emilia. I can see why. I know women twice your age who would've fallen apart at much less than what you've weathered."

Emilia brought the teacup to her lips but paused before drinking. "Once I learned he was in Harlow, I should have found a way to leave."

So why didn't I?

The brief and inane conversation about lutefisk and local manners said enough about why. Then again, nothing in that exchange had been inane. At least, not to her.

Aggie leaned forward and narrowed her eyes, as though making sure she had Emilia's full attention. "Hush now with your naysaying. The past is done, but there's a lot to do about the future. What counts is that you got spark, child, and you'll be okay. So will Blaine."

Emilia took a sip of her tea, unable to fully invest in Aggie's offer of hope. So much had gone wrong. She'd had over a decade of one thing failing after another. Sometimes it was hard to understand how her heart kept beating every day and her lungs still breathed.

"About Blaine," Aggie spoke again, her habitual smile creating multiple small brackets on either side of her mouth. "He's a good man who'd never go outta his way to hurt anyone. He's also not one to get angry about much, which leaves me thinkin' where there's anger, there's also passion. You understand what I'm sayin'? His gettin' upset speaks on his feelings for you."

Emilia opened her mouth to protest, but Aggie held up a hand, interjecting. "Now wait one minute, I'm not done, and I betcha I know what you're thinkin'. You're thinkin' the timing is all wrong, and maybe that's true, but don't let something like that be the reason you lose the love of a good man."

"But I don't think—"

"Oh, Sweet Jesus, Mary, and Joseph. Yous guys think too much." Aggie shook her head and stabbed a bony finger in Emilia's direction, her brow set to an angry glower. "Don't fool yourself into believing you got more time on this planet than you do. I've seen enough births, deaths, and marriages to know the biggest mistake anyone ever makes is to waste a chance when it's given. I never heard a couple in love say they wished they'd met later than they did, have you?" Aggie raised an eyebrow and scoffed when Emilia didn't produce an answer. "Darn tootin'! And you were lucky to leave one regret behind in LA, so don't go making another one by passing up this chance with Blaine."

Emilia's cheeks turned cold, providing the sensation that all the blood had drained clean out of her. Aggie's advice hit like a slap to the face. "But Blaine's engaged. You said so yourself."

"Geez Louise, I know what I said, and either way, yous guys got a lot to figure out amongst yourselves. And that means Sarah too. You heard what I said about love and mistakes and regrets." Aggie leaned forward and groaned as she pushed herself up.

But Emilia didn't *love* Blaine, at least not at this point in her life. She maybe cared for him… felt an attraction… But for all she knew, he was a completely different man from the one she'd known so long ago. And hearing Aggie mention the word "love" so many times filled her heart with a wrenching panic. Whoever this Sarah woman was, she loved Blaine enough to marry him, and Emilia would not get in the way of that.

"This is for you." Aggie passed Emilia the green-filled spray bottle. "It'll keep the pests off those plants I gave you, though I don't suppose plants'll be enough of a distraction now I know what you're dealing with. So, I've got something else that might keep you busy."

Emilia accepted the spray bottle but frowned at Aggie's last statement. "What do you mean?"

"I mean you're too idle here." Aggie's eyes twinkled again, which Emilia already gleaned was not a good sign. "That kid workin' for me at the nursery. He's got too much schoolwork lately and is cuttin' back his hours, so I need more help. Hows 'bout you come by tomorrow and do some work for me?"

"Oh, no. I'm—"

"You're what?" Aggie held a stern, direct focus; one that somehow still managed to contain a level of humor-filled challenge. "Unable to help an old lady with a bad back? Besides, what with settin' up this home, couldn't you do with the money? I'll even pay cash if you're worried 'bout that husband of yours."

Emilia gnawed her lower lip, holding back a desire to point out that she wasn't exactly the figure of strength and muscle Aggie probably needed. In fact, at just a few inches taller than this woman, it'd be a case of the short leading the short at the nursery. But maybe Aggie had a point. The extra cash wouldn't hurt, and it was nice of her to accommodate Emilia's need for financial secrecy.

"Good." Aggie nodded, already turning away as if she'd read Emilia's thoughts and made the decision for her. "I'll see you tomorrow afternoon, okay? And promise me you'll think 'bout all that other stuff I said too."

Twelve

ANTHONY SCOWLED at the gilded antique clock behind the black marble desk; forty-five minutes and Luciano Conti still hadn't emerged. Everyone knew Luciano never arrived anywhere late, especially not within his own damn building.

Anthony ground his teeth together and curled his fingers into tight fists over his chair's armrests, pounding at the brown leather with a satisfying thud. Thanks to Emilia, his social standing had taken a catastrophic hit.

"So, Mr. Stucco." Luciano's voice startled Anthony into ceasing his armrest beating, the mafia kingpin striding across the plush crimson carpet before plonking his plump and aging body into a chair behind the desk. "To what do I owe the pleasure?"

His gaze glided over Anthony's wrinkled clothes while a slow smirk bent the outer corners of his lips upward. The muscles at Anthony's jaw strained as did his fists. He looked like a homeless bum, and Luciano—with his classic leather shoes, crisp beige suit, and slicked black hair—looked just as polished and pristine as Los Angeles's most powerful crime boss should.

And yet again, thanks to Emilia, "homeless bum" was pretty much who Anthony had become.

"I have a business proposition." He held back an urge to bare his teeth and snarl at having to ask Luciano for help. An animalistic response, sure, but he'd spent eight days struggling to tame the wild rage within. "A proposition that will make you lots of money."

Luciano slumped way back in his chair, fingers adorned in heavy gold rings and interlocking over his rounded belly. "Of course you do, but I have a lot of money already. And from what I hear, you're broke as fuck."

"You've heard?" Anthony raised a brow, stroking Luciano's ego.

The man had eyes and ears all over LA. Of course he'd heard.

Luciano shook his head, slow, unimpressed. "You know I have, and I'd never waste my time meeting a client who can't pay. I'm only here because we have history. So, what is it you think you can get from me today?"

Luciano's flippancy. His downright disrespect. It lit a sense of searing violence that clashed within Anthony's stomach, his nails biting into his palm as he tried to subdue that clashing.

There'll be time for violence and rage. Later. I have to remember where I am.

He cleared his throat and took a second before responding, "I'm not 'broke as fuck.' My funds are tied up at the moment. That's all. With your help, there'll be plenty of money to go around."

"You know, I don't want to return to the days of throwing my clients in the river, Mr. Stucco. So maybe you understand why I don't provide services based on *if* someone can pay." Luciano leaned forward and flicked open a flat wooden case on his desk. "Your accounts are frozen, and you didn't have the foresight to hide your money in other places." He pulled a cigar from the case and pointed it at Anthony. "That was stupid."

Anthony shifted in his seat, pulling his posture up and pushing his chest out. The insult's sharp sting cut against the fact he'd spent yet another night sleeping in his car. As much as he wanted to lunge across the desk and smash Luciano's wrinkled old head into the unforgiving black marble, he again vowed to channel his fury into something else. Someone else. *Emilia.*

Luciano flicked at a silver lighter. "So, let's say your plan, whatever it is, doesn't work. You know the big bad world of business, Mr. Stucco, and you know I still have to pay my men. What would you do if you were me?"

Anthony's pulse pounded in his neck, and he watched as Luciano lit his cigar, taking short, sharp inhalations before tossing the lighter onto his desk.

Anthony's life had become a series of near misses, including his escape the day Emilia ran away. If he hadn't turned back to the apartment on his way to work, all because he'd forgotten to take a second shirt for his night out with friends, he would never have returned home in time to see the stack of papers fanned across the kitchen counter.

There'd been photos and multiple documents, and right then he'd known he had to run. *And why?* Because that stupid bitch had gotten all het up over one little fight the night before.

By the time he'd peered outside the apartment's city-facing windows, five squad cars were already weaving toward the building. He'd got outta there as fast as he could, leaving with nothing more than the shirt on his back and a few hundred dollars in his wallet.

He glared at Luciano and extended a smirk of his own, painfully aware he couldn't fuck this up. "If I were you, I'd take a calculated risk."

Luciano sputtered out a smoke-infused laugh, gray plumes circling the air above him. "The keyword is 'risk.' You think it's my problem you couldn't manage your ill-gotten funds?"

Anthony slammed an open palm on the desk and leaped out of his seat, his face hot while sweat trickled down his temples. "You've gotten soft, you fat, lazy bastard."

Luciano didn't so much as flinch, and still, Anthony needed to prove he had the balls to stand up to this asshole. "You're talking shit, Luciano, you know it. If I couldn't see both your hands right now, I'd guess you're jacking off under that ugly desk of yours since hanging shit on me is about the limit of excitement in your life these days. Am I right? You built your career on taking on risks. How many times have I hired you? How many loaded friends have I steered your way? I helped you become what you are, you dumb fuck. You owe me. You. Owe. Me."

Luciano flicked ash off his cigar and into the red crystal ashtray beside him. The lag in his movements said Anthony's outrage didn't perturb him in the least. "Stop being a shit, Anthony, and sit the fuck down while you're at it."

Anthony sat down and made a point of not breaking eye contact with Luciano. "What I have in mind is an easy job for you, and it could be your biggest pay day yet. If you turn this down, you'll be the biggest fucking limp-dick this city's ever known."

Luciano chuckled and stubbed out his cigar before narrowing his eyes at Anthony. How long had it been since someone had the balls to call this man a "limp-dick," much less a dumb fuck? Likely not since he'd been a pimply teenager with nothing more than a pastrami sandwich to fill his pockets. Most people these days found him downright terrifying.

Luciano was Anthony's creation. His connections and his money had dragged this fucker from a two-bit drug pusher to a corporate monolith. It'd be a cold day in never before Anthony let this shit stain forget that.

Luciano leaned back in his chair, and his demeanor settled. "I can't believe you couldn't control your missus. I've seen chihuahuas more vicious than her."

He laughed, but Anthony didn't join in.

Luciano soon shut up, and he eyed his cigar, twisting it between his fingers as if the action was his idea of meditation. "Fine. I want numbers. How much money are we talking 'bout?"

"You mean, you don't already know?" Anthony put forth his best smug grin, again giving Luciano a chance to showcase his knack for insider knowledge. Money had always been his weak spot.

"I hear millions." Luciano smiled like he could already see the cash piled on his desk.

Anthony nodded, reeling the man in. "Millions upon tens of millions. But only if you're down with my plan."

Luciano finally stopped eyeballing his cigar long enough to meet Anthony's gaze. "What do you need?"

"Hide me from the police and find my wife. I'll make sure she returns my money."

"That sounds like a very loose plan. Besides, what's my cut?"

"Just let me worry about the details. And your cut is ten percent."

Luciano spat out a thick and throaty laugh. "Don't be a dumb fucker. I want thirty and you take one of my men with you. You're as slimy as I am, and that means I don't trust you. So if the scheme you're hatching in that hollow head of yours doesn't work, you best believe your family will be footing the bill."

Consequences be damned, Anthony rolled his shoulders back and rose from his chair, already taking on the confidence of a new man—a man about to show his two-faced wife kind of enemy she'd created in leaving him with nothing to lose.

"Twenty-five percent and you have two weeks to find her. That's my last fucking offer."

Thirteen

EMILIA WOKE at midday to the soft tap of rain on her bedroom window and muted light spilling in through the white drapes. Once again, the house's every creak and groan messed with her sleep, and she'd failed to close her eyes until the early hours.

More than a week in Harlow, three days since the call with her dad, and still freedom hung on her like an ill-fitted dress. She kept expecting Anthony would pop out of nowhere to exact his revenge.

Compared with the new daytime distraction of working at the nursery and Aggie's quirky hot-takes on life, the quieter nights were when Emilia's racing thoughts returned and her nerves fared worse. She couldn't remember her last night of decent sleep. She pushed the bed covers away with a sigh and resigned herself to yet another day nursing a dull, sleep-deprived headache.

At least I have a bed and a day off from the nursery…

Yes, there was that. And positive thoughts felt better on the soul than the constant sense of doom that followed her, so she stood and padded toward the kitchen, her bare feet cold atop the wooden floors.

She made a cup of tea and took it to the front veranda, her pulse quickening at the new buds on the plants Aggie had given her. The rain-dappled growth brought a promise that this garden might be more than a simple side project, that maybe she could succeed where she'd always assumed she'd fail. That maybe she *would* be around to watch her flowers grow, and Blaine's appearance and Anthony's disappearance didn't have to defeat her.

Tall brown grass swayed in the light wind, emitting a gentle rustle while a blue-green glint flashed in her peripheral vision. She focused on that glint, narrowing her eyes to an object poking from her letterbox.

Who'd be sending mail so early into my move?

Dread rippled over her skin and churned her stomach as she raced over the veranda's weathered timber boards, her bare feet soon stinging on the crushed gravel path.

Before long, a glossy emerald green envelope glistened in her palm, tidy ink swirls spelling out her name, embarrassingly un-terrifying. Then again, looks could be deceiving.

She worked a finger under the seal and tore it open, raindrops chilling her bare shoulders, the cool wind adding to that chill. Star-shaped sequins fluttered in a slow spiraling dance to her feet. She laughed. Someone had put a great amount of effort into this particular creation.

Inside the envelope was a peacock blue card; she pulled it out and read:

Dearest Emilia,

You are cordially invited to the annual **Harlow Moonlight Soiree.**

This year's theme is A Midsummer Night's Dream.

Dress up. Wear your dancing shoes. And bring a plate of food to share.

Best Regards,

Aggie McKey xox

She pressed her hand to her chest and smiled, her doubt even more on the ridiculous side now. Aggie, the mischievous town matriarch, had mentioned nothing about a soiree, and the dressed-up invitation hinted that this event would be a big deal.

Emilia bit back a wide grin and ran toward the house, the gravel path once again making her regret placing mistrust over putting on shoes.

Inside her bedroom, she collected her phone and called Ally. "Did you get an invite too?"

"Oh, is this for the soiree?" Ally's voice sprung forth even brighter and more excited than usual. "Not yet, I'm at work, but Mom's probably got the invite taped to the fridge by now. What's the theme this year?"

"A Midsummer Night's Dream."

Ally unleashed a high-pitched squeal, forcing Emilia to pull the phone from her ear. "What? What is it?"

Ally sent forth a series of staggered breaths before she replied, "My idea. They finally picked my idea. Geez Louise, this is so exciting. The soiree is like the biggest event of the year. It happens every spring, and everyone in town comes along before the place gets swamped by tourists over the next two days for the town fair. It's something Blaine started five years ago to get more people into town. You know, to help local businesses. It's grown every year since."

Emilia's heart beat a little faster at the mention of Blaine's name. "Oh, really? Tourists?"

"Ya, but just at the fair. The soiree is mostly townsfolk and their guests. It's the best. Oh, can you sew? We should make costumes together."

Emilia laughed and kept Ally waiting, overrun with the memory of nights at her mother's side in their tiny kitchen, the smell of sunflower perfume enveloping her at the even tinier dining table. Her mother had taught her how to work the old sewing machine there. Back when she'd known nothing but simple comfort and a cohesive family.

She cleared her throat from the huskiness forming and answered Ally. "I can work a sewing machine with the best of them."

"Oh sh—" Ally's voice dropped to a muffled whisper. "I have to go. The boss is coming, and like usual lately, he's not too happy. I'll swing by your house around eleven tomorrow and we'll talk soiree details then."

The line went dead, so Emilia headed back outside to finish her tea.

Ally's mention of Blaine's recent prickliness mingled with Aggie's advice about moving on from the past. The soiree would be one step closer to the future Emilia wanted. Another chance to make new connections. All she needed to do was stay brave and keep showing up.

Late afternoon came, and the light rain from that morning turned into heavier sheets of water over the darkened valley outside Emilia's kitchen window. Since Blaine had stormed off *before* starting much work, she peeled potatoes at her dilapidated counter, two of her overhead cupboards a partially demolished mess.

Aside from that, her day had gone to plan, in that, there'd been no plan. No interruptions. Nowhere to go. No unforeseen dramas... *Pure heaven, really.*

The gloomy sky grew darker still and so did the light in her kitchen. She tore her gaze from her peeling knife and looked out through the window, to the misty landscape half-obscured in the torrential downpour. Since that day in Blaine's driveway, when Anthony had changed the course of her life forever, she'd developed a terrible association with rainy weather and storms.

A clap of thunder roared over the valley. She jolted, dropping her knife to the counter and pressing her hands to her ears.

Breathe woman, it's just noise and water.

Rain pinged like stray bullets against the cottage's metal roof, the ruckus providing a chance for her to work on her vow of being brave. So in a moment of daring, she made her way out the back door and onto the landing.

The icy air nipped at her nostrils, the smell of wet earth and damp hay filtering through; the once bone-dry grass was no longer dry. More lightning fired across the plain, and she jumped, this time at the almighty crack of her gutter detaching from the edge of her roof.

A large chunk of metal hit the concrete edging, the boom ear-splitting; still, one end remained attached to the roof, threatening to pull the rest of the guttering down.

Clearly, she wasn't the only one overwhelmed by rain.

Storm phobia aside, she had to act or the damage would get worse. What with her half-kitchen, the last thing she needed was to lose a section of her veranda too.

She bolted across her yard to the back garden shed, and her loose white shirt became sodden in seconds. The booming sounds continued, this time the thunder and not her gutter, and once more her nerves frazzled.

A rickety old ladder lay within the shed. She hooked it under her arm, pocketed a screwdriver, and then headed back into the pummeling rain.

Sharp chills penetrated her bones. She positioned the ladder against the roof's edge and climbed up each rung, wanting this ordeal over as quickly as possible.

She'd never been the handy type, which made twisting at screws ever more terrifying atop the feeble ladder. The whole thing wobbled if she twisted too fast, and her hands turned numb from the cold. Her shivering made dismantling the gutter about as easy as performing brain surgery with a wet piece of dental floss.

The screws were stiff in their holdings, and she grunted at the effort of loosening the three that needed to come out. Every passing second added to her shivering and the anesthetized sensation in her fingers. Anyone would have struggled, but for a girl from the sunny West Coast, the frosty conditions took her breath away.

The last screw gave, and she fought back a joyful sob, the damaged section of gutter falling to the ground. Now all she had to do was climb down seven rungs and be free from this cold nightmare. All she wanted now was a warm bath and then to go to bed.

She took the first rung. The ladder wobbled again and breathing got harder. Why couldn't she breathe? Despite the cold, she needed to stop and get her bearings. *Because* of the cold, stopping seemed like a terrible idea.

She gasped for another tight breath, her ribcage somehow way too small for the air she needed. She tried for another rung, her eyes fluttering momentarily closed.

Oh, God. I know what this is. Not now. Please, not now.

For some reason, she thought someone called her name, but she couldn't be sure. Maybe she would be lucky. Maybe that someone would help. Dizziness had well-and-truly taken over, and nothing she did seemed enough.

She made for another useless attempt to breathe. The world around her tilted and muddled. Somehow, she'd have to make it inside the house, but not right now. Right now, she just wanted to sleep.

Fourteen

BLAINE STOOD helpless as Emilia's eyes drifted closed, and she lost her grip on the ladder, her body landing on the muddy earth with a sickening thud.

He ran forward and soon huddled at her side, holding his fingers to her lips while waiting for her warm breath to hit his skin. *She was still breathing.* Next, he slid his hands under her and caught a palmful of mud as he lifted her out of the rain.

He'd come here thinking he could get some work done since he'd mostly be inside and away from the elements. There'd be a few awkward glances here and there, but for the most part, he'd ignore her and any emotions she might draw.

The last thing he expected was to arrive just in time to see her pass out.

And what the hell was she doing up a ladder in the rain, anyway?

His insides churned at her slight body sprawled across his arms, her head curved back, and her eyes shut. He nudged the back door's handle down with his elbow and stepped into the kitchen. Thanks to their run-in the other day, he knew where the bathroom was.

He stormed through the house before laying her down on the tiled floor; where he propped her legs up on the edge of the bathtub and sent more blood toward her heart.

Over the years, he'd made a point of keeping his first-aid skills current because as a carpenter with multiple employees, accidents happened. The first thing he noticed now was that her color was off. Her honey-toned complexion was mostly gone, and a purple tinge took over in places.

He had no idea how long she'd been out in the cold wearing no more than a t-shirt and shorts, but her icy skin indicated it had been a while. If she didn't wake soon, he'd call an ambulance, but being remote meant help would take a long time. He would have to assist her as best he could.

He tugged at the tight waistband on her denim shorts, his movements jerky and matching his racing thoughts. Restrictive clothing would hinder her circulation, and as uncomfortable and inappropriate as touching an unconscious woman felt, his actions were necessary.

Her white t-shirt lay caked in mud, her arms and her left cheek not fairing any better. A white bra glowed from beneath the shirt, one he'd need to unclip in the hopes of getting more air into her lungs and waking her up.

He paused, not wanting to touch her in that way. "For fuck's sake, Blaine. Pull yourself together."

So, he stopped mumbling out loud and leaned in again, sliding his hands either side of her body and under her back, his face hovering inches from hers while he wrestled with the clip.

Not wanting to eyeball her anymore, he turned his head to one side. But of course, the second he got the clip undone and faced her again, she was blinking up at him with an unfocused frown.

"W... what are you doing?" She slurred her words and lifted her head, attempting to get up, but sinking and quitting just as quickly.

He snatched his wet hands back from under her and wiped them on his jeans. "You fainted and feel like an ice block. I need to get you warm."

"I..." She lifted her head again, groaning. "I can get myself up."

She tried to use her left elbow for leverage, only for her face to contort and a pained hiss to break free. He put a hand between her shoulder blades and helped her lay down again. "I saw you land on that shoulder. Best not to use it just yet."

"I fell?" She kept her eyes squeezed shut. "Oh, that's right. I did."

Every other part of her shook now, her teeth clinking together. There was no point drawing this out.

"I'll run a hot shower for you. A bath would be better, but I'm not having you pass out on me again, and I don't much like the idea of having to fish you out of the water." She didn't answer, so he reached across her and twisted the shower's faucet. "While we're waiting for the water to heat, let's get you out of those wet clothes."

She flung her eyes open and shook her head furiously. "I am not getting naked in front of you."

He wanted to laugh at that, to point out it wouldn't be anything he hadn't seen before, but she needed his help more than his humor. Frankly, their interactions so far had been disastrous, so he understood her need for privacy.

"I'll make you a deal." He leaned over her again, slipping his hands under her and lifting so she could sit without having to bear weight on her shoulder. "You okay?"

She gave a quick nod, still shaking, her gaze wide and darting over his face like she didn't know what to make of all this. "What's the deal?"

"You keep your underwear on, but with a busted shoulder and all the shaking, there are things you'll struggle to do on your own. So, I'll stand behind you and look away while I help you undress. Once you're in the shower and holding onto the rail with your good arm, I'll keep my back turned so you can warm up. Sound all right?"

Her gaze held his, and for a quick moment, he thought he saw tears gathering in her eyes, perhaps a hint of how vulnerable she felt. Whatever he saw, she blinked it away all too quickly.

"Help me stand then."

He got to his feet and hooked his arms under hers, hoisting her up, his dove gray t-shirt collecting water off her in the process.

"Oh. Wow." Her good arm clasped around him harder than the other. "This feels really weird."

"How's your head?"

"I'm dizzy, but it's fading. Still, I feel terrible."

Her stance seemed stable enough, so he eased back a little, giving her a chance to take her own weight. "What's your full name?"

Her brow twisted in an *Are you joking?* sort of expression, but she answered, anyway. "Emilia Bonacci."

He shifted behind her and slipped his fingers around the hem of her shirt, tugging the sodden material up, a hard task since it insisted on clinging to her. And even as he kept his promise not to look, his blood stirred at having his lips poised so close to her neck, a soft lavender scent breaking past the damp and earthiness on her skin.

"What town do you live in now?" Even as he spoke, his voice took on a raspy edge, one he hoped he hid well.

"Harlow." The abrupt softness in her reply hinted a change in her too, though he refused to analyze what that change might be.

He finally slipped the shirt over her head, trying in vain to not think about how he was slowly undressing her, diverting his focus to asking another question that might confirm her state of mind. "Am I a penguin?"

She broke out with a laugh. "Given how cold I am, I'd say *I'm* the penguin."

He chuckled, getting down on his knees to help with her shorts. Enough questions. She clearly hadn't lost her marbles in the fall. His fingers skimmed her hips, and it was his turn to squeeze his eyes shut.

She jolted out of his hold again. "You better not be looking at me."

"Trust me." He reached for her again, albeit blindly. "I'm not."

He tugged her shorts over the curve of her hip. "These should be loose enough to shimmy out of. Need any help getting into the shower?"

"No." She shimmied as suggested. Again, he looked away. "I'll use my good hand to hold on to the wall."

"Good." He turned his back to her and pried his phone from his pocket. "I'll stay to make sure you don't pass out again, and in the meantime, I'll see if Dr. Richards can drive over and take a look at you."

She didn't answer, but he heard the flow of the shower change, a sign she'd gotten in.

He waited for the doctor to pick up, all while his heart hammered and his fingers trembled. That tremble extended to his voice once the doctor picked up and asked for a summary of the situation.

What if Blaine hadn't walked by when he had? What if no one had seen her fall? And seeing her unconscious. *Being here now...* Every moment of that slow uncertainty finally caught up to him, burrowing deep into his core with two inalienable truths. She'd scared him. And this incident changed everything.

He didn't want to give Miss Bonacci more space. He didn't want to continue his caution in order to spare his heart. He'd spent years separated from her and wanting her all the same. No matter where either one resided, the pain of not having her followed him, anyway.

So why not try to figure out her missing pieces? To fill in the blanks in her story? He'd seen enough today to know he didn't want to leave Emilia to survive alone.

Fifteen

"TELL me where you are right now and what your name is?"

"Oh no." Emilia swung her good arm over her eyes and groaned at Dr. Richards beside her. "Not you too."

She lay on her teal couch, a pillow tucked behind her head, a fluffy white bathrobe on. The balding doctor bobbed down on her left and squished his brows together. "I'm sorry, did I miss something?"

"Just answer the question." Blaine stood, arms crossed before the fireplace—a fireplace she hadn't used yet because she didn't know how to light a fire. But of course, he did know how to light a fire. Now flames filled the room with a subtle orange and flickering glow.

"Fine. I'm Emilia Bonacci. I'm in my house in Harlow. And no, Blaine is not a penguin."

The doctor spun around to Blaine, no doubt giving him a look that said, *Is she usually this odd?* Blaine rolled his eyes, a shadow of a smirk curling his lips. "I have no idea what she's talking about. The fall must have done more damage than I thought."

If she didn't have a hugely painful shoulder, she would have ripped the pillow from under her head and tossed it at him. All she could do was flare her eyelids and give him a mouthed scalding for throwing her under the proverbial bus.

The doctor chuckled, seeming to catch onto the inside joke, while using his hands to gesture for her to sit up. She did so with a great deal of awkward shuffling before he held onto her elbow and set about checking her arm's range of movement. Occasionally, she'd hiss from the pain, the lines between Blaine's brow growing deeper each time.

The doctor looked up at her. "Wriggle your fingers for me?"

She did as she was asked, no pain generated from that particular movement.

He tapped on her good shoulder, gesturing for her to lay down. "So, it appears you had a fainting spell, likely a form of cold shock from exposure to the elements minus the appropriate clothing. Perhaps you panicked a little too, which caused some hyperventilating and then passing out. There's no sign of concussion but, Miss Bonacci, you do understand this isn't California, yes? It might be early spring here, but the weather in these parts can change quickly. You're lucky Blaine found you when he did."

Her cheeks burned, and she jolted as a piece of coal exploded in the fire, the flames casting a sunset outline around him. His gaze landed on her, but she turned away, unable to stomach whatever he thought about her impulsive actions during the storm.

She gave her attention to the doctor instead, his kindly brown eyes a million times easier to deal with. "And the shoulder?"

"Well, you were lucky there too." He pushed to standing. "I don't suspect any dislocation or a break, just a bad sprain. I'm going to leave enough strong pain relievers to last you the next twenty-four hours, but you might need some over-the-counter stuff for a few days yet. All things considered, my recommendation is you go easy for a bit and see how you do day by day. On the small chance that you do have a concussion, I also don't want you to be alone tonight. If Mr. Callaghan here isn't staying, you should call someone else to come down."

A tight laugh burst past her lips, and she looked from the doctor, to Blaine, and then back to the doctor. "But it's not necessary, right?"

"What she means to say is"—even though Blaine spoke to the doctor, his stare fused with hers—"thank you for coming over in a storm, and she'll be sure to follow your advice to a tee."

His brow raised in a dare for her to challenge him. *Challenge accepted.*

She scowled at him again but held back on her urge to hiss like an angry cat. *Traitor.*

The doctor chuckled again and took his first steps toward the door. "If either of you require anymore advice tonight, just call. Otherwise, Miss Bonacci, I've left my card on your mantle in case you need further care in the next few days."

She let out a sigh and closed her eyes, allowing the two men to exit the room and leave her alone with her thoughts. Soon, soft murmurs wafted from the hallway; no doubt she had a starring role in the conversation.

If only she knew more people beyond Aggie or Ally, neither of which lived on her side of this sprawling town, making it a huge ask for either to come over so late at night and in bad weather. Then again, anyone had to be better than Blaine…

The only reason they'd survived so long tonight was that she'd hidden in the living room, while Blaine kept ducking out to the kitchen to check on the pot of soup he'd insisted on making. Why was it that everyone jumped to making soup whenever someone was in any way unwell? She didn't have a cold; she'd fainted and fallen off a ladder. Heck, did soup even help a cold?

Oh, I should probably just shut it. I'm being an ungrateful brat!

Yes, that she was, but being ungrateful distracted from the all-powerful awkwardness of having the love of her life in her house—watching her like a hawk—staying the night… Whatever happened to enjoying her privacy and a day off?

She eyed the fire, its warm heat radiating across the space and adding to the hot sensation behind her eyes. She hated being reliant on anyone else, being so vulnerable, and to a man of all people. As if she hadn't spent her entire life thus far being all those things. She'd worked too hard the past weeks to take herself away from all of that.

"Are you feeling any better?" Blaine broke her mental ramblings. He leaned against the doorway, watching her. Again.

"I'm okay." Her husky tone made that statement sound like a lie, probably because it was.

He strolled over and nudged her legs, making room for himself on the couch beside her. Meanwhile, his skin radiated the scent of leather, wood, and subtle musk. A uniquely *him* smell.

Her throat clogged, his unbridled masculinity overwhelming and hard to escape. "Ummm. Thanks for helping me today."

"I didn't expect to find you like that." The deep lines returned to his forehead, and his hand rested on her knee. Maybe an unconscious move to him but still suggestive enough to send warm tingles up her body. "I'm just glad you're okay."

She offered a soft smile to compensate for his worry. Searing attraction aside, she didn't like being his cause for concern. Besides, they were stuck together now, and he really had done an amazing job looking after her. She couldn't imagine any other person being quite so attentive, not that she'd had a whole lot of attentive people in her life to compare him to. Still, she might as well try to get along with him.

"Will the soup be much longer?" She made a show of tracking her gaze over his torso. "You could do with a decent feed. You're looking skinnier these days."

He threw his head back and laughed, the rich rumble an inviting sound. He'd grown a great deal taller and broader since their days together, though any softness of youth had faded in favor of harder planes. Country life had been outright good to him, and his laugh indicated even he knew that.

The peridot in his eyes continued to glint. "Just like you've gotten a whole lot more agreeable?"

She scoffed, maintaining eye contact. "Agreeable hasn't served me all that well."

His lips parted like he wanted to ask her something, to explain further maybe, but explaining meant talking about Anthony, and she didn't want to do that. She looked away, her voice dipping. "Let's just leave it at trouble follows me, okay?"

He pushed a loose curl from her face, the shock of such tenderness forcing her gaze back to him. "I don't mind your brand of trouble, Emilia. And I like your new sass."

It was her turn to lose her speech, which unfortunately gave Blaine time to rise from the couch. "I'll get that food for us and be right back."

A childish part of her didn't want him to leave, to cling to him like a toddler would a parent. But she lay useless and eyeing his breathtaking silhouette as he walked away, soon resorting to staring at the ceiling and its unexciting white plaster that echoed his absence.

Her father had been a provider, not a nurturer. Anthony was neither. She couldn't recall a time he'd even so much as offered her a glass of water. While Blaine had pulled her unconscious from a storm, been discreet in helping her into the shower, got her medical care, built a fire, and cooked.

Each kindness pushed him deeper under her skin, just like in the past. He forced her to care and prodded emotions she hadn't touched in years.

She gnawed on her lower lip, certain she couldn't let his kindness extend past tonight. She definitely couldn't let him get too settled in her world, even if a huge part of her very much wanted him to.

Creating space for him would be a cop-out. She'd done helpless and hopeless. Never again. Now was the time for getting on with her life *alone*.

The measured thud of his footsteps filled the room, and he walked in holding a tray with two steaming bowls balanced on top. "Sorry, I'm not much of a cook, but I gave it my best shot. Do you want help sitting up?"

He lowered the tray onto the small table he'd procured from the kitchen, a half-smile twisting at his lips. She held a hand to him. "Yes, I could do with some help here. And let me be the judge of your cooking."

He stepped closer, his face lowered way too close to hers. His hands clasped under her armpits, palms pressing into the sides of her ribcage until she sat on the couch's edge. She tried to ignore the stall of her breath and the heat rushing her skin.

His gaze lingered on her, but he took a step back; she cleared her throat, focusing on the food. "This looks good."

He smiled, pushing the table so it stood within reaching distance from her. "The proof is in the tasting, right?"

He sat perpendicular to her, ignorant of her galloping pulse. From the corner of her eye, he soon tucked into his meal, lifting spoonfuls of soup to his mouth, though the metal spoon itself was small compared to his large, work-worn hands. And those hands brought back memories…

"Eat." His stare bore into her, forehead knotted in a question.

She jolted, only now realizing she'd slipped into full-on gawking at him.

She curled her fingers around her spoon, those fingers burning to reach out and touch him.

Bad idea. Bad idea. What is wrong with me?

She peered down and shuddered at his other hand resting on the table, long fingers curved into a relaxed sort of fist. That hand sat not too far from hers. Moments passed, and she managed to eat some food while he occasionally peered over, probably making sure she ate.

Her hand began to shake, so she put down the spoon, her mind muddled with the rising heat of rebellious desire.

"Emilia?" He took hold of her elbow, the one with the spoon in it.

"I'm okay." She nudged his hand away. "Don't worry."

"You don't look well."

She barked out a manic kind of laugh. He shuffled closer, stirring her discomfort. Another coal burst in the fire, and she flinched. With that, her nerves reached the limit of what they would take.

"Actually, there is something you could do." She leaned away from the table, tucking the arm attached to her injured shoulder close to her body. If she needed a sudden exit, she didn't want to risk supporting herself on it. "You could leave. Seriously, you've done so much for me today, and I'm sure I'll be fine till morning. I'm just going to sleep the rest of the night, anyway."

He stared at her, a small muscle ticking over his temple.

She glanced away and at her soup again. "Thank you, but I need you to go."

His posture grew straight in her peripheral vision, his enveloping energy scrubbing at her habitual timidity. "That's not going to happen. Doctor's orders, remember?"

"It was a suggestion more than an order." She fidgeted with the tie on her bathrobe, breath hard to come by, maybe because she heard how stupid her excuse sounded. "And I have a right not to take that suggestion."

"Not on my watch, you don't." He leaned closer, not helping her jitters, though a softened edge somehow shone through his tone. "Emilia, please don't fight me on this."

The heat from his body crossed the small distance between them, or maybe that bit was just her imagination. Either way, her nails dug into her palms, and she sucked at every proceeding breath.

Being nice had never worked for her, and Blaine here wasn't listening. Her earlier sense of dizziness stirred once more within her head, this room and this man too much for her.

"Damn it, Blaine, just go home." She looked down at her lap, her last bit of control imploding. She'd fought tooth and nail for solitude and anonymity. Why did so many who encountered her want to take those things away? "I don't need you."

"You don't need me?" He reached out and caught her uninjured shoulder. "Look at you, you're shaking and listing to one side. Emilia, slow down and breathe."

Tension swelled in her head, his words bringing awareness to the prickling on her skin and the overly hot sensation burning her from the inside out. She gasped for a breath, feeling like a trapped bird in a far-too-small cage. Why did he have to be right?

"Emilia"—his fingers pressed into her with a gentle sort of pressure —"take a deep breath down low into your stomach. Go slow."

She shook her head, her entire body shivering. "I can't. It's not helping."

"Here." He slid his hand down her arms. "Take your index finger and trace the outline of my hand. Go slow and breathe along with it."

She pointed her finger and started at the base of his thumb, doing her best to forget this was Blaine she touched, whilst focusing on the task of essentially drawing around each of his fingers.

"Even slower." He glided her hand, drawing out her movements, her breaths falling into sync. "Has this happened to you before?"

Tears pricked her eyes, but she forced a low breath, not brave enough to look at him directly as she gave a small nod. "A few months now. I was about to get help in LA, but then things changed. No one else knows."

She took another full breath, even though a buried sob filled the space in her chest. Despite the topic and the swelling sensation, her heart rate came down, the residual adrenaline in her body taking longer to rid her of all jitters.

"Might be something to see Dr. Richards about. It can't be easy for you settling into a new town and all."

She gave a shaky laugh, her attention involuntarily reconnecting with his. Something about the "and all" he mentioned, suggested he knew there was more to her general fragility today. "There's been a few shocks for me here in Harlow, yes."

A gentle smile took over his face, like he understood her reference to meeting him again after so many years. He closed his hand, capturing hers so their fingers interlaced. Despite the intimate gesture, the open look on his face suggested a show of solidarity more than him wanting to pressure the truth from her. "Would it help if we stopped pretending nothing happened between us?"

An alarming sort of shiver swept over her skin, though ultimately, she relaxed and appreciated his direct approach. "I don't know, and I'm not sure I want the whole town to know."

He shook his head. "No, I don't either."

A quiet moment passed between them, one that was easy and pleasant. A reminder of why she'd fallen in love with him so long ago. Before all her family's interference. Before the surprise of running into him in Harlow.

Being around Blaine had always been easy, with his innate ability to just let her be. Something a lot of people had failed to give her, especially in the years following her mother's death.

For all he'd given her, he hadn't received much in return.

"Blaine"—she squeezed her fingers around his, absorbing the rare moment of connection with someone she'd once considered a kindred soul—"I'm so sorry. I don't even know where to start apologizing. Do I go back ten years, or just forget that and start with you having to save me from fainting spells and ladders?"

He laughed, his grin adding an extra glint to his eyes, the skin over his cheekbones crinkling in unison. "I don't know. The list is so long now we could be here all night. Maybe you could settle on getting rest instead."

His smile dropped, the corner of his lip trembling just a fraction. She peered down at her lap, nodding to herself. Indirectly or not, she'd hurt him.

"I want you to know I didn't come to Harlow to torture you with my presence." She snapped her attention up, wanting to give him *something* in light of what he'd done for her today. "I can't change our past, but not a day goes by where I don't feel guilt over what they did to you. If I could, I'd go back and erase everything."

The pressure of his hand around hers eased just a little. "Even the part where we met?"

She tightened her grip on his hand instead, making up for what he couldn't seem to give her right now. She didn't blame him. The fact he even spoke to her at all was a miracle.

Besides, she'd had a desire to reach for him earlier. Now she had that, she wanted him to know, as temporary as his presence had been in her life, he'd made a huge difference. "I'd only erase the part where we got hurt. You make up my best memories, Blaine. I would never give those up."

Tight bands constricted around her ribcage, and his gaze danced over her face, the lines between his brows reappearing. Had she said too much? Heck, what she revealed surprised her too.

He turned his face to the fire, its vibrant glow illuminating the pale green flecks in his eyes. The more she looked at him, the more she ached to hear his thoughts—to slow her racing concerns over the million ways he might react.

Despite the distance and the years, he'd lived on in her heart. No matter how many times she tried to compress the memory until it almost didn't exist. But almost wasn't enough. What they'd shared. Those brief months. They'd haunted her. Especially at her loneliest moments.

Now that she'd given him a glimpse of that truth, did he feel the same? Or had she just handed him a chance for revenge? His golden opportunity to hurt her back.

Sixteen

"You just made my heart shrink a few sizes." The husky edged to Blaine's tone had Emilia pulling her hand from his.

Maybe telling him that he made up her best memories was taking things too far. Maybe she'd read the moment all wrong and merely sounded pathetic. He had every reason to move on, and it wasn't his fault that she hadn't.

"I'm sorry." She forced herself to finish the apology, even as he pulled his gaze from the fire and onto her. "You came here to work, not get sucked into helping me. Now my big mouth is making things even worse."

"That's not it." He gave a small scoff, attention falling to the table with their half-eaten bowls of soup. "I left my whole family behind at nineteen. My parents had to stay with my sister in LA, so she could finish her final years at school. Hell, I wasn't even allowed to go back to visit because everyone was so afraid of what would happen if the wrong people saw me in town… I had no choice but to carve out a new life here in Harlow. You were gone from my life without so much as a goodbye, Emilia. I figured you'd moved on to someone better, someone your dad approved of. I was just some scruffy kid you dated a little while, right?"

"I'm sor—"

"I swear to God, you better not be about to say you're sorry again." He lifted his gaze, shaking his head.

She frowned and peered down at her lap. "I do that a lot, don't I?"

"Too much for my liking." He shifted beside her, and a moment later, his fingertips touched her chin, directing her attention back to him. "Not a single one of us gets to choose our family, got it? I don't blame you. I never blamed you. But it's a hard punch to the gut to hear you say the last ten years could have been a whole different story."

Her brows tightened, and he must have seen the confusion on her face because he spoke again. "If I'd known, I would have come back. You know that, right? I would have found a way to get you out of there."

Her jaw fell slack, and she turned from him, her hand taking on a life of its own and landing over her mouth.

Now she was the one feeling the force of that gut punch, a genuine pain growing in her tummy and absorbing her ability to think clearly. She wanted to say she'd tried to find him, but his family had frozen her out—understandably believing she'd only bring him harm. But what was the point of sharing that news? Of presenting more things to be upset about that could potentially lead to a family rift?

Her throat swelled, and she held back from talking, even as Blaine's hand found hers again, pulling it away from her lips, shifting her entire body toward him.

As if by instinct, she leaned in, meaning to rest her head on his shoulder in some kind of show of mutual comfort. Before she understood what happened, his lips were on hers.

Her entire world stopped. Her heart seemed to stretch and strain within her. She couldn't be sure if this was what she wanted, but then her eyes slammed shut, taking the decision out of her hands.

Gentle warmth spread through her chest, and the earlier tension in her muscles eased at the softness of his lips over hers. He tugged her closer, and her last threads of self-restraint snapped as the kiss deepened.

An unexpected moan escaped her, and she broke free, this kiss marking ten years since she'd felt so utterly wanted and alive. She stared at him for the longest time, the flames from the fireplace adding a beautiful contrast to the angles of his face, the woodsy scent of him drawing at her senses. If she wanted to say something, she couldn't, her voice all too thick and raw for escape.

He leaned forward and captured her lips in his again, and for a second there, she gave in, only for the unfamiliar dull ache between her legs to awaken her from his spell.

She wrenched her mouth away, breathless but certain she couldn't go on. Her head was a muddle, but not enough to hide the fact she wasn't in the right frame of mind. "We need to stop."

Blaine's brows knitted together. "Your shoulder?"

She nodded, but the ache around her heart warned of her main reason, one so much more familiar, a line she'd already crossed and would now have to wear the guilt over. "And Sarah."

Blaine's cheeks hollowed while any tension at his jaw dropped away. "Emilia—"

She gave a slow shake of her head, not wanting to talk about it or argue, her guilt expanding like a growing weight on her chest.

She stood up, wobbling for a moment before she steadied on her feet. "I'm going to bed. Blaine, I refuse to be the other woman."

Seventeen

BLAINE FORCED his eyes open and sat up in the chair he'd pulled into Emilia's bedroom, his back a jumble of pain in numerous places. He hadn't wanted to sleep on the couch, since that meant leaving her unwatched overnight, and sharing a bed with her had been out of the question.

After their kiss and her mention of Sarah, she'd simply locked herself away and refused to speak. She needed to rest, so he hadn't pushed for more conversation, though his ability to sleep had died in the process.

This chair, although one of his creations, hadn't been designed for sleeping in, that much was certain. And then there'd been his intrusive thoughts over the talk he would have with Emilia today.

"Hmmm…" She gave a small groan and rolled over, facing him, her eyes slow in fluttering open, before they snapped completely wide.

Even across the room, he caught the quick dilation of her pupils, suggesting she'd forgotten his presence. Her face took on a sudden hard edge. Like she'd also just remembered her problem with him.

The thin strap of her white nightgown intersected her warmer skin tone, threatening to slip off her slender shoulder. He frowned down at his lap, trying to focus on something other than how much he wanted to finish what they'd started last night.

She's right, though. There's Sarah. Explain to Emilia, and then I need to talk to Sarah too…

He shifted his thoughts to easier ground for now. "How's the shoulder?"

"Still sore." She sat up, her voice croaky.

Even with her sleep-tousled hair, her skin glowed, and she appeared well rested. Probably more rested than he'd seen since her arrival in town. *At least one of them was.*

She stared at him through the weighty silence for a while, that stare reminding him that he wasn't wearing all that much besides the wool blanket he'd stolen from the couch and his briefs underneath. Mostly because he'd come here in his work clothes and didn't want to sleep in them.

The fact that he didn't rush to cover his bare torso seemed to push her gaze from him again, as though she sought to ignore him. "Don't you have a shop to run today?"

The way she pulled herself from the bed, sheet draped over her shoulders, along with her terse tone and choice of words, more than implied her desire to have him gone.

"I've got more important things to do." He held court in his chair, refusing to shrink away, tempted to push for a more direct chat about what had passed between them last night. "Like dole out pain meds to you all day and help where I can."

She gave a sharp laugh, a sexy mess of dark ringlets tumbling about her face as she jerked her attention back to him. "Oh no, no, no. That's *not* going to happen."

She leaped out of bed and threw open her wardrobe doors, only stopping to wince and hiss because she'd clearly forgotten all about her bad shoulder.

"You have to go." She ground her words past her obvious pain.

He sat forward and scowled at her. "and you need help today."

A hard knock came at the door, followed by an overly bright, female voice calling Emilia's name. Emilia slammed her stare into him.

"Oh, no. I forgot." She jammed her arms into the sleeves of her bathrobe, wincing once again. "Ally's coming over this morning. She can't see you here."

He gripped the blanket, just as she powered over to rip it away. "I'm not sneaking out the backdoor if that's what you're asking."

Emilia narrowed her eyes like she might actually launch herself at him if he didn't let the blanket go or get some clothes on.

His lips twinged. Maybe her launching herself at him wasn't such a bad thing. Maybe that would force her to face reality with him. So he let go. Her eyes flared as her end of the blanket sprung back, revealing his body, bare except for his black underwear.

She turned away, her cheeks red. "Please. Just get up and put me out of my misery."

He strode over to her, turning her to face him. "Cancel your catch-up with Ally. Tell her something came up. I'm sure falling off ladders counts as 'something.' We have stuff to sort out, Emilia, and I'm not happy about leaving you here alone all day."

"Dr. Richards said I only needed monitoring overnight. I'll survive without your help, Blaine." She turned from him, picking up his pants and jamming them into his hands. "Besides, this isn't just about Ally. This is just too much... too much—"

"Too much what?" He pushed his legs through his pants, tugging them over his waist, pissed that he even obliged.

"Too much reality." She crossed her arms over her chest, her shoulders rising. "I don't want anyone to know about last night."

"You think I'm the type to broadcast something like that?"

"I don't want anyone to know about us, either." Her gaze swung away from him, and she gnawed on her lower lip. "And what happened last night, it can't happen again."

A cold wave hit his bare skin, his blood itself seeming to cool. Her approach was so impersonal. Insulting. Cruel. *No.* He'd seen real caring in her eyes last night. She'd confided in him and made him believe he had a real chance here. A chance worthy of handing over his trust. She'd felt something, just as he had. For some reason, she wouldn't admit to her feelings. But unlike her, he wasn't about to run.

Fuck. I sound naive. Delusional. Maybe she just doesn't care.

If that were true, why kiss him back last night?

He stepped in front of her, blocking her ability to walk away. "What's the real problem here?"

She squeezed past him and stormed from the room, her voice sailing behind her. "We're not teenagers anymore, Blaine. We'd be crazy to take this further."

He followed, momentarily stunned as she hurried about the living room collecting stray pillows and blankets and all evidence last night had ever happened. "We share a connection and a past. We'd be crazy *not* to try."

She barked out a shot of laughter, one that dented his already bruised heart. "Whatever you're expecting from me, I'm not ready, and things are way more complicated than either of us deserve. Trust me, I'm doing you a kindness here. You need to go."

And just like that, her father's words from years ago echoed in his head. A woman like Emilia didn't belong with someone as ordinary as him. Maybe the trouble here was that she'd come to believe the same shallow bullshit her father had worked so hard to instill.

Maybe she wasn't so ashamed of their tender moment last night, as much as having to admit to the outside world that she had any connection with him. She'd just said as much, hadn't she? Except, he was willing to throw himself completely into being with her, and he didn't want to be her secret all over again.

White-hot hostility cracked his restraint. *Time to face the truth. I don't know anything about her anymore, do I?*

Well if she wanted him gone, he'd go, but not before he said his piece. "I might not be in the same income bracket as the crowd you're used to, Emilia, but I've worked damn hard for the life I have. Last night meant something to me, and you led me to believe you felt the same. We both know things aren't simple here, and I can deal with complicated, but I'm not someone you use for kicks and then toss aside."

She stopped clearing bowls from the table still in the living room, her pupils suddenly dark pools. "Blaine, I—"

He shook his head, not letting her continue. "I'm not ashamed of my damn feelings, you didn't use to be, either. You've let your dad get to you."

Another knock cut through the house, followed by Ally's voice yelling for Emilia to hurry up. She broke eye contact and stared out the living room door, her jaw hanging open and a moment of silence passing.

He shook his head and marched away to the bedroom, snatching up his shirt from the back of his chair and shaking it out. By the time he got dressed and reached for the front door, a dull ache pulsated through his chest, his emotional pain taking on physical form.

"If this were about money..."

He turned at her voice, her hands raised and gesturing to the old walls around her.

"Do you think I'd be living here? Alone? Driving that busted-up Pinto?"

His fingers tightened around the door handle, yet he failed to pull it open. Hope sprung eternal when it came to this woman, though he wished with every fiber of his being that it didn't. "If this isn't about money, tell me what this *is* about?"

A flash of something took over her face, her cheeks slackening before she turned away. He swore under his breath and followed her back to the living room, refusing to analyze why exactly he couldn't just let her go.

He let out a sigh at her continued retreat, not wanting to say what he had to say next but needing to, anyway. "This time you have a choice, and I'm asking you not to leave."

She stopped but kept her back to him.

"I didn't *leave* last time, and this is my house." She spun around, glaring at him, her eyes rimmed in red, her entire face contorted and pinched. The volume of her voice confused him. Maybe he hadn't known her all that long, but still, he'd never seen her so angry. "I'm asking *you* to leave, and don't you dare imply I'm the only one with secrets when you haven't been all that open or honest, either. You have Sarah, Blaine. Even if you're willing to pretend you don't, I'm not."

An icy ball formed in the pit of his stomach, his muscles suddenly slack. Of all the things she could have said...

"Emilia. That's not what's happening here." He stalked toward her, his voice husky. "I'll talk to her. She'll understand."

"Oh God." She clapped a hand over her mouth, her eyes turning watery again before she gave him her back. "You too?"

She stormed past him, swiping at her face, not sparing him a second glance. "Get out of my house, Blaine."

Eighteen

THE DOOR HUNG OPEN, and Emilia stepped back, making room for Blaine to leave, his attention lingering as if to beg her to reconsider. Meanwhile, Ally stood on the veranda with her lips parted like she meant to ask about what happened, only to fall short a few words or ten.

Emilia shook her head, signaling for Ally to drop the questions, at least for now. All shocks aside, the one thing holding her together was the small concession that at least this house was hers alone to occupy— something she hadn't had with Anthony—and she, therefore, enjoyed the power to decide who stayed and who left. *Blaine included.*

Ally stepped into the hallway, her gaze in the direction of the living room. "I'm going to take a guess here that you don't usually keep your kitchen table and chairs in this room. What the heck happened?"

As much as Emilia would have loved to have moved everything back to its rightful place, she had no hope with her injured shoulder.

She turned to close the door, catching the last glimpse of Blaine and his truck, the windows still covered in condensation from a night in the cottage's driveway. There'd be no point in lying to Ally now that she'd seen him.

"I fainted yesterday afternoon, in the rain, of all places. Blaine happened to be there to help, and Dr. Richards asked him to stay and keep an eye on me overnight."

"Hmm…" Ally's gaze searched Emilia's, but nothing about her expression gave much away. "Are you okay now?"

"I landed on my shoulder, and it hurts a lot, but I'm sure I'll be fine." She faked a serene smile, unwilling to go into as much detail as she had with Blaine last night about her history of stress-induced fainting spells.

"Let's make tea and take it to the living room." She gave a nervous chuckle as they entered the kitchen. "You know, since that's where the table lives for the moment."

"Ya, sure." Ally headed toward the electric kettle on the counter. "And I can move the table for you later if you like. By the way, I'm glad you survived, but maybe next time check the weather report before taking an afternoon swim, okay?"

Emilia dragged out an ironic laugh, even though what she really wanted to do was collapse on her bed in a torrent of tears. "I'll keep that in mind."

I'll talk to her. She'll understand.

Blaine's words about Sarah lingered in Emilia's ear, and a wave of nausea hit her belly. She didn't want him to make Sarah understand anything. Emilia knew all too well what it was like to have a man try to make her "understand."

Betrayal was betrayal—no matter the spin—and the guilt of her kissing him would be something she'd have to wear, regardless of how confused she might have been at the time.

So even now, as Blaine's absence hung like a heavy stone around her neck, she took a deep breath and did what she always did. She stifled her feelings in favor of not making everyone else miserable with her problems. At least for the moment, anyway.

"So…" Ally smirked from beside the stove, only stopping to pull out a frying pan from one of the doorless cupboards. Clearly, breakfast was also in order. "Blaine was your knight in shining armor, huh?"

"Ally." Emilia dragged out the name, her weak version of a warning.

"Oh, come on. Dontcha know, life gets boring around here, and I'm good for keeping a secret? Pleeeeassse."

Emilia leaned against the doorframe and stared at the floor. What *had* happened? She'd taken a tumble, and in a moment of rapture invited Blaine back into her life—the most thrilling, foolish, and temporary decision she'd made in years.

The man had a way of making her revert to being an impulsive and overly emotional teenager again. But an impulsive and overly emotional teenager she was no longer, which meant she'd need to find a way to take responsibility for her actions last night. Even if Blaine wouldn't.

"There isn't much to say." She strolled over to the fridge and handed Ally a carton of eggs. "Blaine took care of me, and now I'm sort of okay."

"And I don't believe you." Ally cracked an egg into a bowl. "It's okay to want to keep a secret, but you, Miss Emilia, are not the best liar."

Sure, fair enough, even the fact she allowed Ally to call her "Miss" *was* a lie. But some lies were needed. Like Ally being Blaine's employee meant Emilia would not mess with this relationship of his, either. Even if last night and this morning upset her. Even if she did want to tell her version of events.

Then again, what was the point of her new life if she spent the entire time avoiding confrontation? Hadn't she done enough damage control for other people over the years? And if she wanted to know if she'd wronged Sarah, if she wanted to know if closing her heart off to Blaine had been the right choice, well maybe sometimes a wrong could make a couple of things right.

She squared her shoulders and steeled her nerves for further disappointment, before turning to Ally. "If you must know, Blaine and I had a fight, and I think I need your help."

"Oh cripes, really?" Ally poured scrambled eggs into the pan and then angled away from the stove. "What was the fight about?"

"Many things." She toyed with her robe, gnawing at her lower lip for a beat. "Though I guess you could say the deal breaker was Sarah."

Ally let out a gasp. "*Oofdah!* You two fought about Sarah?"

Emilia shrugged, trying to pretend the memory didn't bother her. "Not directly but to be honest, we kind of ran out of time to get all that stuck into the topic."

"Oh, you mean, before I showed up?" Ally cringed, a silent offer of apology while she pushed eggs around the pan. "All I can say is, Blaine might be stubborn, but he's not a liar or a cheat. Maybe you could give him a chance to explain."

"Actually, I was hoping you might know something." Emilia headed for the kettle and the two teacups already waiting nearby.

Her pulse surged. She didn't just *want* to know about Sarah, she *needed* to know, at least so she could gauge how guilty to feel. Fainting and shoulder injuries, coupled with intimate encounters with ex-boyfriends, weren't exactly a springboard for clear thought. Still, she blamed herself for letting Blaine get so close before clearing up the whole Sarah thing.

Blame the rain. And the fainting. And the potential concussion…

No. All that was a cop-out she refused to succumb to.

Ally pushed the cooked egg into a clean bowl and passed it to Emilia. "I'm sure you know, Blaine isn't exactly an open book when it comes to anything, much less his personal life."

Sad truth was, Emilia had been the cagey one both last night and this morning, while he'd been the perfect example of an open book. Well, again, except for the whole Sarah thing…

She chewed on a forkful of breakfast, thankful for Ally's company and help, all while coming to terms with one further reality. For whatever reason, she wanted to believe Blaine wasn't totally out of her reach. "Maybe I'm better off getting the truth from Sarah."

Ally gasped and reached for Emilia's forearm, causing the bowl in her hand to wobble and almost topple to the floor. "You can't. Sarah won't take too kindly to anyone poking in her private life, much less someone she's never met."

"It's a chance I have to take. I know if I were in her position, I'd want to know."

And the fact was, she *had* been in that position, many times, so she *did* know.

Ally let go, looking genuinely disappointed. "But why not give talking with Blaine another try first?"

Emilia took her last mouthful of food and worked over that question in her mind, recalling how pointless such conversations had been with Anthony. How her terrible relationship *might* have ended sooner if someone, *anyone*, had backed her up and told her that she didn't have to live her life by such low standards.

"No, that won't work." She put her bowl in the sink and reached for her purse sitting on the counter. Sarah worked at Maynard's, and if she wasn't there, surely she'd be easy enough to find since everyone in town knew her. "I need to do the right thing. I need to talk to the one person who has the most to lose."

"Blaine Callaghan, get your sorry butt out here!"

Blaine wandered from his workroom to find Ally sprinting toward him, the heavy glass door slamming in her wake. This had to be the only time he'd ever seen his sales assistant inside Oak Tree Furniture on her day off, much less with such an animated entry.

She stopped before him, hunched and panting for air. "And for cripes' sake, why don't you ever answer your phone?"

If one angry woman wasn't enough for the day, of course, Ally had to join the fray. He frowned down at her through a narrowed gaze, skeptical of what she had to say since he'd last seen her at Emilia's. "What's happened now?"

"I don't know what took place between you two last night, but you need to speak to Emilia, now! She's on her way to see Sarah."

His heart pounded, his shoulders drew with sudden strain, and just like that, his last shreds of calm fell to pieces. "I thought I told you I didn't want you talking about my private life?"

Ally jabbed a finger in his direction, her brows slamming together. "Oh no, don't you even try to blame this one on me! Why didn't you talk to Emilia when you had the chance, *before* she got all upset about your vague relationship status? Geez, aren't you and Sarah meant to be engaged? What the heck is happening right now?"

He growled, frankly done with dealing with so many angry people in one day and unwilling to explain anything to Ally.

He marched toward the exit, not wanting to waste more time. His pounding heartbeat grew faster, and the thundering throb filled his ears while an unsettling hot prickle burned at his skin. He could understand Emilia having regrets. Maybe she'd said more than intended, invested more than she could afford.

And yes, things on his side of the fence weren't exactly neat and tidy either, but she'd blocked any attempt he'd made to explain. Now, she hurtled toward involving more people in this issue, all of whom *weren't* him.

Sure enough, he didn't have her trust, but now he questioned whether he could trust her too.

Ally's loping footfall trailed behind him. "Where are you going? What about the shop?"

"Damn the shop." He threw a hand into the air, plowing through the exit, the bell above the door clanging in protest. "Assuming Emilia has decided to track Sarah down at work, I'm going to Maynard's. I have to fix this mess once and for all."

Poor Sarah. She didn't deserve any of this. He had to get to her in time. Had to prevent the deluge of undue pain and drama barreling her way.

Whatever Emilia had to say, she'd crossed a line, one that would blast a hole straight through their already tumultuous relationship. She most certainly had no right to drag a complete innocent like Sarah into this disaster.

Ally continued after him down the street, almost like a stray puppy nipping at his heels. "Mind if I come with?"

He pulled open his truck door and threw her an angry glower. "Ally, I love you, but this is none of your business. Stay away from Maynard's."

He slid into the driver's seat and slammed the door shut, blocking any chance for her to protest.

He checked his watch and did the math. It was just past noon, and Harlow was a widespread town with Emilia's cottage closer to the tavern than his shop. If she'd gone straight to Maynard's after speaking to Ally, chances were he'd get there too late.

Nineteen

THEN

From: Emilia Bonacci
  To: Emilia Bonacci
  Subject: I want my life back!

It's been a week since it happened. Since dad told me he was sending me away, and worst, since Anthony attacked Blaine and tore us apart. Dad refused to let me out of the house until he could get me onto a plane. I'm in Pennsylvania at Aunt Pina's Place now.

Even at my aunt's, everyone who visits, especially other relatives, keeps giving me these glares. Aunt Pina looks at me like I've ruined the family name. Maybe I have. People here barely talk to me, not that I want them to, but okay, I get it, they're all judging me. Can they just let it go already?

. . .

I still haven't heard from Blaine. Does he not love me anymore? I can't blame him after what Anthony did. Oh God, I can't stop thinking about that night, and the blood, and I feel so guilty. Dad took my phone away and gave me a new one with a new number. I didn't memorize Blaine's number. I wish I had. The only thing I can do is email him. And I did that the moment I got my new phone. I even tried to call his parents through a landline number I found in a local directory. It's been five days and still nothing. All I can do is keep trying.

I don't understand. This can't be the rest of my life from now on, can it? The only other time I've felt worse than this is that day when mom had her stroke on the drive home from school. I still remember the car crumpling around the tree. I cried sitting on the curb. I cried every day for months after because, even at thirteen, I knew life would never be the same. I can't believe it's been five years already. I still feel just as helpless.

My dad and Anthony got what they wanted, and now everything hurts. My head hurts all the time because I can't stop the tears, and my heart... I'm losing yet another person who means the world to me, and I feel like my heart might just give up altogether. I know my dad hasn't been the same since Mom died, but she would never have let this happen. She would never have sent me away. Does he really think he's fooling anyone into believing he's okay? Besides, her dying hurt me too. Can't he see that?

I want my life back. I want Blaine back. Please don't let this be all that's left for me.

Emilia shifted in her seat at the bar, her focus trained on the orange-vodka drink in her hand, the sweet-astringency having long lost all appeal. She still waited to speak with Sarah. Every time the woman approached, all Emilia could muster was a weak nod in a silent request for yet another drink.

Pathetic. Truly pathetic!

She was on her fourth drink now, and as a general non-drinker, her movements were getting clumsy and slow, the glass against her palm uncomfortably cold and wet.

She drummed her fingers on the bar and released an overly loud sigh. Perhaps she should just head home. Did she need to be the one to tell Sarah? Maybe she could insist Blaine do that. Then again, maybe she should take some time to sober up first. A few more minutes, or knowing her, a few hours. Oh heck, she was never going home.

A panicked laugh burst from her lips. The few people around her turned, expressions pinched in probable confusion or annoyance.

Okay, so maybe she was stuck here regardless of how much she didn't want to be. Maybe she could make use of her time and talk to Sarah, anyway.

How would she start? "Hi Sarah, are you really Blaine's fiancée? Gee, I hope not, cos, well, last night we kinda sorta kissed, and then he slept over."

Another manic and, this time, pitchy laugh broke free. More people turned, and she shuddered in an attempt to shake off her current spate of involuntary actions, almost knocking over her boozey juice in the process.

Oh, what a slew of consequences she'd woken up to today. There'd been the forgotten catch-up with Ally. A catch-up meant for discussing the soiree, only for that to get swept away with the whole pushing Blaine out the door debacle, and having to deal with the notion that another woman's relationship lay in ruins. Then there was the issue of Emilia's now questionable reputation in this town... and her sobriety...

Sheesh! What had she done?

"Seems like you're struggling to finish that one." Sarah stood at the opposite side of the bar and nodded toward Emilia's mostly untouched drink. "Want me to take it away?"

Emilia pushed her glass forward, her ribcage suddenly refusing to make room for much breath. "I swear, I don't usually drink."

Sarah gave a light laugh and leaned in, resting her elbows on the bar, her flaxen locks skimming her toned and tanned shoulders. "You'll get no shame from me. We have some serious heavy hitters around here, and you're nowhere near one. My best guess, though, you've got something playing on your mind. Am I right?"

Emilia shook her head, and her booze-addled brain made her wobble slightly in response. *Fiddlesticks!* This was her chance to say something, to help this woman maybe escape one huge life mistake, and Emilia simply couldn't find her words.

She'd watched Sarah flit from one patron to another, making easy banter that made grown men nearly fall apart with laughter. Her personality sparkled amidst the busy setting. The woman exuded confidence, while Emilia never had.

"No. Ahh… I'm fine. It's just been a crazy twenty-four hours." She forced a taut smile and went about drawing circles on the countertop with her forefinger, paying way too much mind to the minute bumps in the treacle-colored woodgrain.

"It's the middle of the day, and you're here alone getting messy on vodka and orange." Sarah's scoff brought Emilia's focus back to the woman's amber-green eyes and her barely hidden grin. "Now you're just insulting my intelligence."

Emilia's heart palpitated, and she rubbed the heel of her hand over her sternum, trying to erase queasiness filling every corner of her torso. "No! No! That's the last thing I would do. And I'm not 'messy,' I'm just… just a little unpracticed in the art of drinking. Besides, you're the one who picked my drink."

Sarah barked out a laugh, her demeanor easy and controlled, and she pushed a glass of water Emilia's way. "Yeah, because you took too long deciding. And if the drink was so bad, why did you order three more?"

Emilia sipped at the water, using the sip to delay her reply—a reply she didn't have. Meanwhile, the silence introduced an unwelcome idea, that Blaine would use her to double-cross a woman as feisty, and ridiculously beautiful, and sharp-witted as Sarah. Not that anyone deserved to be cheated on.

Oh God, what if this wasn't the first time? What if the years have turned him into a serial cheater or something?

Now that would most definitely bury an axe in her years of pining after him.

She lifted her attention to Sarah, who swiped Emilia's purse from the bar and fished out her car keys.

Emilia startled and flung her arms forward. "Hey, you can't do that!"

"Well, I just did." Sarah tucked the keys under the counter and out of reach, her following light shrug conveying zero remorse. "And since you're not fit to drive, I'll keep you company here until you are. In the meantime, you're welcome to tell me why you look so sour."

A nervous chuckle fell from Emilia's lips, and she stared at her fingers now digging into the bar top. This was her invitation to admit everything, but *wow*, she didn't want to.

"Actually, I came here to talk to you about Blaine." Her full disclosure materialized as though some unknown entity possessed her body and spoke for her. A good thing really since she seemed to lack the ability to speak up otherwise. She straightened and channeled "the entity" again, entity channeling probably not the best form of fake courage for a born and raised Roman Catholic. "Before you decide this is none of my business, I probably should explain that something happened between us last night. Something... kind of physical..."

Okay, wow, that sounded worse than intended, though maybe things *were* that bad.

Sarah's grin fell to a hard, flat line, and from her leaned position against the bar, she now stood bolt-upright, her shoulders rolled back and all stiff. "You slept with him?"

Emilia cringed, her chest suddenly tight while time stood still, and she lamented living in a town so far from a hospital. "Umm... probably not in the way that you're thinking... I had a fall yesterday while he was over to do work on my cottage and he looked after me overnight. We kissed, but he slept on a chair *next* to my bed. Nothing else happened. I swear."

Sarah's easy expression twisted, and the slow bob of her throat hinted at heartache. "Sounds like whatever you two have together is serious."

"No. I mean, I don't think so." A nervous laugh escaped, and she cringed once again, the hardwood over her seat adding to her discomfort. "This whole thing kind of took me by surprise. Honestly, I just got so swept up in the moment last night… Oh, I really should shut up. I feel terrible."

Sarah leaned in, her stare hard and cool. "You knew about me and still kissed him?"

Emilia's mouth fell open, but for the longest time, nothing more than a broken croak came out. She took a deep swallow, the sides of her throat painful and bone dry. Really, what was she supposed to say except for "yes"? She was guilty as charged. Whatever revenge Sarah had for her would be justified.

A strong hand gripped her upper arm. "What are you doing?"

She jumped at the snap of Blaine's voice, loud and abrupt and gouging a deep pit through the center of her stomach.

"I'm *doing* the right thing for everyone involved here." She tugged her arm away, his searing glare inches from her own. He had no place trying to intimidate her. "Unlike you, I refuse to hide from the truth."

"I offered you the truth this morning." He pushed the words through gritted teeth, his tone tight and buckling under the strain of his jaw. "You pushed me out the door, remember?"

"I wanted to speak directly to Sarah."

He barked out a sardonic laugh, a scowl still fixed on her, the planes of his cheekbones hard, and his entire body tense. "Well, that's a hell of a lot of pressure to put on someone you've never met. You had no right bringing her into this."

"Really now?" Sarah crossed her arms, one brow raised. "I'm not so sure about that."

"Yeah." Emilia shrugged; a shrug that was probably everything but unmoved. "She *is* your *fiancée*, right?"

A muscle ticked on the edge of Blaine's jaw, and for the longest time, he didn't even blink. Meanwhile, she couldn't *stop* blinking, and she felt somewhat faint again.

He turned to Sarah, his expression unreadable. "She's been drinking?"

Sarah pulled Emilia's keys from under the bar and jangled them in the air. "Featherweight drinking at best. You got here just in time, though not before I heard the more interesting details."

She threw him the keys. He spun around to Emilia, his eyes

narrowed like he inspected her anew. "You fainted yesterday and are on strong pain meds, and now you're drunk?"

"Who's drunk?"

Everyone turned to Ally, already squeezing sideways between Blaine and Emilia.

Blaine stared down his assistant. "I told you to stay at the shop."

Emilia curled her fingers around Ally's arm and pulled her closer. "Quit being a bully. She's with me."

"Fine." Blaine shoved the keys into Ally's hand, though his glare now latched to Emilia. "Since she wanted to be part of this, she can look after you." He turned to Sarah, the tension over his brow releasing. "I'm sorry you had to find out this way."

Her lips pressed into a straight line, and she gave a stiff nod, her eyes taking on a subtle sheen. "I'll speak with you tonight. After that, you can get to talking to her." Sarah nodded to Emilia, though her focus stayed on Blaine. "You owe us that much."

Twenty

EMILIA WOKE with a head full of regrets and the sense her life had well and truly unraveled. If a botched truth-giving mission wasn't bad enough, the time on her phone stated 5:30 a.m. and there was no chance she'd fall back asleep.

She pushed her white cotton bedspread down her waist, and the cold morning air hit her exposed arms, all while the same thought played over and over in her mind. *She shouldn't have gone to Maynard's!*

Her thin nightgown lay in a pool of cream silk at the end of her bed. She crawled over and shrugged the garment onto her shoulders, today designated to hiding. If she were truly lucky, she'd find peace here at home, far away from the outside world where she tended to get into trouble… Well, as long as she managed not to pass out and require help again.

The quiet of her kitchen beckoned and so did a warm cup of tea, so she made her way down the house to boil the kettle. While she waited for the kettle, she stepped out into the brisk dawn air through her back door—a thick mist lingering in plumes of swirling vapor down the hill, the grassy basin below filled with early morning mystery and magic.

Something about that dancing opaque air and its slow-moving patterns painted a picture of unexpected beauty. It drew imaginings of fairies and gnomes taking one final frolic before the humans began their day.

She chuckled to herself and sank to the cold veranda boards, crossing her legs beneath her so she could enjoy the scene a little longer. This sprawling landscape made her troubles with Blaine seem so small. An entire world stretched out there, and she was just a tiny part of it, her freedom still largely unexplored.

A gust of wind nudged the detached piece of gutter still in a mangled heap at the end of her porch. Somehow that chunk of metal had unleashed more havoc on her life than she could already contend with.

Oh, don't lie. I did this all to myself!

A bitter tang coated her tongue. That she had. She'd dragged Blaine and Sarah, and even Ally, into her whirling drama. For what? The tense stare-off between Blaine and Sarah, the woman's lack of vengeance, plus his storming off *again*, left Emilia with the strong sense there was something she didn't know.

A loud knock boomed across the house. She rose to her feet, careful not to push off her still-injured shoulder, eventually making it to the front door.

"Ally and I decided I should drop these off."

Sarah waited on the door's other side, a lopsided smile on her face, and Emilia's car keys dangling from the tip of her finger. Emilia's heart twisted, and her stomach churned. *So much for hiding!*

"The pub's closer to your place, and I had to get up early for the breakfast shift, anyway." Sarah's head tilted to a spot behind her, where Emilia's rusty clanger now waited on her driveway.

"Ahh." She cleared her throat and shook her head, trying to get her brain into gear. "Thanks. You didn't have to trouble yourself."

Sarah shrugged. "Seriously, no big deal, I like a morning run, and the bar's an easy enough journey from here."

Emilia trekked her gaze down Sarah's fitted fuchsia sports jacket and moss green leggings. Even in activewear, the woman looked a picture of strength and Amazonian beauty.

Not content with being idle, and in light of Sarah's kind gesture, Emilia pushed the door wider in an invitation for this woman to step in. "Are you sure? I'd be happy to get changed and drive you to Maynard's."

"Hmmm…" Sarah sent forth a dubious side-stare. "Okay, but only if you let me get you breakfast when we get there."

Emilia raised her brows, still not sure why this woman insisted on being so kind to her, given her confession and immature showdown at Maynard's. And the fact she wasn't unkind, again shot holes through her theories of Blaine being a coldhearted cheater.

Sarah pushed past and into the hallway. "Are you feeling better today?"

Emilia gave a nervous chuckle and entered her bedroom, leaving her door ajar so they could keep talking. "I'm okay, but I really shouldn't have drunk so much. I'm sorry about my lapse in judgment yesterday. As you can see, I'm not adjusting well to the whole independent country living thing."

She pulled on a pair of jeans and a red, cable-knit sweater. By the time she stepped out to the hallway, Sarah leaned against a wall, her posture annoyingly relaxed. "No need to apologize. You didn't have all the details, and as far as I'm concerned, you made an honest mistake."

Emilia frowned, even as a flutter of hope unfurled deep within her chest—because of course, she wanted to believe Blaine didn't have it in him to lie—even if that made her outburst yesterday uncalled for.

"I don't understand." Her mouth ran dry, and she took a prolonged swallow, delaying whatever news awaited her because even the best-case scenario meant dramatic things for her. They meant her suspicions about Blaine were wrong, which meant she'd have to face her feelings for him *and* do something about those feelings. "Does that mean there isn't something between you and Blaine?"

Sarah peeled away from the wall and ushered Emilia outside. "Well, there is something, but life isn't always so simple, now is it?"

Emilia paused on the veranda's edge while Sarah spun around from up ahead, her shoulders slumped and expression gloomy. "We tried to make it work, but…"

"But"—Emilia's stomach churned—"you're both engaged, right?"

"*Were* engaged." Sarah lowered her chin and shook her head at the ground. "I tried really hard to hate you at first, but if I'm honest, you didn't do anything wrong and neither did he. Blaine's a good man, Emilia. Maybe too good, sometimes. As in, so good he'd ask a woman to marry him out of some misguided sense of right and wrong."

"Why would he do that?"

"Because for three years we were happy enough, we both wanted children, and getting married seemed like the thing to do." She gave a shrug. "There isn't a heck of a lot of options in a town like Harlow. Wow, saying that out loud sounds so stupid now. He loves me. I know he does. Hell, I love him too, but love isn't enough. Not in this instance, and not in the way either of us needs."

Emilia stared at the dusty ground, her tummy heavy like she'd swallowed a basket full of rocks. Not only had she put on an angsty show yesterday, but she'd busted up an engagement. *For fudge's sake!* Next, she'd learn she'd had an unwitting hand in killing someone's much-beloved puppy...

"I'm so sorry, I didn't mean—"

Sarah scoffed, one side of her lips ticking up. "No, you didn't. You didn't break us up, okay? Well, technically you did, but Blaine told me the minute you arrived in town. He told me about your history together. Told me it wouldn't change anything between us. Except, no matter how much he wanted to play the hero here and continue the loving fiancé act, I knew right away where his heart really lay."

Emilia's blood ran instantly cold. She moved to speak but couldn't produce a word.

Sarah gave a soft chuckle. "You look more devastated than me. Listen, I was the one who said we needed to take a break from each other, that I would step back until Blaine came to a decision on his feelings for you. I've always felt like something held him back, like he'd been trying to let go of some last threads of hope, that he would have settled down way earlier if that weren't the case. And now I know what held him back. Or should I say, *who?* So maybe your emergence has spared everyone from making one really big mistake. God, I hope so."

Emilia's mouth slipped open, her ribcage slamming tight, so much so the air in her lungs fell through her lips in an audible sigh. Hearing

Sarah's take on all of this was an out-of-body experience. "W… why would you step aside like that?"

"You mean besides him telling me he'd never gotten past the idea of what could have been?" Sarah quirked one corner of her lip, a mischievous glint entering her eyes, like maybe she'd had a little more time to find the humor in all of this.

Meanwhile, a cold shiver crept into Emilia's bones, and she marched past Sarah and toward the Pinto, hiding a flush of guilt and her desire to be away from this tough conversation.

"Emilia?" Sarah's hurried footsteps crunched over the rocky path, her voice lifted. "Are you okay?"

"Yes, yes, I'm fine." Emilia kept her face angled away, half choking on her reedy words before spinning around to look at the woman whose life she'd just wrecked. "I… I'm sorry, I'm not sure I heard you right. Lots of people have a 'one that got away,' but that doesn't stop them from moving on. You're saying Blaine stalled on getting married because… because of *me?* It's been ten years, and look at you, you're perfect. You have so much more going for you than I do. Isn't this all just a bit crazy?"

Sarah gave a light shrug, the planes of her face smoothing out. "Aggie's husband died twenty years ago, and she's never moved on. She's always said she never had the desire to. It's not unthinkable Blaine might feel the same about you."

Sarah's even tone jarred against Emilia's rattled nerves. She shook her head, balling her hands at her sides to keep from clapping her palms over her ears. "No. No. That isn't right. I'm sure Aggie spent decades with her husband. We were together for just over six months, and I ruined Blaine's life. There's no way—"

"Seriously, what is wrong with you?" Sarah stepped closer, the muscles around her amber-green eyes drawing into a tight squint like she studied Emilia in some kind of new light. "The man's spent years pining for you, and you just happened to have the extraordinary chance of meeting again. The other night, he slept over and looked after you. He clearly likes you, probably *loves* you, so you can't just bow out on him now like there's absolutely nothing special about any of this."

Emilia drew back, her voice catching as she tried to speak. "We were just two kids with a farfetched idea of what we thought love was."

And if anything, her disagreement with Blaine and her hesitance now proved she wasn't ready to tackle a new relationship. Heck, she'd treated him so poorly, and twice in one day, she deserved his hate. It wasn't as if she was confident or forward enough to ask for his forgiveness, let alone another chance.

Sarah stalked closer, her long and spindly fingers wrapping around Emilia's forearm in a gesture demanding undivided attention. "After talking to him last night, and given the look on your face right now, this is more than 'just two kids' with no idea what they're doing."

Emilia's throat constricted, but she croaked out a reply as best she could. "You deserve him more than I do."

Sarah threw her head back and barked out a laugh. "I'd rather be alone than compete for his love, so whether you want him or not, I'm out of this race, got it? Neither of you will find any peace until you prove once and for all whether you can make this work."

Unshed tears prickled the corners of Emilia's eyes, her shoulders rounding forward and dragging her usually perfect posture down. She wanted the peace Sarah spoke of, the peace she'd set out on this journey to find, only to be thrown from one ugly surprise to another.

Sarah turned toward the Pinto. "Anyway, we should go. As promised, I'll organize breakfast for you at the bar, but I'll say this last thing… If Blaine's happiness isn't with me, I hope he finds it with you. So once you're done at Maynard's, do me one favor and go to Oak Tree to speak with him."

Twenty-One

EMILIA KEPT the Pinto idling outside Oak Tree Furniture, her fingers wrapped tight around the steering wheel, a distinct tremor working through her arms. She'd been here for ten minutes, but heck, the details of Blaine's broken engagement—that she'd been at the center of it all—still shook her to the core.

So many years apart, so many missed opportunities, and now she had a choice: play dumb or do something to stop even more time going to waste.

She fought an urge to slam her palm onto the horn and hold it there, rage bubbling like hot lava in her belly. Rage at the people who'd held her back for so damn long. Those same people were the only ones to benefit from her misery. They'd kept her and Blaine apart, kept her from realizing so much…

Sarah and Aggie were right. By not exploring her feelings for Blaine, she was selling herself short. The time had come for things to change.

She sat a little taller, her sallow reflection bouncing off the rearview mirror, complete with wary eyes and a forehead creased in worry. She looked a mess, and still, that wasn't enough to divert her from her plan.

She rushed out of her car and across the pavement, the wind whipping at her back as Oak Tree's glass doors gave way far too easily at the push of her hand. She called out to Ally's turned back. "Where's Blaine? I need to talk to him."

Ally wrenched her attention from the customer beside her, her cheerful grin wavering. "He's out the back, but I'm not sure you'll want to talk to him, he's a bit—"

"I'm a bit what?" Blaine held a solid gate across the showroom, his unreadable glower pinned on Emilia. He stopped beside Ally's customer, glower softening by the smallest margin. "Leave now and I'll give you twenty percent off next time you come in."

The older man eyed Emilia, then gave Blaine an easy salute before turning for the exit, throwing Emilia a jubilant wink on his way past.

Blaine tore a twenty from his pocket and handed it to Ally. "Early lunch for you, and don't come back for at least an hour."

"But it's only 10 a.m. and—"

Blaine must have given her a death stare to end all death stares because she dropped her shoulders and turned from him too. "Ah heck! Fine! I'll go."

Emilia watched Ally leave, half-wishing she could follow. Then she recalled every event that had brought her to this moment, and she forced her focus back to Blaine.

He stabbed his thumb over his shoulder, back toward wherever he'd just come from. "Let's take this to the back. Whatever's brought you here, I don't want anyone else seeing this."

Fair enough, the store had giant street-facing windows, and she'd already put him through a public display yesterday. His distrust here was warranted. Besides, whatever did happen next had the potential to be humiliating for her too, so maybe a private talk was a good idea.

She bowed her head, nodding, following Blaine away like an obedient puppy. They entered a room at the back, a workshop with a heavy-duty workbench in the center and stacks upon stacks of unpolished furniture edging the walls.

The thick and bitter scent of lacquer and sawdust punctuated the air, the polished concrete floors speckled with beige wood shavings. She'd sure as anything strayed far from her usual surroundings, and still, she waited for him to face her, her spine straight and words scraping past the dry prickliness in her throat. "I spoke to Sarah. I was wrong."

He gave her what she wanted and spun around. Even with his full attention, he didn't move or speak, just stood about six paces away, maintaining a peeved scowl.

She eyed the room, not fighting his cold reception since she kind of deserved it. Then again, he'd been the one to invite her back here, so was he really going to say nothing?

She took a small step forward, trying again. "I knew the second you walked away at Maynard's I shouldn't have gone behind your back. I know I should have come here sooner, but—"

"But what?" Nothing about his hard stare shifted. "You were a bit too drunk?"

Her jaw dropped a little, somewhat insulted.

"I was going to say I was stupid to involve other people and didn't think you'd want to hear my apology, but sure, let's go with drunk." Her forehead strained as she held back her own scowl. "I want to sort out our differences."

Again, she got nothing. No longer able to maintain direct eye contact, she settled her attention on his gray flannel shirt while the sound of his footfall drew nearer, causing her heart to thump.

"I think you missed a few things. What about how you kicked me out of your house and refused to let me explain? One moment, I'm your knight in shining armor, the next you're treating me like some underhanded villain. It's one thing to self-sabotage, but did you need to take me down with you? And despite what you say, you're not stupid, Emilia. Impulsive, maybe, but not stupid. You knew it was wrong to drag Sarah into your little intervention."

She inched back, her palms clamming with sweat. "So now you're looking for a complete inventory of what I did wrong?"

"Oh yes." He nodded, stepping forward again. To Emilia's dismay, she found herself backed up against the workbench. "And I hope you also gave Sarah one hell of an apology, just like you're about to give me. Knowing the troubles she's been through, you can't imagine how much I didn't want to add to them."

She pressed her lips together, pained to hear there might be even more to Sarah's story, adding yet more fire to the hell she'd already created. "You're not going to make this easy, are you?"

"Should I?" He raised a brow, his smoldering gaze swirling the contents of her stomach and sending her generally off-kilter.

"I've made a heartfelt effort to come here and say I'm sorry." She forced her gaze onto him, her defenses winding her nerves to within snapping point.

"And what, you figured that 'effort' deserved an automatic reward?" He leaned over, his hands pressing to the bench on either side of her, caging her in. The heat coming off him made her own temperature rise, and she wasn't sure if she was supposed to kiss him or fight him. "Ever since you arrived in Harlow, you've been little more than trouble to me. I like having the upper hand for a change."

Her fingers dug into the bench's timber, counteracting her desire to run, like a deeper part of her wanted to see where this confrontation led. With Anthony, she'd been deathly afraid of confrontation, not with Blaine. *How strange.* "You're the one who waltzed back into my house and kissed me. You're the one who started all of this."

A tiny hint of a smile wobbled the edges of his lips; lips she was having trouble not staring at.

"Oh, so now it's back to my fault again, is it?" No doubt he had fun watching her squirm, though in the quiet moment that passed, his gaze searched hers, suggesting he did a fair amount of squirming too. "Some apology this is."

He pushed off the bench, turning his back.

The lump in her throat settled deeper, and she frowned, confused and anguished at his flip-flopping brand of resistance. Her situation was far from ideal, and yet, she'd come here, open to at least allowing him back into her life if only in some small way.

But if Blaine wasn't sure, if he wanted to be another man in her life expecting her to grovel, then she wouldn't give him that satisfaction.

A barely audible growl abraded through her throat, and she forced herself forward, charging toward the exit, set to leave. What had happened to the endearing boy she'd once known?

"Couldn't my word have been enough?" His voice boomed across the space, and she stopped at his words. Words that echoed and reverberated. *Words. Words. And more words.*

"You think *words* mean anything"—she gave a tight laugh and refused to turn around—"to someone like me?"

Maybe Blaine did have nothing to do with all the years of lies and control, everything that had rotted her life and left her with nothing to show for her pain. But he'd been privy to enough of what she'd lived through to guess that trust couldn't be an automatic thing. *Not now. Not ever.*

"I told you." His voice lowered a little, like perhaps he'd read the subtext in her statement. "Sarah wasn't someone you needed to worry about. I understand you've had some shady characters in your life, but you have to—"

She spun around and glared at him, daring him to finish that sentence so she could let herself off the hook and finally walk out of his life forever.

Instead, his face paled, and he pulled back. "Oh, geez. I'm sorry."

She'd taken all the hurt for those "shady characters," and he'd been witness to the manipulation. He'd lived a small moment of her torment.

She marched toward him and grabbed the front of his shirt in both hands, not allowing him to step away, her skin prickling with a need to be heard. "I don't want your apology, and I deserve your anger, I get it. I exposed you to all the horrible things around me, and yes, in recent times, I've led you on and failed to give you a chance to explain. If I had, there wouldn't have been that scene at the bar. I'm sorry, okay? I'm sorry. And I'll never stop being sorry when it comes to you. I've messed you around since the very beginning, but none of it was intended. In the years you haven't known me, things have only gotten worse. I'm an impulsive mess. I can't remember the last time I had a thought not muddied by what-ifs and second guesses. But this is my life right now, Blaine. Take it or leave it."

She released her grip and sagged back.

To her astonishment, he didn't step away. The muscles in his jaw bunched as he ground his teeth together, denoting some kind of deep response he wasn't yet ready to share.

Twenty-Two

"I'LL TAKE IT."

Blaine's tone held a solid edge of finality, those three short words unashamedly direct within the open space of his workshop. He stepped up to her, his palm landing on her overly hot cheek, making her heart thunder in her chest. "I'll take you, and whatever it is you say is making you an 'impulsive mess.' I want the mess, Emilia." His irises lit up like lime citrine caught in the sun, the skin around his eyes creasing with a smile. "Besides, you didn't do all that much leading the other night."

An inescapable wobble took over her mouth, and a broken sort of laugh rushed through the taut muscles in her throat. "I'm pretty sure you saved my life the other day, and all I did was flip out on you. I should have let you stay. I should have canceled my plans with Ally. Should have let you talk. I don't know why I—"

"You've had enough on your plate with your move and the accident." His thumb continued its gentle brush over her cheek, that simple gesture enough to make time stand still.

Another laugh burst free of her. He didn't know the half of what filled "her plate," though she couldn't blame him for his ignorance, not when there was so much she kept unsaid. "My faith in men is rotten to the core."

He held a stillness she only wished she could have too, but all he said was, "I've figured that much."

Her thoughts darkened, and she focused on the dip at the base of his throat. "Sarah told me about the breakup. I'm sorry."

When she lifted her attention, his gaze didn't meet hers, the strain on his face returning. "I didn't want to hurt her."

"I don't think you did, not really. She's smart enough to know that sometimes you have to disappoint others, no matter how unintended. In fact, she said pretty much exactly that. It's a lesson I should have mastered a long time ago. Also, she said something else." Emilia lifted her hand and pressed her palm over the wide expanse of his chest, the soft fibers of his shirt and his warmth slowing the fevered rhythm of her heart. "She wants you to be happy."

Blaine gave a slow nod, his focus flicking back up to her. "And I want her to have the same."

"Also…" Acute awareness rippled over her skin, a tingling that felt like an electric current bringing attention to every inch of her body. Now that Blaine had forgiven her, it was her turn to take a chance. "She wants us to be together."

His sharp stare narrowed as if his emotions balanced on a knife's edge. "And your thoughts on that are?"

She sighed, her own emotions teetering on a precipice, one that lead to an almighty fall into unforgiving, stony territory. How many more chances could this relationship take? There wasn't any room for her to fail Blaine again, but she couldn't promise she wouldn't fail, either way. Not with all the chaos in her life.

"Well, for a small town, things in Harlow sure do seem to move fast. This is—*you* are—a lot to take in." She paused, and as predicted, Blaine gave a lopsided smile at her observations about Harlow and him. "I keep telling myself that being around you is one huge mistake, but for all the risks, I don't want to stay away. I can't decide whether my whole falling off a ladder thing was fate or stupidity, but we've been apart for so long that now we're in the same place, I'm a little glad my lapse in judgment happened. I don't think we should waste this opportunity, do you?"

He dragged his knuckle over her jawline, his gaze poring across the details of her face, the tenderness causing her muscles to turn all weak and trembly. "Given your already 'rotten faith in men,' do you think you could come to trust *this* man?"

She kept her attention locked on his, wanting to ignore the sense of emptiness taking her over. "I want to. Believe me, I want to."

His spare hand moved to her elbow, sliding her sweater sleeve up till he touched her bare skin. A shimmer of heat spread through her body. How could such a simple touch have her holding back a groan?

"Then the answer is easy. We'll go slow." Though his soft drawl spoke of a desire to go anything but slow. "It's been a long time between now and back then. Let's get to know each other again."

Light flooded her eyes, only then alerting her to the fact she'd had them closed. So much for hiding groans; she wasn't half subtle. And even with his offer to get to know each other again, another part of her acknowledged that perhaps no one had ever known her all that well to begin with. The sad truth being that Blaine, in their brief months together, had been the one person to get the closest.

She cleared her throat, hoping to clear her wandering mind in the process. "How do you suggest we do that?"

His hand moved from her elbow to her waist, and he pulled her in, her pulse, along with her next breath, skipping.

She'd warned herself not to let anyone close. But here she was, breaking her own rules, forgetting all her reasons for caution, and luxuriating in the caress of this all-too-lovely man. So much so, she made a conscious effort not to sniff at his cool scent wafting over her.

He pressed his nose to hers, his reaction to her melting into him. "Come with me on a date."

The command was a rumbling whisper in her ear, one that reverberated through her entire body and left her mumbling, "Haven't we already passed that phase?"

She felt his smile against her cheek. "I'm happy to sleep over again, but in your bed this time if that's what you're after."

Her face burned, his words and the tantalizing rub of his body making it hard for her to think. She'd gotten disastrously swept up with this man more than once, and always to bad effect. Maybe the slow approach wasn't such a terrible idea. "Umm. A date it is then."

A chuckle rumbled through him and lightened the mood, awakening her to the emersion of yet another unique opportunity. "And I have a condition."

His hand slipped from her waist, down to her hip, but she dropped her hand over his, stopping his slow exploration. He tilted his head to one side in a quizzical sort of stare.

A wayward smile pulled at her lips. She had a chance to turn his toying with her, back on him. "I haven't been on a date in years. I want you to pick the place. I want a surprise. I want romance. I want a *real* date."

Despite the levity in her request, her shoulders dropped because the last time she'd been this excited to go on a date had been with Blaine, too, only ten years earlier. Which meant, for ten years and almost all of her twenties, no one had cared enough to get enthusiastic about taking her out.

Oh, there'd been the lavish parties and dressing up for big events, but that was all about putting on a show. An exercise in making Anthony look good. He'd rarely spared her a second glance. And even when he had, it wasn't with any soft appreciation, only a razor-sharp look of scorn. The kind a snake leveled before devouring its prey.

Blaine's hand shifted on its determined journey to her hip, his light touch bringing her back to this moment and his gaze on her lips. "I can manage that."

He leaned in as if ready to kiss her, and she pressed her fingertips over his mouth, causing him to laugh.

"What now?" he mumbled through her fingers.

She dropped her hand, her next words a smoky quiver. "Wait."

"You mean, ten years wasn't enough?" His smile grew.

Despite the laugh that escaped her, and her desire to cave to his seductive efforts, it wasn't fair to let him get ahead of himself. "There's a lot you don't know about me."

His fingers inched up her hip, to her waistline, then under her sweater, teasing the naked skin at her side. "I figured that much. I want to talk about it, but not here. Not now. Can we just enjoy making up for a while?"

His lips found the side of her neck, and she squeezed her eyes shut, surrendering to the pleasure.

"Aren't you afraid of what I might say?" Her breathy tone was so unlike her, which made her love the sound even more. Anthony was on the loose, and so much of her life was still in limbo, but damn Blaine, he could make her forget. And hadn't he already agreed to "take" all of her and her chaos?

His excitement pressed to her tummy, and the sensation lit a fire throughout her body. Pure instinct and need had her yearning for his lips on hers.

But he didn't give her that. He kissed her jawline, followed by the side of her neck. She arched her head back, giving him better access, and he obliged, making her legs quiver in the process.

She held on, curling her fingers into his shoulders; a total sucker for whatever he gave, this seemingly small exchange momentous for them as a couple. But for her, as a woman too.

She needed this. Needed him. Needed so much of what she'd missed. This basic human experience.

His lips touched hers, only grazing the corner of her mouth. He made her want to burst into flames to escape the slow-burning tease and maddening assault on her heart.

"You smell incredible, like sweet vanilla and lavender." His voice was all husky desire before he straightened and pulled away, his taut stare an odd mix of pained regret and grace-saving humor. "We already decided to take this slow, didn't we?"

She eased back too, letting her hands fall by her side. "Yes. Yes, we did."

They did need to stop if for no other reason than Ally would return —but holy smokes—Emilia didn't want to.

"I need to make some calls for our date." The glint returned to his eyes. In fact, he looked lighter than ever. "In the meantime, try not to look so sad. I'll pick you up at seven tonight."

Twenty-Three

"You look amazing." Blaine stood with Emilia outside her front door and placed a tentative kiss on her lightly blushed cheek.

Her soft floral scent matched her coy smile. To be fair, so much rode on this date, his face probably betrayed the same nerves.

"It's a miracle I got ready in time." She took his hand, and he led her to his waiting truck. "Aggie had some super-urgent, last-minute thing to do and called me to fill in at the nursery. I only arrived home a little while ago."

"Good thing you made it." He opened the passenger door and helped her in. "I know this isn't exactly a horse-drawn carriage, but I promise the date gets better from here."

She chuckled, squeezing his hand, all while he damn-well hoped the date "got better." He'd waited ten long years for this day, emotionally invested the second she'd agreed to give this reunion a chance. So yeah, there wasn't a great deal of room for error.

She flattened out the flared skirt on her pale pink dress. He closed her door, rounding the truck in his tan chinos and sky-blue sweater, a white t-shirt poking from atop the V-shaped collar. The outfit was more than a few steps up from his usual sawdust-covered flannels.

"So, where are we going?" Emilia blinked at him while he climbed into the driver's seat, the low tilt of her chin setting forth a challenge. One that said, *I have high hopes for this date too.*

He presented a smile, though his stomach churned. "You'll have to wait and see."

"Because I wanted a surprise?"

"Regretting that choice already?" He backed out of her drive.

The warm evening air flowed through his open window and brushed along his arms and face, carrying with it the grassy scent of the sun-heated fields. Meanwhile, Emilia's face still held a great deal of strain.

He reached out and placed a hand over hers on her knee, allowing the breathtaking scenery to work its magic, to melt away any lingering first-date jitters.

I keep telling myself that being around you is one huge mistake, but for all the risks, I don't want to stay away.

As much as he wanted to purely revel in the beauty of those words and what they meant, a menacing sort of omen hid in the middle. A warning that refused to let him go.

But for all the risks…

What risks?

He wanted to believe she referred to the usual perils of falling in love, or more precisely, getting her heart broken; for some reason, he doubted that. Maybe because he'd known her.

At one time, Emilia had been the sort of woman to throw herself all in. She'd been big on emotions and fearless toward love. Something had changed. She'd already mentioned there was more to her story than he knew.

"So, how's the new garden?" He asked the question, vowing to shelve his suspicions, and at the same time acknowledging his right to feel safe too. Maybe he wouldn't press for too much information just yet, but eventually, he wanted answers.

"There are new shoots and flowers each day, and so far, nothing has died. I can't complain. Though"—she turned to him, a mischievous grin lighting those large doe-eyes of hers—"while the garden might be coming along, I can't say the same for the inside of my house. There's this guy who was meant to complete the work on my kitchen, but…"

She shook her head and let out a dramatic sigh, not bothering to complete that sentence.

He laughed, glad for her more easy-going approach. "Sorry about that. From what I hear, he got caught up saving a damsel in distress."

He omitted the part about that same damsel booting him from her house, cornering his ex, and getting wasted off a measly few drinks. No point in stirring up old mud, right?

"Are you sure she wasn't just trying to hold back production?" Though her smile held, her cheeks flushed. "You know, making excuses to keep him around?"

He squeezed his hand over hers, heart shifting at her endearing admission. "Pitching herself off ladders was the wrong way to go about that. All she has to do was ask."

Blaine steered the truck around a corner, the sky darkening, its sapphire peak fading down to a fiery orange horizon. "Do you see that?" He slowed down and pointed at a small tin shed to her right; behind it stretched a sea of purple flowers.

"Is that lavender?" Her voice pitched upwards, suggesting the surprise element of this date might work out after all.

He turned the wheel again and steered down a narrow driveway leading into the field, vivid color and fragrance answering her question. Aggie stepped into view from beside the shed, waving her hand in an unneeded effort to gain his attention.

Emilia turned to him, brow raised in an expression that asked, *What did you do?*

He merely pulled the hand brake and pitched forth an oblivious smile. "Should I give you a little help getting out?"

She drew out a sidelong scowl and swatted a hand to say she could manage on her own. Meanwhile, the ever-uninhibited Aggie McKey sidled up to his window. "Good to see you made it here without drawing each other's blood."

He pushed his door open, and the old woman drew closer, planting a kiss on his cheek the moment his feet touched ground, before making a point of tweaking his nose. Something she'd done since he was a little boy.

He grumbled, still undecided as to whether he appreciated the nose tweaking or not. "Thanks for your help today."

Emilia squeezed in next to him, and he wrapped an arm around her waist.

Aggie winked, her upturned face revealing a distinct sparkle to her faded seafoam-colored eyes. "Just make sure I get a front-row seat at the wedding, okay?"

Emilia jolted in his hold. He pressed a knuckle to his lips, holding back a laugh.

Aggie pulled a set of keys from her pocket. "I've done everything on your list, Mister, so I will let you two get reacquainted." She dropped the keys into his hand, already trudging toward her own truck. "Just remember, no fightin', ya? Dontcha make me drive all the way back here to turn the sprinklers on yous two."

She winked again, her low-level chuckle accompanying her exit.

Emilia peered up at him, her eyes wide and expectant. "This is Aggie's place?"

He took her hand, guiding her along a small path leading to the field's gated entrance. "The McKeys have run this land for five generations. These days, Aggie's grandkids manage this place, and she runs the nursery. Though, as you can see, Aggie can still pull some strings from time to time."

"Lucky for us." To his joy, she closed her eyes and took a slow, deep breath, the field's aroma unmissable either way. "This place is beautiful. Thank you for organizing this."

He leaned in and pressed a light kiss to her neck, right where she tended to place her perfume. "I've taken a recent liking to lavender."

She turned her gorgeous smile toward him, her thick black lashes fluttering and making his heart thud. "You planned all this based on my perfume?"

He tried not to smirk, the sky having changed to a radiant flamingo pink, the color mixing with the lavender behind her like some kind of pastel aura.

"It's just one detail in a long list of things I like about you. Come on." He pulled her along again, deciding that dealing with Aggie's childlike tendencies had been worth Emilia's awestruck reaction. "There's more to this date than flowers."

That much was true. He wanted to do more than flatter her with observations on her perfume; he wanted to give her a whole host of reasons to love Harlow. A host of reasons to stay.

They strolled through the lavender rows, the heady sweet scent dancing around them, her knee-length dress swaying in the breeze over her nimble steps, her delicate fingers extended atop the bobbing flower heads.

Potent pride warmed his blood. She seemed happy. All he'd ever wanted was to see Emilia happy, so much of their relationship marred with uncontrollable interference and heartache. For this brief moment, it was just them. He could finally take credit for a few of her smiles.

She spun around, her warm-chocolate eyes glittering as she pointed down the row. "What's that?"

He raised his chin, prompting her to keep walking. "I told you there was more to this date."

She stopped, despite his command, and bounced on her heels where she stood. "Is that a table? We're having dinner right here in the field?" She beamed at him. "Mr. Callaghan, I had no idea you had it in you…"

She laughed and pranced away, looking over her shoulder as she did so, the overjoyed light in her eyes making his heart squeeze once more. Since when did Emilia Bonacci prance?

"I'll to need you to define what 'it' is exactly." He strode after her, taking his time, savoring this moment, folding her ease and adoration up and locking it away safe in his memory.

"Romance, Blaine. I never took you as a romantic." She'd stopped at the table, the surface covered with a white linen table cloth.

He hid his smile a little. There was probably a lot about him she didn't know, sentimentality and preferences on romance included. The whole point of this date was to get reacquainted. If he were truly lucky, there'd be many more dates, and an entire lifetime to "learn" each other throughout their many seasons.

She took his hand, pulled him into her, and stood on her toes. "It's been a long time since someone did anything this thoughtful for me."

Though her ensuing kiss caught him off guard, her words had the deepest impact; ones that introduced yet more pain to his heart, even as her lips held his. He imagined her alone, or worse, with someone who hadn't looked out for her, and the thought alone tortured him.

He pulled back, looking over her anew, reminded just how much about this woman remained a mystery. What had the last decade entailed for her?

She slipped back and took a seat; he followed and forced himself to find something meaningful to say. Like how much his minimal effort today was the bare bones of what she deserved...

"Do you mind if I unpack?" She pointed to a wicker basket beside her feet, opening it before he had a chance to say anything. "I can't wait to see what we have here."

The moment to speak up had gone, and he gestured for her to go ahead, his gaze falling to the already laid out china plates, crystal glasses, and stainless-steel cutlery.

Despite his simple requests, Aggie had gone above and beyond, especially since she'd skipped the plastic picnicware and used real crockery instead. Maybe he'd continue to grin and bear her nose tweaking. She only ever meant well, and he definitely owed her big time for today's favor.

He reached across the table and poured two glasses of red wine, occasionally glancing at the black ironwork candelabra and vase full of field flowers—both small touches he might not have thought of himself.

Pretty soon, Emilia had pulled all the items from the basket: an assortment of fruits, cheeses, dips, and salads. They sat and sipped on wine, making idle chatter about his work and the interesting characters Emilia had met so far in town.

Before long, a heavy quiet fell over the table, and he couldn't help but notice the way she twisted one of the white, cloth napkins around her index finger.

He lowered his fork. "Is something wrong?"

She jolted, dropping the cloth to the table as though completely unaware of her fidgeting.

"Oh." She jerked her gaze away to some point in the field. "I just got a bit lost in thought, that's all."

Her brows pressed together, dipping at the center, hinting maybe that "thought" still stuck around.

He leaned back, making it clear she had his full attention. "Want to talk about it?"

"It's just." She frowned down at the table, focus bouncing from one item to the next, like maybe the bowl of salad or the vase played an instrumental part in forming her next words. "I always wondered what happened to you. Why you chose to come back to Harlow of all places. Why you never once tried to find me…"

Now it was his turn to peer down at his plate, his mood dragged beneath a slew of old memories of being helpless and lost. "I had no other choice. Neither of us would have been safe if I'd stayed in LA. Same goes for if I'd tried to contact you. So when Frank offered me a place to live after your father and Anthony forced me out, I took him up on the offer."

She let out a small gasp, and when he peered up, her eyes were wide and her posture poker straight. "My dad and Anthony forced you out?"

Dull strain pulled at his cheekbones, and he inspected her every move, his body heat rising. "You mean, you didn't know?"

She shook her head furiously, her fingers coming to her lips in a slow and trembling movement. "No. What are you saying? What did they do?"

"I assumed—" He cleared his throat, pulling himself taller, this date getting a hell of a lot darker than he'd ever intended. Though now this line of conversation had arrived, there didn't seem much point in trying to avoid it. "That night, after you came to my house wanting to run away, and my parents found me in the driveway. They called the police and reported Anthony for property damage and assault, but when he got hauled in, your father bailed him out."

"My father?" Her face went sheet white, quite a feat what with her soft sienna skin tone. Her fingertips no longer hovered over her lips, her entire hand now clapped over her mouth. "Why? Why would he do that? Why would he get involved?"

He gave a barking laugh. God, they'd done a beautiful job of keeping this woman naive. "Because Anthony convinced your dad I'd been in the process of kidnapping you. He told everyone, including the police, he'd been the one to stop me."

"But…" Her entire body began to shake, and her gaze darted about, as though the alternate truth she searched for might be anywhere but sitting directly in front of her.

"Emilia, please don't pass out on me in this field."

She held up a hand, a sign she could handle the news, though her heaving shoulders filled him with doubt. "I just don't know how… How could he? How could anyone believe Anthony's story?"

Blaine reached across the table for her hand and hoped the contact would help her settle some. "All I know is, once the legal dust settled, I had orders from your dad to leave the city. In return, he wouldn't press charges, and you and I would go on with our lives as if we'd never met. I wanted to contact you, believe me, I did. But I was afraid of what might happen to you if anyone found out."

She bit her lip, nodding like she understood, and yet the hurried movement said the truth hurt her all the same. "I…" She turned her hand, so her fingers grasped his. "I tried to find you. I even spoke to your parents not long after that night, but they wouldn't say much. I figured you'd all decided I was bad news, which I guess no matter how you spin it, I am."

"Emilia, we're not teenagers anymore." He gave a weak smile, his thumb caressing her smooth knuckles. "And I know you tried, but my parents didn't tell me until a couple of years ago. They lied out of fear your dad or Anthony might retaliate. By the time I found out, I was seeing Sarah, and I figured you'd probably moved on too. I didn't want to bother you."

She squeezed her eyes shut and sucked in a shaky breath. "You didn't have to leave LA alone, if—"

"No, Emilia. I did." He pulled his hand back and sent forth a stern glower, mostly because he didn't want to play the what-if game. A game no one at this table could win. "Even if I'd known you'd contacted me, my parents had to stay in LA for work, and my sister needed to finish her last years of high school. I couldn't put them at risk by staying, as much as I couldn't risk you getting hurt if we got caught trying to leave again. Anthony and your father already made it clear what they were capable of."

She slumped back, her fingers slipping from the table. He hated the deflated roll of her shoulders, the way her gaze no longer met his; while the truth hurt, not facing it hurt even more. Denying what had happened. Pretending the past didn't bother him. Those things had held him captive for far too long. Maybe denial had done the same to her too.

He blew out a hard breath, feeling like a total bastard for shooting down her hope. The truth of what her own family had done maybe spelling the end to this date. "Look, we both got a raw deal out of this. Anthony never paid for his crime, and your father got to keep you under his control. Seems everyone benefited from breaking us up, except us. So, it's not your job to carry around the guilt over what Anthony and your dad did, got it?"

"I feel angry more than guilty." Her chin remained pointed down, but she peered up at him through long, thick lashes, those deep brown eyes drawing him in. "I thought there was something wrong with me." Her voice fell to little more than a whisper. "Like you'd moved on, and I was the one left behind."

"No." The muscles in his jaw clenched, and he took a deep swallow, trying to work up to what he had to say next. "I carried you with me, even when I wanted nothing more than to forget you."

He gave her a moment to process what he'd said. The fact that he sat across from her now—that he'd gone to the effort of forgiving her insecurities and overreactions thus far—added credibility to his words.

And on that note, since he'd bared a little of his soul and illuminated part of their story, he gave a curt nod, seeking a little payback. "I have a question for you now."

He leaned in and gave her a direct stare, elbows on the table, ensuring she didn't sidestep out of this face-off. Given the line of discussion, given what he'd been through and what he knew of her life, he had his hunches and wanted them confirmed. "After my confession, I think I deserve an answer."

Her posture turned rigid, cheeks taking on a hard set, though at least she wasn't yet shying away. "I'm not going to like this, am I?"

He shook his head and braced for the worst, though some things had to be done, precisely because he meant to avoid "the worst." "Probably not."

She bit her lower lip and gave a steady nod, a woman unsure, but open to accepting her fate.

So, he poised to ask his question, almost certain they'd both regret it when he did.

"Why are you in Harlow? And what are you running from?"

Twenty-Four

EMILIA TRIED to escape the hot sensation burning up her skin, Blaine's stare pinning her with an unspoken challenge to answer the question.

Why are you in Harlow? And what are you running from?

How did he know? Did she make her fear and caution so obvious? Of course she did. She'd warned him about her having secrets, hadn't she? Though maybe she could laugh his question off. Deflect and pretend she didn't know what he was talking about.

Maybe she could straight-up suggest he was way off base, that she merely wished to leave the city and indulge in country life for a while. She wouldn't be the first.

Then again, she was the one still very much married, even though she'd flipped out at Blaine over Sarah. Maybe she could be forgiven for her intended deception. Chances were better than great that Blaine and Sarah had a relationship far closer to a functional marriage than she and Anthony did.

She released a pent-up breath and loosened her posture, deciding she had too much respect for Blaine to lie. He'd saved her life, forgiven her mistakes, been more compassionate toward her than anyone else besides her own mother. And he was right, he'd answered her questions, so maybe it was time to answer his.

How much worse could talking to him make her existence, anyway?

"I couldn't live that life anymore." A raw and brittle voice escaped her mouth, one she barely recognized; but she forced herself to go on with the truth, claiming a morsel of ownership over what had happened to her. "Everything looked so beautiful from the outside, perfect even, but my spirit had died years ago, and most days, I felt like I was on some kind of life support. The people around me had drained any spark I'd once had. I'd wake each morning just wishing I could be somewhere else, that I could have some kind of control over my life. I had to get away because if I didn't, the other options running through my mind terrified the hell out of me. Day by day, my thoughts got darker, and then the anxiety-induced fainting started. If I didn't leave, I'd end up doing something drastic."

Blaine's hard glare melted, and he gave a slow, incredulous shake of his head. "But you got out, and you did it alone."

"Sure." A tight laugh pushed past her lips. "And I wouldn't have had to do anything alone if my dad and Anthony had just butted out and not driven you way."

The glare returned. "So that's who you're running from? Your dad and Anthony? That guy is still meddling in your life?"

Her gaze fell. Each new bit of information she offered only fueled more questions, but did she want to go into so much detail about Anthony? Not just the threat of him finding her, but the stuff that truly hurt, the stuff that seared her with pain and shame at every single reminder or mention of his name.

She could barely fathom telling Blaine she'd married Anthony, much less any of the other stuff, so she pinched her lips together and shook her head, aiming for a vague reply instead. "I wish things had turned out differently, that's all."

Blaine pulled his jaw shut tight, nostrils flaring, while his stare drove into her, hard and unforgiving. "You didn't answer my question, Emilia. Is Anthony still in your life?"

Her chin trembled, and her throat swelled while she gave a quick shake of her head. "Not anymore."

Not a complete lie, but not the total truth, either.

"Emilia…" Her name was a growled warning, and his momentary pause hurt more than when he spoke. "Talk."

"Blaine…" She whispered his name, a last-ditch plea before she slammed her eyes shut, not wanting to see his face when she told him. "Anthony is my husband."

Air rushed into her lungs, and she recoiled at the admission; she wanted to be sick. But the prolonged silence said more about how much pain she'd inflicted on Blaine.

"Why him?" His deflated tone made her stomach twist and her eyes sting, the roiling crush of shame worked its way through her body. She wanted his anger more than she wanted his disappointment. "Of all people, why him?"

She opened her eyes to find his cheeks sunken and pale—like the truth sucker-punched him in the gut—though the shifting ache in her belly suggested maybe she'd been the one to take the hit.

"What was I supposed to do?" She didn't like any of this. She didn't like it one bit. Her loud, hard voice built the emotional wall she needed to get through this conversation. Better for Blaine to hate her. "You were gone, and I had no way of making it out of there on my own, I was ju—"

"So you married *him*?" Blaine's words lashed back, his eyes flinty, his sunken cheeks now locked with tension.

"My dad controlled my education, my money, my entire life. I did what he wanted because I had nowhere else to turn."

"You could have said no, Emilia! You could have said no and gotten the hell out of there."

"I was seventeen when you left, remember?" Her voice rose, throat constricting around her argument. Now she really did want to cry. How dare he judge her. How dare he assume to know what it was like. To be a girl in that scenario. The support and scope for who she wanted to become so stupidly limited.

Not everyone had a Frank and Maureen to run to when things went bad. Not everyone lived in a culture where something as arbitrary as gender didn't have to determine how competent one was to make it in the world.

She'd felt so helpless at the time, raised to leave anything that pertained to "the real world" for the men to handle, and her helplessness had only gotten worse with each year. Her life had been a socially engineered prison so few women in her community ever escaped. It had taken her years just to see what was happening.

"Did you expect I'd hightail it out of there to live on the streets until I turned eighteen and finally had some legal right over my life?" She swallowed back her tears, refusing to shed them. "And unlike you, I had no other family or connections to support me."

"Damn it, Emilia. That's not fair. I never *left*. I was run out of town. I had no choice, just like you." He shot from his chair, the entire thing falling back and slamming to the dry dirt behind him, sending out a small plume of dust.

He turned and stormed away a few paces. More silence came. His stance excluded her from gauging the reactions on his face.

Once more, he left her alone with their past and her guilt.

"So you're married?" His back remained to her, like the only way he could ask that question was if he didn't have to look at her.

She gave a small. "Yes."

This time, he spun around. His eyelids flared in a way that said she wounded him yet again. "Then why come on this date? What was with the last few days of jealousy and drama?" His voice echoed across the field, and she flinched at the semi-manic laugh that escaped him, his hand dragging through his hair. "Why give me hell over Sarah if you're the one who's already taken?"

Her mouth wavered, in part because she knew she deserved his rage. And still, rage, no matter how many times she witnessed it, turned her tummy rock-hard and brought an instant debilitating ache to her chest. "I…"

"Say something." He barked out the order.

She flinched again, and her mind blanked. She wanted to answer him but simply couldn't.

"Nothing makes sense." He strode forward and stood over her, voice still lifted, so she buried her back deeper into her chair, trying to hide.

"Tell me what I'm supposed to think." He leaned in. *"Tell me!"*

"Stop yelling at me!" This time her voice was the one to shatter the field's peace.

She jumped to her feet, shoving both hands at his chest just to get him out of her space.

To his credit, he did move, his face falling slack like he hadn't expected her retaliation. *Well, good!*

"I'm so sick of men yelling, and ordering, and getting so damn uppity every time I fall short of expectations." She gave him a searing glare and backed up even more. "You call us the 'hysterical' sex, but look at you." She thrust a hand out in his direction. "Every single one of you is a goddamn mess too."

Holy cannoli… Did she just say, "damn" followed by "goddamn"? Each of her dead Roman Catholic ancestors would be rolling in their graves…

Blaine's gaze flicked over her like he didn't quite know what to make of her reaction. He didn't seem angry at least, just… confused?

Something shifted in her chest, and her temper cooled a little.

"My marriage was hell, okay?" Not that she'd never mentioned her bad marriage before. Time and time again when she had, she'd been told to stop complaining, to put on a brave face, to "adjust" to her misery because she was probably at fault for everything wrong in her life.

"You really want to know why I came to Harlow? I filed divorce papers, Blaine. I didn't lie. I'm free to do whatever I want now, okay? Including dating. And if you *must* know, I left LA to get away from *him*."

Blaine worked his jaw from side to side, grinding his teeth as though that might bring about his next thought. "And let me guess, your dad and Anthony don't so much agree about you leaving?"

"I ran, Blaine." She wrapped her arms around herself and lowered her voice. "I planned as best as I could. I hadn't figured on leaving so soon, but the night before I left Anthony and I got in a fight, and I couldn't stay any longer. So, I ran the very next morning."

It hurt to look at him while relaying this, but she did so, anyway. She needed him to understand. Needed him, and everyone else, to just go easy on her for a while. "I'd decided on Harlow weeks before I left LA and sent an email to Frank and Maureen about renting the cottage the night Anthony and I fought. I had no idea my escape would lead to you. You have to believe me, Blaine, I didn't set out to hurt you."

The strain across his face dropped, the hard line of his jaw easing. "That fight you got into with Anthony." He jutted his chin toward her hand still wrapped across her body. "Is that why you arrived in town with busted knuckles? Did he hurt you?"

She didn't need to peer down at her hand to know those cuts and bruises had mostly healed by now, so she merely peered ahead for a moment and gave Blaine a shaky nod. "He tried to touch me that night and I said, 'no'."

"Emilia." Blaine's voice was husky, and he took a step forward.

She held a hand out, signaling for him to stop. "Let me finish. Maybe you need to hear this part of my story, and maybe I need to tell it too."

Twenty~Five

EMILIA DREW A HARD BREATH, unable to believe she was finally talking about this part of her life. A part so all-consuming, yet she'd been forced to hold on to it in silence. All because so many people didn't want to hear.

"For years, Anthony and I had an agreement. Can you imagine what sharing a bed with that man entailed?" She blinked, and to her dismay, a fat tear rolled down her cheek.

She swatted the trail of water from her face, trying to ignore the heavy weight pressing on her lungs, a weight that made every one of her ensuing breaths shake.

"For the first few years, he forced himself on me a lot. He was rough, with zero care for what I wanted. Almost every encounter resulted in bruises somewhere on my body." She gave a shuddering laugh, a silly reaction really, though one she couldn't stop. "But we were married, and having sex was his right and my duty, or so they say."

They being the people in her community. She'd tried to talk, to seek help, only to receive ridicule and dismissive statements about how a husband was supposed to "chase his wife." How she should be flattered over his "passion" for her.

She wanted to vomit just thinking about all the things she'd been told to accept, to be *thankful* for. Hot bile pushed against the already swollen muscles in her throat. Nothing of what Anthony inflicted on her could be classed as passion. Control, yes, but not passion.

She'd experienced passion. With Blaine. And passion then had extended beyond the physical, encompassing genuine respect and freedom, especially when one's partner said, "no" or "stop."

What she'd had with Anthony had been something else entirely. Each incident was his chance to exert his power, to prove himself important at her expense.

"This went on for years, though less and less, until I stopped being enough for him." At least, Anthony had wanted to wait until their thirties before trying for children. Subjecting a child to that situation, much less leaving with one in tow now, would have been a nightmare. "Maybe in most other marriages a husband turning his attention to other women would be cause for devastation, but to me, Anthony's infidelity was a relief. He didn't much care when I moved out of our bedroom. I gave him open permission to bring other women home after a certain hour, as long as they stayed in his room and away from me and the rest of our house. The deal was, I'd keep his secret and play at being his wife, all on the proviso he never touched me again."

Blaine stood quiet for a moment, the lines on his forehead bent, his gaze shifting about her face in a hint that maybe he didn't know what to say. This in itself provided relief. There were few "right" words to say to someone who'd just admitted to surviving ten years in an abusive marriage. And if there were any right words, none of them included making excuses for Anthony or describing his behavior as "to be expected," enough of which she'd already endured.

"Until that last night?" Blaine flexed his brow in a small, pinched sort of manner like he still hadn't processed all she'd said. "I'm not sure I want to know, but you should probably tell me, anyway."

She gave a taut smile. No one else knew about that last night. Maybe she should have told her dad. Maybe he should wear a portion of the darkness his knuckle-headed decisions had lumped on her. Maybe then he would be less inclined to expect her to return. *Though, given all the things he had known about, maybe not…*

"Anthony had been extra erratic those last few months, and I figured out why. He was attempting to get away with some shady dealings regarding his work for my dad. I played dumb, allowed him to believe he had me fooled too, all while lining things up so I could escape and destroy him in the process. That last night, he came into our apartment wanting to prove something, either to himself, or me, or both. He stank of cigarettes, sweat, and booze. He came in ranting that one day soon I would have nothing. That I'd be begging him to touch me just so he'd throw some loose change my way. He wasn't too happy when I replied that I'd rather starve to death. As usual, I figured he just needed time to sleep off his drinking, so I left for my room. But he followed me."

Blaine winced, a distinct tension drawing at his upper lip like he knew this story would only get worse. And because of his visible pain, she pressed on, wanting to get through this hard retelling as soon as possible for both their sakes. "He wrapped his hand around my throat and pinned me to the bed. Through my panic, I could hear the clinking of him loosening his pants. I can't tell you what I thought at that moment because there wasn't much time to think. I just swung at him, and his nose made this audible crack. I might have broken it. I don't know. I hope so. His blood gushed all over me, and he let go quickly after that. I must have looked like something escaped from the pits of hell, all covered in his blood, so I ran with that image, and I screeched and screamed. I said he needed to leave, or I wouldn't stop screaming until I woke up every last neighbor in our building, and someone called the police."

The tension on Blaine's face relaxed some, and he spoke again. "And that worked?"

She nodded, peering down at her hand, the one that had sported bruises, fingers clasped but fidgeting all the same. "Long enough for me to lock my door and hide. I would have left right there and then, but I didn't want to risk running into him again, especially not while he was drunk. So, I stayed awake the entire night, researching, watching my door. I waited for him to leave for work the next morning, so I could print off all the incriminating evidence I'd collected over the months. After I did all that, I left for myself."

"Emilia." Blaine stepped forward, holding his arms out and then dropping them as if he'd wanted to hold her, only to second-guess the action.

She nodded, letting him know it was okay. Anthony might have left scars, but she'd only ever felt safe around Blaine. He swept in close and wrapped his arms around her in a tight embrace, his palms encasing the back of her head.

Maybe words weren't the best remedy for what she'd revealed, but his tender touch, a stark contrast to what she'd experienced with Anthony, made her feel a million times less alone.

Blaine kissed the top of her head, his quiet strength seeping into her bones. "Does Anthony know you're in Harlow?"

She shook her head against the soft blue of his wool sweater, savoring the warmth, her hands wrapped around him too and pressing into his back. "At least, I hope not. I hope I never hear from him ever again."

"I wish I'd known about this earlier," Blaine spoke into her hair, and she closed her eyes at the comfort of his soft rumble.

"When?" Something painful shifted in her chest, the sort of shifting that threatened to reawaken her tears. "Between us fighting, me kicking you out, or you storming away? When was I supposed to tell you?"

He stepped back and inspected her through a frown as though he didn't know where her defensive reply came from. Neither did she. A deeper part of her knew his statement was nothing more than a turn of phrase, but perhaps on some level, there were things she still wanted to hash out with him.

"How about that night you fell off the ladder?" He cocked his head to one side, extending an unimpressed facade. "Before you decided to rip into my personal life?"

"Would knowing about me and Anthony have changed things?" She peered up at him, softening her expression and peeling back from her more abrasive approach. "Would you have kept your engagement with Sarah instead of being here on this date with me?"

"That's the dumbest thing about all of this." He scrubbed a hand over his face and growled to himself, but not in a way that made her feel in any way unsafe. "You know I'd still be here."

No matter the stakes, he would choose her every time. Yeah, she knew that much. And he was right, maybe none of that made any sense, but the "dumbest" thing was that she'd do the same for him too.

She lowered her chin, kicking at the crumbly earth beneath her pale-pink ballet flat, wishing things could be different, about a billion times different and far less complicated. Blaine deserved uncomplicated. Heck, so did she.

"I didn't choose this life." Her voice came out a hollow whisper.

He held a long silence, leaving her to wonder what went through his mind, or whether he would even say anything. "Neither did I."

Her shoulders eased with that revelation, her defenses taking a backseat. The course of his life had been pushed offtrack because of her.

No. Not because of me. My father and Anthony did this. But I need to clean up the damage either way.

"I have to see this thing with Anthony through. I have no idea how long that will take or even what will happen. I hope in the end, I'll be free and you will be there with me, but if you want to go, I—"

The inside of her throat turned thick, and she abandoned the end of that sentence. She'd been about to say she'd understand. And that much was true. She could understand him wanting to leave, to save himself, more than she understood him wanting to stay. But making out like there'd be no hard feelings? That was the disingenuous part. Losing Blaine twice would crush her.

"You know I don't want to go." He stuffed his hands into his pockets and frowned at the ground, his forehead twitching as though that honesty hurt him. "I just don't want you to give me more hope if it doesn't exist."

"I'm doing everything I can to free myself from that man." She stepped closer, wanting to reach out and touch him, though his taut stance left her uncertain if she should. "Bear with me, okay?"

The skin over his exposed collarbone was a mottle of flushed red and white, his overall strain still very much there. "I want to kill that man for what he did to you."

His fists clenched at his sides, hinting that if Anthony were here right now, he'd be fielding a solid punch to the face.

She understood Blaine's anger and wanted to defuse it all the same. This date was for her and him, not Anthony, not her dad. Two men who'd stolen enough joy.

So, she lifted a hand to his cheek, where an extraordinary heat wafted off his skin in a physical expression of buried rage. His gaze snapped down to her, somewhat conflicted and heartbroken too, suggesting her touch pulled him from something.

He pressed his hand over hers, and he turned his head, kissing her palm with a tenderness that had her heart palpitating, and her eyes ready to weep again, but for a whole other reason.

"Let's take this one date at a time." Her lower lip trembled through her smile, no doubt making her attempt to reassure him not all that convincing. "I know this is nothing like what either of us ever wanted, but I want to focus on the positive. I'm here. I'm free. I have a whole new life to get used to. And I want to get used to it with you."

"Then thinking positively"—his arms enfolded her, one corner of his lip lifted, and the wrinkles over his forehead flattened—"I might avoid a prison sentence if I just pretend that husband of yours never existed."

"You do that." She tipped her head down and pressed her cheek to his chest, the light thud of his heartbeat soothing her own. "And I might give it a try myself."

They stood there for a while, the lavender rustling and emitting its calming scent, the night air cooling, and Blaine's arms offering a warm contrast to that cold. She huddled into him, some of her problems shared, but their impact on her life not halved.

"Blaine?" She tilted her head back and drank in the light in his eyes. "Take me home."

Twenty-Six

THE TRIP back to Emilia's house consisted of little conversation, right up until they pulled into her driveway with the red Pinto parked ahead. She'd overwhelmed Blaine, that much was obvious. Despite the silence, she didn't feel judged or less for having revealed the truth, only that she'd given him a lot to think about.

She opened the truck's door and took the long slide down to the ground, the vehicle designed for someone much taller than her. Blaine trailed not far behind, and she headed for her front porch, a low-level tension drawing at her tummy and suddenly stopping her in her tracks.

She spun around to him, and his brows pressed low under the force of a frown, a frown that questioned her abrupt pause. Only for him to speak first.

"I don't want the night to end like this." He spoke the thoughts already running through her mind.

She wanted to say she didn't like the silence, that she appreciated the effort he'd put into the date, and maybe they could try again sometime soon. "Neither do I, Blaine, I—"

He shook his head, gaze dipping, before rejoining hers once again. "I mean, I don't think this night should end at all."

For a second there, her world stilled, and she figured she'd heard wrong. Maybe he implied far less than where her mind went. But then she closed her mouth and reconsidered her next words. She didn't much mind *what* he meant either way.

She stepped toward him, the hard lump in her belly turning into a tickling flutter of butterflies. "No, tonight shouldn't end here."

She reached for him, burying her fingers in the hair at the nape of his neck. He met her in the middle and pulled her closer, his lips snaring hers.

Maybe he'd meant that he'd merely wanted to join her inside to talk a while longer, but the firm heat of him felt just right. It melted weeks of uncertainty. He was her blissful distraction. Her choice. Her moment of control when for so long she'd had none.

She broke the kiss and slid her hands down his arms, interlacing her fingers with his and pulling him along. Soon, she had her front door open, and he paused in her hallway, his earlier dark frown returning. "There's something I need to clear with you first. Something you said that's been playing on my mind."

The butterflies in her tummy disintegrated into dry ash, and her shoulders fell slack right along with them. Still, she nodded, allowing him to speak.

"I have emotions, Emilia. Sometimes they're going to come out." His pale green stare held hers, stirring the earlier memory of her snapping and calling him her equal when it came to being "hysterical" and "messy."

Well, she didn't exactly deny or regret that. She'd long ago learned that men could be just as wild and irrational, perhaps sometimes more so. Maybe it was the societal pressure to express little more than anger and happiness. An absurd pressure that made emotions harder to control when they eventually did break loose. Either way, she'd attributed negativity to his expression, and for that, she did have regrets.

"I'm sorry." She stepped back, making it clear he was still welcome in her home, despite the heavy topic. "I want you to feel whatever you feel, believe me, I do. But when you yell, I just can't take it."

His eyes narrowed, his unspoken way of asking her to explain.

"Anthony… he…" She slammed her eyes shut, refusing to bring her soon-to-be ex-husband into this moment. "Just don't yell at me, okay? It scares me. Can we just agree to be a whole lot gentler with each other from now on?"

Blaine drew closer and cupped his hands to her face. "You're right. I'm so sorry." His voice dropped to an intimate whisper, one that held a wounded huskiness. "I won't raise my voice like that again. I promise. Okay?"

She gave a shaky nod, wanting to move on, to chase away the darkness, at least for a short while. The night sounds of cicadas pulled her back to the moment, those sounds full of mystery and promise. They caused the corners of her lips to ascend into a genuine smile. "Good, now close the door. Before a wild coyote or bandicoot, or whatever other wild creature is out there, barges in."

His gaze didn't leave hers, though his weight shifted as he extended a leg to the side and kicked the door shut. The loud slam sent a crack of laughter rippling through her, and he followed suit, his hands still caressing her cheeks.

And even though her bedroom stood just to her right, she spun away and lead him to the left—to her living room and the couch— where she wouldn't have to deal with her negative associations with beds and bedrooms.

She would create new memories tonight. The kind of memories she should have had from the very beginning. Memories with Blaine. *Of* Blaine.

With any other man she wouldn't be so sure, but she *knew* this one. He'd never once tried to control her. To cause her pain. He'd only ever offered protection and the truth, even when it wasn't easy. She'd be safe with him. She trusted him.

She stood him before the couch and allowed him to kiss her, her tummy butterflies taking flight again and igniting a deep-set tingle throughout her body. Her skin felt alive, and it begged for his touch.

His hands pressed either side of her face, directing the kiss; her hands wandered lower, to his tummy, pulling at his sweater, only for his firmly tucked shirt to thwart her attempt to undress him.

New laughter took over, and she folded forward a little, the kiss breaking while she wrestled to free the material from beneath the waist of his pants. Blaine took a second to help, chuckling as he did so, soon throwing the shirt to the couch as if its minor protest offended him.

The muscles over her face sank, and all she could see was the stunning man before her. His beauty. The physical expression of what he meant to her. Raw, wild, and powerful. Yet somehow vulnerable and tame.

She'd seen him shirtless before—that morning she'd booted him from her house—but having him this close and *knowing* without a doubt where this would go... His semi-nakedness was familiar, yes, but so different from the young man she'd been with years ago. He was safe and known, and someone new, all in one, and the crush of how much she wanted him stole her breath.

"Wow." The expression fell from her with what felt like the last sound she would ever muster.

"We can stop." His voice brought her attention from his broad chest and onto his eyes, now dark pools in the dim of the room. "Emilia, just tell me and we can stop."

She shook her head, swamped by his willingness to put her first. Words now totally lost, she raised her hands and slid her dress's thick straps from her shoulders, allowing the outfit to fall to her feet with a light thud.

His fingertips connected with the sides of her waist, and he tugged her in, his heat-stoking gaze stirring an inferno low in her belly.

Her heart thundered, and her ears filled with the loud rush of her blood, her legs weak while she warred between wanting to cry and wanting to leap into action. She hadn't ever felt so joyfully out of control.

"Kiss me again." She held his gaze as she spoke, only for her vision to fall to darkness, her eyes slamming shut the moment his lips took hers.

Five years. Five years since she'd been with a man, and that last time had been *nothing* like *this time.*

She kissed Blaine back, desperate to get to him, to make him feel her desire. She wanted to lose herself in everything that being with him meant to her. To reclaim their years apart and all they'd been through together.

She pulled at his belt. He kicked off his shoes. She freed him. He unhooked her bra. Neither one stopped the fevered exploration of the other, and soon enough, they both stood bare.

She pressed at his shoulders and sat him on the couch, allowing his gaze to dance over her nakedness, his chest unmoving like maybe he forgot to breathe. *Well, that makes two of us.*

She stepped in and lowered herself to his lap, his warm and hard surfaces surrounding her in strength. But she could be strong too. She'd survived, hadn't she? She'd learned to be all she needed. Her strength had brought her here, where she rewrote her story and recovered who she was always meant to be, gathering all that had been stolen from her.

Including Blaine.

She sank over him and guided him into her, taking time to adjust to the hot sting of his length and width. He seemed to notice her physical discomfort and pressed his hands on either side of her ribs, supporting, guiding.

She used the moment to appreciate this man and his quiet confidence, that his strength extended to letting her decide her place with him. That appreciation had her relaxing and luxuriating in the feel of him, had her wanting to weep at the tenderness of it all. At his steady stream of kisses over her neck and his soft touch over her skin.

A force grew within her, urging her to move, to take him—to celebrate her freedom to live and love as she wished. Her heart surged with that need, and she rose and fell over him; his long fingers clenched at her hips, pressing her down and adding to the sumptuous pressure.

Not once did his mouth leave her body, his lips brushing a nipple, his teeth scraping a shoulder. Her hands traveled up the thick muscle of his chest, worshipping his heat until her fingers found the nape of his neck, and she grasped at his short waves there.

She rocked against him, slow at first, then building speed. One moan after another poured from her, each movement taking her closer to a climax that had eluded her for so long. His capable hands held her tight, and she arched back, her moan exploding into a guttural cry, one that held years of grief, and loneliness, and longing.

He took over now, helping her move atop him and drawing out her pleasure until she feared she'd fall apart from the unrestrained bliss. But fall she did. In so many ways, she fell and let go.

He lengthened within her and joined her over the edge, into a valley of pure and heart-stopping connection. For the longest time, she stayed in his lap, her arms locked around him through the silent reverie.

Save for an awareness of his smell, all rational thought escaped her. The leather and wood, his skin's added musk from their heated love-making. She wanted to stay like this forever. She hoped they would get that chance.

Sometime after midnight, Emilia lay in her bed, unable to sleep, her arm tucked under Blaine's head. She slid away, leaving him to rest, pausing a moment to sit on the mattress edge because a sense of overwhelming guilt had her tummy churning.

After what they'd shared, there were things she no longer wanted to keep from him, but honesty would come at a cost. He'd have questions, some of which she had no answers to. Not without learning the latest news from LA.

She pressed her feet to the cold wood boards and stood, the years of lies and secrets having caused so much hurt. Another phone call with her father was the least she could do. She'd confront him over pushing Blaine from her life, over stealing her choices and therefore her happiness, then she'd find out if Anthony remained on the loose.

Perhaps there were new leads. Maybe she'd have an easier story to tell if the shambles of her escape included an ending where Anthony sat locked behind bars.

She threw a crocheted blanket over her shoulders and wandered into the living room with her phone, closing the door while the dial tone to her dad's number rang in her ear.

"Hello, you have reached Vittorio Bonacci. Please leave a message and I'll get back to you."

The prerecorded message left her frowning into the near darkness.

She redialed, pacing the room.

"Hello, you have re—"

She hung up again, a disconcerting gnawing in her stomach.

Despite the message's request, she couldn't leave a message. Not when she'd gone to the extent of using a concealed number. She had to reduce any evidence of her existence. So, she sank back to the couch, one thought bothering her more than the rest.

Her father worked hard. Way too hard. It was midnight in LA, and he wouldn't be asleep right now. He'd probably be tinkering with a new design, maybe a statement piece for a celebrity red-carpet appearance or a commission for some private client.

In all her years of knowing her dad, with all their differences and misunderstandings, there was one thing she knew about Vittorio Bonacci. The one thing that troubled her most…

He *never* missed one of her calls.

Twenty-Seven

"I HOPE you don't mind all this extra work."

It was late afternoon, and Ally's light blue eyes offered a coy apology from across Emilia's kitchen table.

"Honestly, it's fine." She pressed her right foot to the old sewing machine pedal, a machine borrowed from Ally's mother. "I'm glad you came over, actually. I've never made costumes before, and this is fun."

"What the heck?" Ally jerked her head back, her voice muffled under the machine's rapid-fire sound, one hand clutched around a long piece of forest green material, the other around a pair of shiny red fabric scissors. "First, you dabble in gardening, and now sewing is your idea of 'fun'? You're like Aggie McKey in the body of a vibrant twenty-eight-year-old."

Emilia laughed, preferring to be compared to an eighty-three-year-old over having Ally and the whole town of Harlow clued in on just how exciting her life actually was. On-the-run socialite with a missing ex-husband, non-responsive dad, and sex with Blaine Callaghan…

Yep, she'd definitely take sewing and gardening over engaging in any strained confessions with people she still barely knew.

"I don't know. Aggie's dropped enough clues that she's a wild one at heart." She nodded at Ally to stay on task and keep cutting.

"Besides, you won't be so skeptical of this sewing business when we have the best costumes at the soiree. Who knows, maybe Wayne will sit up and notice too."

Ally rolled her eyes and scoffed. "Ya. Sure. Except, I give up on him. The man's clueless and chasing him is way too much effort. Besides, there are always new faces at the soiree each year, so my best bet is to maybe meet someone there."

Emilia gave a shrug of agreement, only for a loud knock at the back door to break her easy mood. She lifted her foot off the machine's pedal, her eyes pulling wide as Ally gaped back at her.

She decided to be brave and make her way toward her visitor, her rattled nerves settling the moment she glimpsed Blaine's unmistakable silhouette through the mesh screen door.

"I wasn't expecting you." She pulled the door open, his mutual smile sending a tantalizing shiver down her body.

"I tried knocking on the front door for a change, but it seems you two were too absorbed in whatever plan you're hatching back here." He nodded over to the piles of fabric on her kitchen table, a small cardboard box tucked under his arm.

His gaze landed on her next and did a slow glide down her body, a sly grin pulling at his lips. As if by instinct, she dipped her chin, sending him an equally wicked stare from under her lashes. Something she would never have dared even just two days ago. Even more unbelievable, she, Emilia Bonacci, was finally having fun!

"I think you should keep letting yourself in. It's been good luck for me so far." She jutted her chin toward the box in his arms. "What do you have there?"

"Aggie stopped by the workshop this morning and insisted I be the one to deliver this to you." He handed her the box. "I have no idea what it is." His gaze flicked to Ally seated just a few yards away. "Last night you mentioned wanting those cabinets installed, I thought I'd come by and do just that."

She backed up and took the box to the table, allowing him room to enter her kitchen. Meanwhile, Ally sat taller, eyeballing Emilia, who'd been eyeballing Blaine. *Just great.*

"Last night, hey?" Ally's mouth stretched into a slow smirk. "Emilia? That must have been one heck of an apology."

Emilia dug her fingers into the box's sides, and her face heated. She shook her head at her friend, a silent plea that her questions go no further.

Blaine lowered his toolbox onto a counter, his attention still on Emilia, as though he put in a deliberate effort to ignore Ally. "There'll be a lot of noise while I work."

She opened her mouth to reply, but Ally shot from her chair, wooden legs scraping loud against the floor. "Oh, dontcha worry. We're just finishing, aren't we, Emilia?"

She extended her arms out and began sweeping large piles of fabric across the table and into a woven basket at her feet, her glinting stare not leaving Emilia as she did so.

She knew. Ally knew!

Emilia distracted herself with ripping the tape on Aggie's impromptu gift, anything *not* to look at her friend. Her heart picked up speed. She had nothing to hide when it came to her feelings for Blaine, but things were so new, and other aspects of her life still so confusing. She didn't want to add being the center of town gossip to her troubles.

She flipped the box's lid open, and a hysterical squeak escaped her at what lay inside. Six knives. In various sizes. A bright yellow post-it note attached to the largest, machete-looking thing.

Hide these around your house, dear. In case your husband comes by.

A quick gasp assaulted her lungs, and she slammed the box closed. Blaine turned to her while Ally gave a scrunched, quizzical sort of look. "What's the surprise?"

Emilia shook her head, jamming the tape back over the open seam on the box. "Nothing. Just Aggie being Aggie."

If Aggie was a deranged serial killer. What on Earth was she thinking sending Blaine over with knives?

She leaned over and stuffed the box under her chair, then crossed her arms with elbows resting on the table in a casual nothing-to-see-here sort of gesture.

Ally stared a little longer, before collecting her purse and rushing toward the back door in long, lolloping steps.

Blaine shifted sideways, blocking her exit. "What are you doing?"

"Just getting on with my day." She gave an overenthusiastic grin; one no one in the room bought. "Got a problem with that, Mr. Callaghan?"

"You bet I do." He frowned down at her, unmistakable fire in his eyes. "Whatever you think you know, you better not breathe a word to anyone else."

She craned her neck and squinted up at him. "And what makes you think I'd do something like that?"

"The fact that I know you, maybe?" He lifted a brow, then stuck his arm out, catching her as she tried to sneak past. "If I hear rumors of Emilia and me being anything more than friends, I'll know exactly who started them."

Ally turned to Emilia, her mouth open in mock surprise. "Do you hear that? Not very trusting, is he?" She swung back to Blaine, lifting onto her toes and giving him a solid kiss on the cheek. The two seemed strangely similar to a couple of squabbling teenage siblings. "Don't worry, honey, Emilia's been my friend about five minutes longer than she's been your... well, whatever you two are. Your secret's safe with me."

She spun and gave Emilia an excited wave goodbye, then swerved around Blaine and out the door. He turned to Emilia, eyes exuding an amused light. "Do you think she'll keep our secret?"

She squeezed her lips together, holding back a giggle, only to burst into a much louder laugh. "Not a chance. Though she did seem to think she's known me longer, so we did fool her there."

He let loose with a soft chuckle and shrugged, his easy steps toward her sending a soft dart of electricity through her body. "I see myself soon becoming the victim of a lot of bribery to keep that girl quiet."

He pulled her up and out of her chair, leaning in until his lips met hers. She melted into his commanding embrace and sighed, his hands raking her hair, his mouth demanding far more than a sweet welcome kiss.

Before she knew it, he'd hiked her feet off the floor, and he wrapped her legs around his waist. Need burned her from the inside out as she locked her arms around his broad shoulders. And still, he was the one to break the kiss, his stare tangling with hers in a long, silent moment.

"Counters." His lips plucked with a new smile. "If I let my body call all the shots here, I swear this cottage is more likely to topple over from old age before I get this job finished."

She caught his lips one last time before resting her forehead on his and offering a reluctant nod. Even as he lowered her, the slide down his body proved a searing kind of hell made of pure yearning.

He drew back, his gaze snagging on her a moment too long, like maybe he wanted to renege on his vow to get to work. But then he shook his head, turning for his toolbox. "Later. Maybe later."

She laughed as he pulled on a set of work gloves, and her sense of duty seeped in. "Can I help?"

He pointed to her still-healing shoulder. "You think that broken wing will keep up?"

"Maybe if you don't ask me to swing a sledgehammer or something."

He smiled and grabbed a crowbar and a second pair of gloves from the toolbox. "Okay, I'll make you a deal. You take on the easier tasks and stop if anything hurts."

She reached for the gloves and the crowbar at the same time. He let her have the gloves but snatched the crowbar back, making it clear that particular tool was not what he considered easy.

"Fine." She slunk back, pulling on the gloves. "And after we're done, you stay for dinner."

Twenty~Eight

THEN

From: Emilia Bonacci
   To: Emilia Bonacci
   Subject: …

I'm marrying Anthony.
   Somehow, he always wins.

By the time Blaine leaned against the kitchen doorway, the sky outside the window had turned black, and he allowed Emilia one final moment to take in the results of their handiwork. "Like what you see?"

She stood ahead and whipped around to face him, her eyes shining like the glossy surface of the best kind of coffee. "The mahogany doors are beautiful. The beveled edges and frosted glass are a perfect match to the cottage's old-time feel." Her gaze washed over him, followed by a smile. "I used to look at my old kitchen and think, 'House from hell, enter if you wish to die,' but this, this says, 'Welcome to my kitchen, would you like a cup of tea?'"

He jolted with a short stab of laughter at her "house from hell" joke; she'd even put on a screechy "evil doll" voice. "That's the best endorsement I've ever had, though you do deserve some credit."

She wandered closer, the scent of her flowery shampoo and perfume warming his blood. "You did most of the work."

"And you caught on fast. I'm proud of you." He couldn't keep from touching her any longer and ran his thumb over the delicate pink of her cheekbones, her soft lashes fluttering as he did. "Maybe you should join me at work every day."

She laughed and pushed him away. "I'd love to, but I have a strong suspicion you wouldn't get much work done. Besides, having me on your turf all day isn't exactly a professional look for either of us."

"Screw professionalism."

"Oh, come on." She giggled, nudging him on her way to the stove. "Our dinner's going to burn, and my kitchen's been through enough heartbreak without us actively setting it on fire."

A smirk pulled at his lips, and he let her go, their game of cat and mouse making him feel nineteen all over again. She seemed less jittery, more open to his touch and willing to make small talk, just as she'd been back then. That knowledge alone made him want to know how long it would be before he learned the last of her secrets; because sure enough, her story lacked details, her small moments of hesitancy indicating she had more to say.

He caught up to her and helped ferry plates to the table, making a point of brushing against her as they found their seats. He wasn't even sure what game he played at, only that he found himself caught between wanting her and wanting to protect her, though the two things went hand in hand.

Her eyes glinted, and she glanced up at him from where she sat. "Are you going to keep giving me moon eyes and bumping into me like a house cat, or do you think you can manage to get through this meal? I don't know about you, but I'm starving."

"Sure." He dropped into a chair and pierced a vegetable with his fork.

First things first, feed the lady, then see where the night takes us…

"So, have you got any new ideas for work besides filling in at Aggie's?" His mouth tugged, but he bit the insides of his cheeks to hide a smile. Even the simple act of sharing a meal gave him a long-lost sense of connection with her. "You know, aside from being my apprentice."

She peered down at her plate, cutting into her meat, movements short and jerky. "I have one idea floating about, but it's still early days."

"Let me guess." He lowered his cutlery and made a show of thinking through his reply. "Sales assistant, utilizing your experience to give Ally some healthy competition… or at least inspire her to slack off a little less."

"Experience, huh?" Emilia chuckled. "You remembered."

Of course, I remember.

"It's how we met, right? You, working in your dad's main store, and me moseying in like an idiot thinking I could afford anything there." He gave a genuine chuckle, but not genuine enough. Truth was, there'd been so little he'd forgotten through the years and way too much he'd replayed over and over again, just so he could keep something of her alive and with him.

Her shoulders bounced with new laughter while her gaze pointed down in a hint that her mind also snared somewhere between past and present. "My plans for the future did involve some sales, though not the sort done behind a counter. I thought maybe you and I could work together, just not in the way you've suggested."

He sat taller. "Well, now you have my attention."

She gave him a side glance, eyes glittering again, obviously finding the intended humor in his not-so-smooth moves. "I have a friend who's originally from LA, but living in New York now. Actually, she's more an acquaintance, really. Her name's Rochelle, and she deals in handmade furniture. I thought… I thought, maybe if you don't mind, I could pitch some of your pieces to her. You know, help your business while dabbling in mine."

"So, you'd be a go-between, like a sales consultant for Oak Tree?" He sank back in his chair, thinking over the business offer, nodding to himself. Her idea didn't sound half-bad at all, and he had nothing to lose from letting her try. "Do you think your friend would be interested in a small country business nowhere near the West Coast?"

"That's the beauty of my plan." She leaned in, elbows pressed to the table, a never-seen-before glow of pride lifting her expression. "I'd spin Rochelle a tale of a quaint, artisan store in a sweet little town— how every sale will help breathe new life into Harlow. She'll love it, her high-end clientele will love it. Your stuff is perfect, Blaine. We could eventually do an entire rebranding mission and push the prestige of your work."

He toyed with the end of his fork and stared into her eyes, a low and hollow pit opening up in his stomach. "And this is all only about boosting sales for me and starting a new career for you?"

He raised a brow, hoping it would be enough to signal he knew something was missing in her explanation.

She pulled her gaze from him and sank back in her chair, a rush of air pushing past her lips in a heavy sigh. "I can't stop thinking about what you said last night, about how my father and Anthony ruined your dreams. I've been in the retail industry my whole life. It seems only fair I would use the skills and connections my dad gave me to help you get back the future he stole."

He stared at her for a while, a feeling of heaviness dragging at the food already in his stomach, that heaviness taking up an uncomfortable amount of space in there. "I didn't open up to you last night with a mind to profit from your guilt."

"I know. I know that." She stretched out a hand and pressed it over his, insisting he listen. "But things have changed. Online commerce and advanced shipping options could offer the business you always dreamed of, and then some, *and* you wouldn't have to leave Harlow. Not if you didn't want to, anyway. And as I said, this town would benefit too."

She drew a hard breath, her hand gripping tighter over his, like a plea for him to sway to her thinking. "There'd be more jobs here. I could start with helping you and then move on to other local businesses. So if helping yourself isn't enough, then think about them, and think about how this might help me too. Not just my guilt. I could use your positive experience to land my first few clients and start my own boutique consultancy business. Something that would take me far away from any reliance on Bonacci Jewelry, or for that matter, what little I make at Aggie's nursery."

He jerked back at that, his muscles suddenly rigid and his skin tingling. Her passion and sense of purpose made what she proposed a done deal. One thing was for certain, he would do anything for her. To keep her safe. To make sure she never had to return to the life she'd had.

Without question, he'd put himself and everything he held dear in jeopardy—including his business—if it meant never losing her again.

Oh hell, I must be losing my mind.

A sudden ache bloomed under his ribcage, one that felt like the land of a bruising punch, but that pain was just the acknowledgment of one inescapable truth. *He loved her.* Not merely the memory of her as he'd loved for all those years, but *her* as she was right now, and who she wanted to be.

He loved the adult Emilia and all her complexities. He loved her in a steady, less fevered way than that of teenage infatuation—the kind of infatuation that runs wild when love is forbidden.

Maybe she loved him too, even if she didn't say as much. Either way, there was *no* going back this time. She was his past. His present. And if he had anything to do with it, his entire future. Knowing what she'd endured in his absence and what they'd shared last night, he'd fallen in love with her all over again.

"You don't look so sure." Her weakened voice pulled him from his thoughts, but he smiled.

Just admitting to his feelings spread a lightness through his torso, filling him with the kind of clarity that had been missing for so very long.

He turned his hand and clasped back at hers, the mountain of buried emotion inside of him pushing to burst free, even though he knew any kind of outpouring would be too soon for her right now. "I'd love to be part of your science experiment."

She gave a soft trill of laughter, the sound mingled with a sigh of relief. "Really?"

He nodded.

She sank back, letting go of his hand. "I wouldn't cause you too much trouble. I'd only need to send Rochelle an email with some photos of your work. I don't have a computer, but if you let me use Oak Tree's, I could get this project started right away."

"I do have one question before I commit."

Her face tightened, but despite his wording, unlike her ex, he'd never seek to hold her back.

"Will your budding business take you away from Harlow?"

Her lips blossomed into a slow smile. "This place is growing on me, for several reasons." Her stare's steady hold confirmed he was one of those reasons. "I have connections all over the country. I could work from the cottage. All I'd need is a phone and a computer. The only thing holding me back right now is—"

Her brows slammed together, and she shook her head as if reshuffling her thoughts. "Anyway, it doesn't matter. Let's get this project up and running, and we'll worry about the details later."

Sharp adrenaline shot through his body, his focus snagging on what she'd diverted from saying.

He reached for her hand again, vowing that one way or another he'd get her trust. When that happened, he'd make sure to handle whatever it was she thought "held" her back. "You're talented and clever, and I've never known a person who's met you and hasn't liked you, Emilia. You deserve to dream big too."

And with that, her gaze dropped to the table, and a frown bowed her lips. Compliments weren't something she was used to. The dark shadows under her eyes said as much.

He reached out and pushed the wild curls from her face, his heart aching for the happy-go-lucky girl he'd known, and what had happened to her to turn her into this bruised and wary woman. "He should have complimented you every day. It would have been easy. You're an amazing woman. If you were my—"

Her wide stare fixed on him, solid and worn. "Don't say it."

Right. Of course, she didn't want to hear about being his wife. It didn't matter that a large part of him couldn't imagine any other future. Emilia, with a world of hurt and a whole new life to build, might as well have lived in an alternate universe.

"Do you trust me?" He cupped his hand over her cheek, reeling a little when she reached up and pressed her hand over his.

"I do, but I catch the way you look at me sometimes, like you don't trust me. and I have myself to blame for that." Her lips twisted into a grimace. "I wish I could offer you more, Blaine. I just don't have the luxury of making plans right now. I can't live up to my own hopes, let alone yours."

"You don't have to live up to anything." His gut clenched at what she'd observed. His suspicion. His desire to figure her out.

"I couldn't make Anthony happy, no matter how much I tried. What makes you think you won't feel the same one day? After everything my family put you through, you'd be right to hold a grudge. I couldn't blame you."

His throat constricted, and a swell of remorse burned through his chest. She'd interpreted his concern over her welfare as a need to "hold a grudge."

"Emilia, Anthony and I are two different people. I hope you can see that I want to help you, not hurt you."

She shook her head, her attention shifting to the far-off wall, but he grabbed her shoulders and twisted her to face him again.

"Listen to me. Anthony was a miserable man long before he ever latched on to you. You don't own his mistakes."

"No. It's more than that." She pinched the bridge of her nose and squeezed her eyes shut. "I'm a mess, Blaine, and that *is* my fault. I'll make you miserable, just like I did him. I can't offer you any kind of consistency. Just put me under enough pressure, and I can't even stay conscious. How much more pathetic can a person be?"

"About that, have you seen Dr. Richards yet? You being a 'mess' is still not your fault, but there might be things we can do to help you."

"And what about your needs? An uncomplicated life. Someone who can support you, rather than the other way around all the time?"

He jumped out of his chair and pulled her up, cradling her face between his hands, their bodies pressed together. Making her look at him. Making her *feel* him. "You have no idea what I need, and if it isn't yet clear enough, I *need* you. More than that, I *want* you. I'm all in, remember? Mess and everything."

She shook in his hold, so he held her tighter, trying to convey that he had her and wouldn't let go. There were a million ways to make a person feel safe, and right now, she needed to know he wouldn't throw her to the wolves like everyone else had.

"These doubts of yours, the criticisms you inflict on yourself—they're not you—and they're not helping." He kissed her forehead, her temple, her cheek. Anything to bring her former joy back. "Something's wrong here, and if you can't tell me, then promise you'll find someone who'll help. Speak to the doctor. Whatever you need to do. But please don't tell me what we have isn't enough to plan a future on. It is. It's more than enough."

She stared at him in complete silence, still shaking, a line of moisture trapped on the shelf of her lower eyelids.

He dropped his voice to a whisper, imploring her to hear him out again. "I don't want more than what you're ready to offer, whatever that is. If your plan is to scare me off or push me away, it won't work. I'm not leaving."

She blinked at him before finding her words. "You have no idea, Blaine. No idea."

Her roughened tone spoke volumes, and he had no doubt what she said was true. There was stuff she kept to herself. That, and her husband had put her through hell. Blaine wasn't so arrogant or foolish to pretend he understood or had all the tools to "fix" her. He'd already figured there was no fixing some things, not on his own, anyway. Emilia's life thus far was a prime example.

"You're right. I don't understand." He leaned down and touched his forehead to hers, attempting to impart even just a fraction of the tenderness she deserved but had never had in all their years apart. "I probably never will understand, not really, but I can still be here for you, and that's one hell of a thing for anyone to have."

She bit down. Eyes red. Chin trembling. "I wish I wasn't like this."

Her weak and breathy tone made his chest sting with a cutting kind of pain. Having him in her life caused her a new host of problems; his presence forced her to see all the ugliness that surrounded her, and he had only a tiny window into any of it. Still, she wasn't pushing him away altogether, and that in itself was a gift.

Her gaze darted about his face, as though seeking a sign or an answer. He ran the pads of his thumbs over her cheeks and dropped a soft, quick kiss to her lips. "Let go, Emilia."

Something in her expression shifted, her cheeks stiffening before releasing altogether, like she fought his words, only to realize she didn't have to.

He pressed another kiss to her, this time on her forehead, then whispered against her skin. "Just for tonight, let me take care of you."

The tension in her body released beneath his hold, and he felt her forehead move up and down against him in a nod. In the next beat, she sagged and gave a soft sigh. He took that as his cue to sweep her up, her arms quick to wrap around his shoulders and her legs draped over his forearms.

"To bed with you, Ms. Bonacci."

And just like that, her light laughter spilled out and filled him with hope.

Twenty-Nine

"WE GET THE MONEY, and then we're out of there."

Anthony glared at Luciano's henchman, the man's arctic blue eyes steeling forward as he spoke, his hands steady on the steering wheel.

The guy looked every bit the big scary mob man, somewhere closer to seven-foot-tall than six and built like a siege fort. *But fuck*, just like ninety-nine percent of the population, he was a walking-talking sack of spineless bullshit.

"And what if she doesn't play along?" Anthony spoke in a low, controlled tone, but his hands coiled into tight fists in his lap. If not for this asshole's size and connection to Luciano, he'd be swinging a solid punch to his skull and getting rid of him.

The man's emotionless stare hit Anthony, and granted, his whole deadpan act drew a shiver. At least the crony would do for intimidation. Emilia, the sniveling bitch, would be soon cowering in a corner and begging for mercy.

Anthony couldn't wait to watch her beg. To watch whatever pathetic pride she'd found in betraying him dry before his eyes. What she'd done. Taking his money. Leaving. He'd take great pleasure in showing her that there'd be no forgiveness. No mercy.

"You listen to what I say. Do what I tell you." The crony was talking again. Anthony made no effort to pretend he cared. "You're not going to hurt her, do you understand?"

Anthony scowled at the road, with its traffic lights and wide concrete pavements, seeing no point arguing with a soft-cocked fool like the one he was momentarily forced to share this ride with.

"What sort of mob member are you?" Even as he grumbled, he kept his cool. For now, anyway.

Luciano had insisted on withholding Emilia's location. His way of ensuring Anthony played by the rules.

"I'm not mob. I find people. I don't kill them. And neither will you. I've never failed a job, and I'm not about to start now." The guy's stagnated phrases signaled his patience wore thin. Maybe because he and Anthony had worked together, and he no longer saw a need to play nice, even though their last job had been something like ten years ago. "And since you've yet to drop a single dime for my hire, maybe you should shut your face for a minute and be thankful for my help. I'm less than one more complaint away from stopping this car and booting you out that door over there." He gave a steady nod to the passenger side door. "And good luck finding your way anywhere, much less your wife or back to LA after that."

Anthony sat quiet for a moment, the muscles in his chest bunching, his fists itching to finally take that swing. His rage had been building for just over two weeks, and every time he sought to unleash it, he was forced to tug that rage back into submission.

Soon, asshole. Save it all for Emilia. I'll have my moment soon.

Yes. He'd lose this deadbrain, then get everything. All the money he'd worked so hard to gather, all the money *she* would get back for him, and all that glorious revenge.

"Have it your way." He took a slow breath and turned to peer out the window and scowl at the rows and rows of shitty suburban houses outside.

For now, he'd play along, his fury heating his belly like a slow simmering pot seconds from boiling over. This crony had one good credit to his name. He'd helped Anthony find Emilia that first time she'd tried to run from him. Far be it from him to get in the way of history repeating.

And until history *did* repeat, he'd find comfort in something else.

"Just get me to my wife." He drew a sharp breath, resting his mind on the surprise hidden in his overnight bag on the backseat. His Glock 1911 and a box full of bullets.

Thirty

EMILIA WALKED the long road into town, an oversized tan wool cardigan hanging off her shoulders and a strong wind pushing into her back. It had been four days since her conversation with Blaine, and it had taken her all that time to drum up enough courage to make the trip to Oak Tree to send that email.

A dull ache wound its way through her body, stealing her breath and pulling heavy at her core. His request for her to involve him in her life wasn't unreasonable, but her past had a strong hold, and she struggled to break free. That lack of freedom meant she couldn't give him all the things he wanted, much less the truth. Not yet, anyway.

Could a relationship survive without honesty? Without trust? In her experience, no. What she held inside would hurt her; it would hurt him too, especially if he once again got caught in the crossfire between her, her father, and Anthony.

The forceful gust turned the ends of her hair into whips that stung her cheeks, the icy air penetrating her clothes and causing her to shiver. Still, the discomfort suited her mood.

Blaine's encouragement grated against her years of neglect. Years of being invisible amidst people who knew her name but not her nature.

More than that, she'd *let* those people overrun her life. Or maybe it was just that passivity had been trained in her from a young age. A little girl taught not to make a fuss. Now she had to pay her dues and the dues of others for their selfish decisions. The loss of her freedom had been the cost of handing over her power, of letting others choose for her, and then there'd been her happiness.

And Blaine.

Her fingers curled around Oak Tree's cold brass door handle, a line of thick gray clouds rolling above like a bad omen. Her long list of unspoken confusions another reason why it had taken her so long to pay this visit. What would happen if or when her past caught up to her?

The bell above the door rang behind her, even as she stepped inside and Blaine's green eyes glinted her way. "Are you alone?"

He nodded, and she padded closer, his hands busy with a pile of receipts at the store's counter, though the clump of paper now hung limp between his finger, and his stare held hers. "The weather's turning, so I sent everyone home early."

"I've come to send that email."

He positioned a dark-wood stool beside him at the counter, then gestured for her to sit. "I'll count receipts while you work."

Her face heated. Maybe it was shame, but she took the seat anyway, nothing but silence filling the space.

He slid an already open laptop before her, the white glow of the screen glaring in her eyes. After a moment she opened the login page for her email, but after that she just stared ahead, nauseated, her heart squeezing, her hands hovering over the keys about to make one stupid mistake.

"Would it be okay if I used the store's email address to contact Rochelle?" She added fake brightness to her tone, disallowing him to see her waning confidence, needing to cover her bases in case Anthony had already hacked into her own email account. "That way Rochelle can respond to you directly."

Which also meant he could still make this deal if something happened to her.

He gave her a sideways glance but crossed the small space to type at the keyboard. The crisp scent of refreshing cologne drifted over her like a light ocean breeze. Cool perfection.

"Thanks." She eased away a little more. "While you're there, do you have photos of your work to attach to this email?"

"There's a folder titled 'inventory photos'." He used the cursor to point out the file he meant. "Pick whichever ones you think she'll like."

He moved out the way, and she took over. The gaping silence drew ever wider while she browsed images—the click of the trackpad and the shuffling of receipts too mild for the distraction she wished for. Before long, she hit send on the email, and the computer dinged to confirm her message was dispatched.

Before she could even look at him, Blaine spoke. "You're scared, aren't you?"

Her heart gave a sharp pang, his perceptiveness something she loved and hated. "Yes."

"Do I scare you?"

She paused and took a second to think over her reply. "No. Not you personally."

"So then tell me what the last few days have been about. I thought that talk in your kitchen changed things between us, but you've been holding back. I can feel it."

He shifted closer to her, but she angled away. "Things *have* changed, but there's a lot I can't talk about."

"We've established that." And even as she tried to gain some physical distance, somehow his gaze still held her as immovably as his hands might have. "Try anyway."

She wouldn't bring him into her troubles. "One way or another, you're going to hurt me, or I'll hurt you. I can't handle being disappointed again. I can't handle disappointing you again, either. And I can't shake the feeling that this won't end well. There's more history and risk to our relationship than either of us admit to. Wasn't one ugly ending punishment enough?"

He stepped closer, crowding her space and caging her in, not much different to a deer trapped in a lion's den. "I've already said I don't want more than you can give. As much as you believe things won't end well, *I* believe the opposite is just as likely. That we'll have a future together. A constant sense of belonging. Of having someone to share all life's moments with. And you're being flippant."

He reached out and touched her face, eyes darkening, his thumb skimming her lower lip and tempting her to press her lips forward and kiss him. Damn the man, he played her at every turn. "Listen, I know you're worried, but stop acting like you don't care. We both know your empathy is what brought us together in the first place."

His husky tone and the reference to that first meeting, the one where he'd been a scraggly teenager in the wrong place at the right time, drew her in.

His eyes glittered now. He saw his effect on her, his ability to pluck once more at her willingness to stand her ground. "Having someone to share everything with, having love, is another worthwhile payoff, don't you think?"

Her lips parted, a piece of her heart melting at his continued touch. *No.*

The very word "love" left a bitter taste on her tongue, and still, she stayed in his hold.

"Blaine, sometimes love doesn't save the day, and not all dreams are meant to come true." She turned her cheek, giving in to her desire to kiss his hand. "My experience of love is that it steals dreams and reduces you to something you never thought you'd be. Just look at us. I'm heading toward divorce, and you just got out of an engagement. Love hasn't done either of us any good."

"And I'd say there's more to love than what either of us have seen."

A pit opened in her stomach, or maybe that pit was more a landslide, or maybe just the sense that she couldn't stick with a decision, her mind flip-flopping between options with each rolling second. "Good thing we're not in love."

The glint in his eye intensified, and he placed one hand on the counter, leaning in, stealing more space. "Are you sure about that?"

Breath escaped her, her resolve faltering as she scrambled for a reply that wouldn't come. Of course, Blaine used her silence as another chance to reel her in. "You loved me once, didn't you?"

Oh God, the low rumble of his voice, the way he wouldn't quit staring her down...

She clamped her teeth together, wanting to cry, wanting to run, wanting to throw herself at him and never let go. Being around him was just too confusing.

"Emilia?"

He closed the final space between them, melting her further, making her believe that maybe they could transcend whatever trouble she was in.

The words finally escaped. A previously unspoken desire, one she hadn't even voiced to herself. "I wish things could be that simple."

He reached out and tucked a loose curl behind her ear, and she let him, even though her brain continued to deny. "They could be."

"No. For the first time ever, I have the life I've always wanted. And I'm stuck somewhere between wanting to run with my freedom and laying down my roots here in Harlow, maybe even with you too."

"Emilia." He took hold of her chin and ensured that she faced him. "I'm not asking you to give anything up. I want to see you thrive. I want to be there for you while you do. So back to the topic of simplicity, all you have to do is say yes."

"Yes"—her heart slowed as if it wanted to stop altogether, but she needed to give him the full answer—"but I don't want you to get hurt."

"Let me worry about my feelings."

This was bigger than feelings. He could get hurt. *Physically hurt.* Just like the last time. And he had no idea about any of it.

"And"—he paused, the dark centers of his eyes turning into infinite pools, while his lips curled into a slow smile—"remember, honey, whatever you're going through, you're not alone anymore."

Her heart shifted again, wanting to deny it, wanting to escape the truth here. He wouldn't leave her, and she didn't want him to.

Maybe Blaine was right. She was being a coward.

A weak, sniveling, wormy coward.

No, I'm not a coward. I'm overwhelmed.

The room went impossibly quiet, and her chest hurt at the first hint that she too could be gentle with herself. She *was* overwhelmed, but not as overwhelmed as the night she'd spent holed up alone in her room waiting for the sun to rise, so she could escape her terrifying husband.

She'd been strong. *Was still* strong. She could be strong *and* overwhelmed at the same time. The two could co-exist. So maybe she could focus on what had brought her here in the first place. Her desire for freedom. She'd fought so hard to choose her own destiny, and right now, Blaine stood before her offering her a new life. One she maybe did want. Had *always* wanted, all along.

She honed her focus on him, no longer needing to second guess her decision, no longer allowing Anthony and the fear he'd instilled in her to hold her back. "Be my date to the soiree."

Blaine jolted, visibly stunned. Maybe she was a little stunned too. She hadn't really planned on asking him, though now that she did, the request felt right.

A quick grin lit his face. "We're going public already?"

"What, ten years isn't long enough?" She laughed, and he pulled her in for a lingering, deep kiss.

The heat of it. The penetrating warmth that went way down low and wrapped around her heart, soothing so much of the ache there. His fingers entangled her hair while tingles ran from her scalp to her toes—confirming the joy of, for once, putting her happiness first.

If only they weren't standing in a showroom with a giant street-facing window, for all of Harlow to see.

She pulled back, another instant laugh barreling through her chest; her heart so light and full because he held her not like a man seeking to control or possess her, but like someone who genuinely cared. Someone who would be both her best friend and her lover.

"I'm going to assume all those kisses are your way of saying, 'yes'."

Maybe things could be as simple as Blaine said. Maybe her dad didn't answer her calls because he was just pissed at her. After all, she'd refused to cave to what he wanted, to return to LA or get back with Anthony. For that, her father punished her.

So, maybe she worried and held back over nothing. Maybe the stuff with Anthony would never eventuate.

Thirty-One

A FEW DAYS LATER, Emilia stood in Blaine's spacious kitchen, chopping vegetables for their food contribution to the Harlow Soiree the next night. This was her first time visiting his house, and while the evening's darkness already stained the skylights above, the kitchen itself glowed with white stone countertops and the cupboards painted in a calming eggshell blue.

"I have to admit, this isn't exactly what I expected your bachelor pad to look like." The entire house was significantly bigger than her cottage, and unlike her kitchen, this one had enough room to accommodate a sizable workstation in the middle.

Blaine wandered over and pinched a carrot stick from her chopping board, her heart speeding a little as the move had him brushing against her. "This house was just a shell when I first bought it."

"Of course." She chuckled to herself. "Doing the place up wasn't half the appeal?"

He propped himself against the counter beside her and bit into his carrot piece. "In my line of work, it'd be shameful to do anything less."

She laughed again, this time leaning over to nudge him in the ribs with her elbow. "I should have just sent Rochelle a photo of this place."

"Ahh." Blaine's face lit up, and he pointed the carrot stick at Emilia.

"Speaking of Rochelle, she got back to me not long after you sent that email."

"Oh, yeah?"

"Yeah, she liked what she saw. Ordered a few smaller pieces to see how her clients took to them, but here's the cool bit. She has a couple of days off coming up and offered to swing do an in-person viewing of what we have."

"Oh. Wow." She didn't mean to punctuate her expression with a drawn-out pause, but she also hadn't planned on having anyone from her old life stop in the town she'd hoped to keep firmly hidden. "Ahh, so when exactly will Rochelle get here?"

"She'll be here for the town fair, so I guess that would be in two days."

"Oh. Okay."

He slipped his hand around to her lower back and pulled her in a little. "Are you all right?"

Well actually, no, she wasn't. Because she had two choices now. Either hide from Blaine and avoid Rochelle at all costs throughout her stay in town, or front up for the barrage of questions and weird looks she'd no doubt receive from someone who'd only ever known her as Anthony's wife. Especially since she'd made no mention in her email to Rochelle about her relationship to Blaine, or even that she was living in Harlow.

Heck, there was a chance Rochelle didn't even know about Emilia's escape—since she now lived in New York—much less the troubles she'd endured in her marriage.

And she had one other choice. One that seemed unavoidable now.

She would have to tell Blaine all about her *other* problem with Anthony, and how her presence in Harlow was more than just a means of escape from a horrid marriage. There was an element of wanting to stay safe. To stay hidden.

"I just didn't expect I'd see anyone from back home quite so soon." A cold sensation hit her stomach. There she went again. Lying to him. Or at least omitting the truth.

She couldn't keep doing this.

"You don't want to see Rochelle?"

"No, I do. I'm just surprised, that's all."

He rubbed her back again, the gesture meant to soothe her, but only succeeding in spreading the sense of guilt, so that it stretched its arms around her and squeezed way too tight.

"If it's a bad time for you, I could tell her not to come."

But the tension across his brows said he didn't want to do that. That this was a big opportunity for him and Harlow, but he'd ditch it anyway if that meant making her happy.

The guilt kept growing, now burrowing deep under her skin.

"No, don't do that." She turned to him and gave a smile, the tightness throughout her face making it one not even she believed. "But what you could do"—she handed him a knife—"is make our dinner, while I get the soiree food done."

His gaze stayed on her for a beat longer. *Yep, totally not believing her.* But he took the knife anyway and extended a smile. "Sure, but it seems I'm not as competent here as you are."

She turned back to her board, her stomach churning, her shoulders tight. Even at times when she kissed Blaine, Anthony's enraged face would spring back to haunt her—a warning to retreat, that she couldn't afford to get too relaxed. But she'd made Blaine a promise, that she was all in, that she'd give this relationship a genuine shot, and right now, she wasn't doing that.

Not when she held the truth from him. Not when fear ate her alive in his presence. The time had come. She had to tell him.

She turned to him, assuming he would have gone to work at his board by now. But he hadn't. He hadn't moved and simply stared at her, his brows lifted and drawn together. Like he *knew.*

She put her knife down again, giving him her full attention. "What?"

His cheeks lifted a little with a small smile. "You look like you belong here."

She let loose with a tiny chuckle. "Are you saying a woman's place is in the kitchen? Because I don't think that's—"

"No" He reached out, his hand slipping to the nape of her neck. "Just that you look like you belong here... *with me.*"

For someone who hadn't belonged anywhere for as long as she

could remember, as far back as her mother's death all those years ago, those were the precise words she'd needed to hear.

And more than hear them, she *felt* them, and Blaine provided the blessed normality she'd dreamed of for so long. So, her heart snagged on the next sad and inalienable truth. Whatever love she felt for him would never be complete until she filled the gap between what he knew of her and all she refused to say.

She buried herself against him, allowing his strong arms to enfold her, support her. She would savor this. Let them have a final moment of being nothing more than two people making dinner and falling in love, then she would tell him.

She would tell him everything.

Blaine's stomach soured at her contradictory behavior. One second, she seemed warmed by his compliment. The next, she retreated, the whole chain reaction a cruel form of silent torture.

A spare chopping board lay on the counter beside him, but he abandoned his task for a moment and opted for a different tack, something that might at least loosen them both up a little.

"Want some wine?" He turned for the fridge, the door already open in his hand.

She'd already returned to her chopping at the counter but called over her shoulder. "Yes, please."

He collected two glasses on his way to sidling up to her. "You sure about that?"

Her eyes narrowed on him. "Yes. Why?"

He dipped his chin, giving her what he hoped would be a mischievous grin. "You're certain now?"

"Blaine, what are you getting at?"

He started pouring, taking his time with putting her out of her misery, enjoying the new levity from his little game and his ability to turn things around. "Just that Sarah told me how little you had before you went all wild and wobbly at Maynard's—"

"Hey!" She dropped her mouth open in mock surprise, then gave his forearm a light tap with the back of her hand. "One bad incident does not count."

He slid a glass of wine across the counter to her. "Easy with this one."

"Fine, I'm a cheap drunk, okay?" She lifted the glass to her lips but failed to get in her first slip before bursting into laughter and pointing at him. "You're not allowed to look at me now. Turn away."

He did no such thing, though she tried to get to her wine again, only for the laughter to restart.

"Seriously, Blaine. If you keep side-eyeing me while I drink, I'm going to keep laughing, which will probably result in me choking on a mouthful of wine. Turn around, just let me get started on this so I can get back to cooking."

A light laugh broke from him, and he did as he was asked. Not so much because he believed turning around would make much difference, but because he loved these small moments with her and enjoyed playing along.

He spoke over his shoulder. "So, still feeling brave about going to the soiree with me tomorrow? The local busybodies will love the new fodder."

Maybe it was the silence or the drum of his heart as he kept his back to her. The farther corners of his mind toyed with the idea that fronting up with him tomorrow would leave her daunted.

"You mean because everyone will expect to see you there with Sarah?"

"No, I didn't mean that at all." He spun around, facing her. The thought hadn't even crossed his mind, though maybe it should have. "I thought, what with your reaction to Rochelle turning up, that you might not be ready for the attention. You've been through so much already. I don't want you to feel like a sacrifice to the gossips too."

She lowered her glass to the counter and sank back on her heels as if what she really needed to do was sit down. If he had to decide between taking her with him and going alone, he would choose to go alone in an instant. Protecting her and her well-being stood way above any need to test the waters of this relationship.

"I have been acting weird, haven't I?" She dipped her chin but flicked her attention to him. "It's not fair on you."

"I only meant that you don't have to do this just to please me."

"No. No, I want to go. Only—" She toyed with the stem of her glass, her stare growing darker, her shoulders slumping a couple of inches under the release of her heavy sigh. "Things are serious between us, aren't they?"

"Have they ever not been serious?"

She released a sardonic chuckle. "You have a point."

She turned to her board, picked up the knife, and held it poised above a stick of celery but failed to drop the blade.

He trekked his gaze to her face, and her eyelids squeezed shut as if she found herself trapped in some deep and bitter anguish. "Are you okay?"

"No. And neither are you."

"Sorry?" He took a step forward and slid his hand over hers, prying the knife out of her fingers before turning her to face him.

Seconds ticked by as her warm chocolate stare drifted over his face, turning dazed and watery. "I thought if I waited, things would sort themselves out. I wouldn't have to say anything. I'm sorry."

"Emilia?"

She broke free of his hold and began pacing ahead of him, her hand thrust into the bramble of curls along her hairline. "I tried to bargain this away, tried to tell myself I'm making something out of nothing— that my life has moved on, so surely everything from back home would too." She shook her head and snapped her attention back to him. "I thought we could just enjoy a few more hours of being a normal happy couple, but I can't do this anymore. I don't warrant your sympathy, Blaine. And I don't want to keep stringing you along or pushing you away. You don't deserve it."

A heavy feeling dragged at his stomach. This sounded like a breakup, but he'd had no clue, no sign it was coming, especially not with all their recent breakthroughs.

Had he really read her so wrong?

"Damn it, Emilia." His fingers dug into the counter's edge; he wanted to reach for her but didn't at the same time. "Tell me what's wrong."

"I hate the state of casual comfort between us, not when it's all built on a lie." Her gaze burned into him now, her forehead a crisscross of anguished wrinkles. "And believe me, I want more. I want to tell you the truth. But when I do, you're going to tell me to stay away from you forever."

"That's not going to happen."

"You can't say that. You don't know what's happened and what might happen. Heck, I'm largely in the dark now too. So before your feelings grow any deeper, I'll understand if you want me to go. You *should* want me to go."

His heart pummeled. What was she talking about?

"You're all that I've ever wanted, Emilia. Trust me, I've tried to move on, but my feelings have never budged from you."

"Oh, God." She stared at him for a beat, before shaking her head and turning away, her palm pressed flat to her forehead. Her cheeks were flushed, and she looked about ready to break a sweat.

He stepped forward and reached for her, but she jolted back again.

"Please don't tell me how much I mean to you. I don't deserve it. I don't deserve it." She paced in a circle, her gaze darting in manic circles around the floor. "My freedom could end at any minute. I don't want to spend what little time I have left running. Lying. I don't want to disappear on you suddenly. I don't want you to think you did something wrong. I just have a bad feeling, and this might be the only time we have left together before…"

She jerked her chin up, and she gaped at him as if she might rescind her burgeoning confession.

Frustration propelled him forward, despite her flicking him away a moment earlier. He grabbed her wrists as her red-rimmed stare locked with his. "Emilia, tell me."

"Anthony has nothing now. Nothing but a huge reason to seek revenge. So if I'm right—and trust me, I know my ex-husband—he won't let go of what I did to him. He'll want to find me, Blaine. He'll want to hurt me. He'll be angry enough to kill me."

Thirty-Two

BLAINE SEARCHED EMILIA'S GAZE, trying to piece together whether her panicked state was something new or something that had been simmering in the background for a long time. He didn't have to guess long, not since he'd sensed her fear from the first moment they'd reunited.

At the time, a part of him had decided it was he who scared her. Maybe that wasn't too far from the truth, but as always with Emilia, she hid more under the surface. More he didn't know.

"Just knowing me puts you at risk." She twisted away, palm reconnecting with her now glistening brow.

"Why? Because Anthony couldn't take no for an answer and ran you out of home?" His hands curled at his sides. Anthony had destroyed everything Blaine loved. The man deserved to hurt for every lie, threat, crime, and stolen second Blaine had dreamed of having with Emilia.

Some men didn't deserve to breathe. Anthony was one of them. And Blaine wouldn't let a bottom dweller like that guy ever stop him again. "I'm not afraid of him."

She shook her head, still not looking at him. "Frankly, if it weren't for my absence reflecting badly on him, I'm sure Anthony wouldn't care if he never saw me again. No. My absence isn't why he'll be out for revenge. It's because he stole money. Lots and lots of money. I stopped him."

Blaine struggled for purchase over his thoughts. Piece by piece, Emilia's words and puzzling behavior fell into place—why she'd kept him at arm's length, why she'd fought him at every turn and, most times, seemed to want to keep to herself.

He'll want to find me, Blaine. He'll want to hurt me. He'll be angry enough to kill me.

Oh God, and *those* words replayed in his head too. He thought she was being dramatic, merely referencing the fact that she'd left. Anthony wanted to *kill* her. *Emilia.* Someone so incredibly sweet and gentle she'd put years of her life aside just to keep the peace. What sort of tyrant would want to hurt her?

Blaine wandered over and placed his hand on her shoulder, gently, God knew she deserved every soft gesture in the world. She spun her gaze around, wide and catching to his.

"Say all that again for me. Slowly." He kept his tone even, controlled, letting her know that he would believe everything she had to say.

"What?" She let out a breathy whisper, her open expression hinting that she'd expected some other response. Rejection maybe. Or anger.

One day, she'd learn that he wasn't a bitter and rude asshole, that he shared no similarities to Anthony, that from now on, she sure as hell would not be dealing with anything alone.

"I need you to start from the beginning. What did Anthony do? How are you involved?"

Her throat bobbed in the wake of a deep swallow. He held her focus, giving her time before she nodded, seemingly resolute. "When I left LA, I took only one suitcase and the clothes on my back. After what he'd attempted the night before, I figured I would well and truly burn my bridges, so during my escape, I left behind a folder for him to find. A folder full of evidence of him having stolen Bonacci funds and, therefore, orchestrating large-scale corporate fraud."

"Whoa. Hang on a minute." He took a second to close his eyes, to let this new information filter through, to take some slow and steadying breaths because he already knew she was right about one thing. Things *were* about to change for them.

He gave her a small nod to continue, not quite ready, but needing to hear the rest of this story either way.

Her attention fell to the tiled floor, her thick curls tumbling about her face as she did so. "Anthony, being the boss's son-in-law and all, held an upper-management role at Bonacci Jewelry. A few months back, I overheard him on the phone explaining a missing transaction to an employee. I've known him long enough now to recognize when he's lying. I didn't even need to see his face for his long pauses and backtracking to lead me to looking into the company accounts.

"He'd abused his senior position to drain huge amounts of company money, writing false bills while claiming missing funds as bad company debt. From what I could find, he'd been at it for years. Meanwhile, he transferred what he'd stolen into a secret bank account, assuming no one would ever notice."

A heavy rhythm pounded in Blaine's head at Anthony's sheer audacity. Not only had he openly cheated on and abused Emilia, but he'd also done it while exploiting his cushy and ill-deserved job.

The man had everything and more than Blaine had ever wanted, which had only ever been Emilia, and still, none of it had been enough.

Anger crushed his confusion—a more useful emotion than simply stumbling in the dark for an unattainable answer. There was no justifying why men like Anthony acted the way they did. All he knew was that his fingers burned to wrap around that rat bastard's throat, to crunch some bones, and revel in the sound of that "man's" strangled breaths.

Hurting Anthony wouldn't make up for the missing years and damage, but hell, it would feel good either way.

"No wonder you ran." Those words were the grossest understatement he'd ever uttered, but he didn't want to scare Emilia with what truly went through his head. His new daydream of subjecting her ex-husband to slow and painful torture...

"How much money did Anthony take, by the way?"

Her gaze met his, almost a little too coolly. "Somewhere over thirty million."

His muscles turned slack before a new level of tension worked through his body. Not a day had passed where he didn't relive Anthony's revenge over what he perceived was Blaine stealing Emilia, even though she'd never expressed any kind of interest in him.

How would the guy react to her foiling his plan to steal thirty million dollars? Thirty million dollars he no doubt figured he'd stolen fair and square, much less the legal ramifications now his secret was out.

"Is that everything I need to know?" The words slipped hollow from his mouth. God, he really did hope that was it.

She shook her head, her arms wrapping around her elbows while her posture shrank. "I wanted my dad to know what being married to Anthony was like, so two weeks before I left, I crept into Anthony's bedroom and took some photos with my phone. It was the riskiest thing I've ever done. If he'd woken…"

She inhaled a sharp breath, and her attention veered to the side, making her seem somewhat embarrassed.

"Let me guess." Blaine drew toward her, the storm in his belly raging anew. "He wasn't alone?"

"And you could tell the woman next to him wasn't me." Her face scrunched into a grimace. "Soon after my escape, I faxed my father copies of all the evidence I'd gathered, those photos, the financial stuff, everything."

Blaine reached out and pulled her close. As high as his stress levels had climbed, hers seemed to have settled, like sharing her problems had given her relief. Her lavender perfume filled his senses, somehow lighting new clarity, the last few weeks suddenly making more sense.

Anthony had used her. Abused her. Stolen from her. No wonder she'd believed she wasn't enough. He'd brought one woman after another into their home. No matter what she gave, he wanted more, and he'd stopped at nothing to grind her confidence down.

Now there stood a real chance he would destroy her.

"I've put us both in danger." She trembled where she stood, but leaned in and buried her face against the shoulder of his light gray sweater. "If Anthony finds me… If he finds out about you…"

He kissed the top of her head, wanting to soothe her. "Wouldn't it be smarter for him to disappear?"

She let out a caustic laugh, arching back so they made eye contact. "The police think he's run somewhere to save his own skin, but I don't believe that. Right now, he's pissed. He'll want his money back, followed by a pound of my flesh. He'll want to hurt me and anyone important to me, which means you."

Blaine's skin prickled, his blood pressure rising. If Anthony came back, the guy would get more than the fight he sought. He deserved a dirty dose of karma, and Blaine would relish being the one to give it to him. "Does anyone else know you're in Harlow?"

"Rochelle obviously, but seeing as she's in New York, I doubt she'll tell anyone. Other than that, as I said, not even I knew for sure I'd come here until the night I ended up booking the cottage."

"And aside from Rochelle, have you spoken to anyone else from LA?"

"Just my dad."

Blaine took hold of her shoulders and walked her over to the counter, sitting her down on a stool. "And what did he have to say for himself?"

Emilia swallowed hard, her expression momentarily crumpling. "He told me about Anthony's disappearance and ordered me to return to LA. Once Anthony was found, he wanted me to go back to my marriage and resume our life, business as usual."

This again?

His stomach muscles drew, gutted, winded, mounting a revolt against the thought of ever letting this woman go. Much less to *Anthony.* "How could he ask that of you? His own daughter."

"If you thought his objection to me getting together with an 'Irish boy' ten years ago was bad, you can probably guess his opinion on divorce is even worse. It's shameful enough that I'm gone and unaccounted for, but throw in officially ending my marriage... It's all about reputation with him, how things will look when it comes to the whole Bonacci-Stucco dynasty he's worked so hard to build. And if I'm not there to hold it all together..."

"But surely you're more important than some trumped-up 'dynasty'?"

"I know, and I'm starting to believe it too, but my situation gets worse. I haven't been able to contact my dad in over a week. His phone rings out, and it's not like him not to answer. I don't know if it's because he's angry with me or because something more sinister has happened." Her voice shook, and her hand pressed to her upper abdomen as if she reminded herself to breathe. "I'm worried, Blaine. I know he doesn't deserve my concern, but I can't keep pretending something isn't wrong here."

"And there's no other way of contacting your dad?"

"I can't call the office or speak to any of the domestic help at his home for an update. They'll all know it's me, word might get out, and I have to stay hidden. I can't call the police, either. Anthony has friends in high and low places, L.A.P.D. included. I don't know who to trust."

"You can start by trusting me." He took her hand and lifted his attention to the white, provincial-style clock on the wall. "Right now, it'll be around 5 p.m. in LA. Maybe whoever works the phone lines at Bonacci Jewelry will still be around."

He fished his cell phone from his pocket. Emilia outstretched her arms, lunging for him. "What are you doing? Don't do that!"

He stepped back and held a hand out, gesturing for her to stay quiet and bear with him. A quick internet search provided Bonacci Jewelry's office line, and he hit the call option, waiting as the dial tone did its thing.

"Hi, this is Detective Henry Murphy from the fraud department." He put on his best official-sounding voice, lying to the unsuspecting lady on the other end of the phone. "I need to speak to Vittorio Bonacci about an ongoing investigation."

Emilia scrambled forward, eyelids wide in clear shock. She pushed at him, fingers reaching and clawing to pull the phone from his grasp. Lucky for him, his arms were much longer than hers, which made blocking her attempts to end the call easy. This whole scenario would have been hilarious if it weren't so damn dire.

He turned to avoid her glare's fiery burn, listening as the person at the other end of the line gave him the answers he needed. In that time,

Emilia gave up the fight, and he peered behind him to find her standing with her arms crossed, and her eyes returned to their earlier red-rimmed state.

"Okay, thank you, just one more question. We've tried to call Mr. Bonacci via his cell phone several times with no success, has he changed his number?"

The helpful lady spilled her answer, one that sent a sick feeling through his gut. He turned to Emilia, and she drew back, her shaking hand pressed to her lips as though she'd read his concern.

He gulped some air and cleared his mind, reminding himself that a person waited for him to speak. "Yes, those FBI guys never keep us in the loop. Thank you for the update, Ms. Rivers. I'll call the office line from now on."

He hung up and whirled around to face Emilia, his chest pulling tight. "You shouldn't be in that cottage alone."

"Why? What happened? Is my dad okay?" She kept drawing back, her hand still over her mouth and muffling her voice, her eyes glistening with fear.

"He's fine, but the FBI took his phone, and someone's been tracing his calls."

"Oh no." She shook her head, slow and disbelieving.

He caught up to her and held on to her arm, keeping her from going too far, imploring her to hear him out. "Listen, this is some serious stuff, Emilia. You need to leave that cottage. It's not safe."

She shook her head again, faster, more insistent. "Anthony has taken so much from me already."

But even as she spoke, her face lost color.

"And he could take your life next. Please, you have me now. Stay here with me."

"No." She hugged herself. "I've made enough sacrifices. I've worked too hard for what little I have. I can't. I just can't."

"Jesus Christ, Emilia. I know this is a lot to get your head around—"

"Ten years, Blaine. Ten years. And I never had my own space. I never had any kind of peace or escape. I want a decent night's sleep, for once. I want to live without fear."

"You'd get that staying right here with me." He let go of her and scrubbed a hand over his face, stifling the irrational need to shake her until she understood just how unreasonable she was being. "Hell, you can have the spare room and all the space you want. I'm at work most of the day. You'll have plenty of peace, and at least I have proper deadbolts on my doors, unlike the cottage."

"You're not listening. The cottage is my one piece of independence. Moving in with you, it's too soon, and it wouldn't be the same."

A mixture of hot anger and insult coursed through his bloodstream, and even as it did, he felt like the world's biggest tyrant. He'd offered her a generous alternative, yet she countered with unbending refusal and rejection. *And still,* he understood why. Why the cottage was so important to her. *And still,* he couldn't let her need for solitude take over the necessity to keep her safe.

"Hate me if you want. You're not going home." He stalked forward, resolute, heat building in his chest. "I'll lock my doors and keep you captive here if I have to. You're staying. At least until Anthony is found."

She jutted her jaw forward. "It's bad enough I'm forced to remain hidden, to conduct any work I might want to do in private. I won't add giving up the cottage to the list."

"Is that so?" He stormed across the room and snatched the keys from the hook beside the back door.

"What are you doing?"

He twisted the key in the lock. "Exactly what I said I would do."

He crossed the kitchen in the opposite direction, striding through to the living room and the front door.

Her voice called after him, hurried footsteps not far behind. "I'll climb out a window if I have to."

"Try it." He twisted the key, almost colliding with her as he turned around. A frustrated growl broke from his throat, but he used her close proximity to stare her down. "You have two choices here. Accept my offer and take the spare room, or keep acting like a spoilt rich girl, and I'll be more than happy to tie you down in my bed beside me tonight."

Her lips parted, but she didn't speak. In fact, an eerie sort of stillness washed over her, followed by a red blush creeping up her neck and through to her cheeks. Then again, even his own body stirred at the racier side of what he'd just threatened.

"I didn't tell you about Anthony so you could hold me against my will." The soft glisten returned to her eyes, her voice weak, hollow, and raspy.

Still, he too could play stubborn. "What'll it be, Emilia? Your bed or mine?"

Thirty-Three

EMILIA LAY restless in the unfamiliar bed, the scent of clean linen all around her. She knew the sheets were clean because she'd watched—arms crossed and scowl pointed at Blaine—as he'd made the bed for her earlier. Now the clock on the nightstand said 3:14 a.m., and she still hadn't slept.

A washed-out blue glow spilled in through her slightly ajar door, frosted moonlight infiltrating from a skylight in the hallway. She shifted under her weighty bedspread, trying for the millionth time to get comfortable, her hair ruffling against her pillow, and a pang of sadness diluting her earlier anger.

She'd been too mad, too stubborn, even as she'd recognized Blaine was only looking out for her. She'd also directed her temper at the wrong man.

And that temper hadn't gotten her anywhere because lying in Blaine's house gave her a sense of relief only surpassed by lying in his arms. She was safe, and she wasn't alone.

Her eyes settled on the gray ceiling, an almighty shudder washing through her body, her insides queasy because she'd have to wait several more hours before she could apologize and put things right with him.

Oh God, and he even threatened to tie me to his bed…

She didn't know whether to laugh at that or succumb to the wild flutter in her heart.

"Can't sleep?"

She startled and turned to find Blaine standing in her doorway, the gentle light outlining his strong and masculine silhouette. He wore nothing but navy-blue boxer shorts and delightfully messed hair, her mouth parched just looking at him. "No. I wish I could. Why are you awake?"

And how long have you been watching me?

"Thought I'd check on you." His smoky tone sent tingles through her body, his crossed arms accentuating his broad shoulders and defined biceps. "Still mad at me?"

To her horror, he strode toward her bed and sat on the edge, a crooked smile on his face.

She turned her chin up, so she could pretend to explore the roof's shadows, trying and failing to still the drum of her heart. "I'm not mad."

He raised a brow, perhaps not all that convinced. "You've got a strange way of displaying happiness."

She blinked into the semi-darkness, her throat scratchy. "I'm not happy, either."

He touched her arm, now bare from the oversized t-shirt he'd made her put on since she couldn't go home to get any pajamas. "I can see that. You know, I'm only trying to help, right?"

She let out a sigh, still refusing to look at him. Again, not out of anger, but because every time he stared at her with that lowered and concerned look of his, she was confronted with the truth that, once again, she'd pulled him into a dangerous situation. "Yeah. I get it."

"Then, what's happening here, Emilia? Get whatever's upsetting you out."

"I feel stuck."

"Because I made you stay?"

"No. But thank you for that, either way." Rough tension abraded her throat, scrubbing at her words as she tried to speak them. "Because for all I've done to move on with my life, I'm still not living. Leaving

LA only fixed some of my problems, but I'm still trapped. I'm still looking over my shoulder and holding myself back because one man can't deal with his grandiose sense of entitlement."

Blaine smoothed her hair, and she turned to find his eyes glittering forest green at her against the low light. "For what it's worth, this standoff with Anthony will end, eventually. And in the meantime, there's nothing wrong with accepting a little help. We all need it, sometimes."

She held his gaze for a long and quiet moment, a smile pulling at her lips. Somehow, his words did make her feel better.

"Thank you." Her gratitude came in the form of a whisper, and she meant every syllable and intention behind it. "The whole process of starting over would have been a lot harder without you, but I can't help but mourn the loss of my dreams. Dreams that will remain just dreams until he's found."

"I know. I know." He leaned in and planted a soft kiss on her forehead. "You're stronger than you think. Hell, you got yourself out of LA, and that's no easy feat. You're going to get through this, just like you got through the rest. And then if we're super lucky, we'll finally be just a normal, boring couple, who doesn't have a deranged man-child out on the loose probably looking to cause us harm."

"Us?" Her voice caught in her throat.

"Yes, *us*. So, it's time you stopped acting like you're on your own." His hand landed on her shoulder, and he gave a firm, reassuring squeeze. "I'm here. Whatever happens, we're in this together now."

"And what if they never find Anthony? What if he gets to me first? I don't want you to get tangled in this."

"It's too late for that. I'm already tangled. I have been for a decade now. You think if I didn't happen across Anthony at any other point in my life, I wouldn't kick his ass simply for what he did to us all those years ago? And whether Anthony is a problem or not, I'd still love you, Emilia. I'm not bowing out just because things are a little rough. He won't hurt you, not if I can help it."

A tear spilled down her cheek, warm relief spreading from her heart outwards. *He'd said he loved her.* When had she last heard that from *anyone*, let alone someone she cared so much about?

She probably needed to acknowledge what he'd said but didn't know how, or whether she was meant to make a big deal of it.

"You're offering too much." She paused, still unsure of what she should say. Maybe his declaration had been a slip of the tongue or simply meant in a far more casual sense than what she interpreted. "I can't ask you to live in the shadows because of me."

"You're not the only one here who values having a choice, and I'm choosing to stay." He took a moment to stare her down, as though pressing the point that he was dead serious about his feelings for her. "We're not giving up on each other, understand? Not over this. Not over him."

She gave a slow nod, unable to pry her gaze from his softened focus. "And how do we get on with our lives when we have no idea what will come next?"

"Like this." His mouth split into a wide smile, one that made his eyes light up as he pulled the blanket back, a cold blast of air hitting her side.

"What are you doing?" She startled and squealed, then wriggled away, his cold legs slipping beneath the covers beside hers.

Powerful arms pulled her in, and he rolled her so that her back pressed to his torso. The heat of his body calmed her to the core, calmed her into stillness, and into embracing her own gentle strength.

She closed her eyes, disarmed and at peace, fragments of defense sliding under the force of his easy presence. He loved her, and unlike most normal people, she still had no idea what to do with that love.

Tuck it away in a corner of my heart, maybe? Never, ever let it go!

He hugged her tighter, his breath stroking the back of her neck, the strange familiarity between them relaxing her. A familiarity that had survived their youth and the hard years apart.

This sweet simplicity. A soul connection that went deeper than vanity and money and reputation. Not a business move. Just a genuine, heartfelt bond. *What she'd craved all along.* Blaine protected her, loved her, gave her a way to finally let go...

Her heart softened further, and she couldn't keep from saying his name. "Blaine?"

"Yeah?"

"Thank you."

He kissed her shoulder, causing her to close her eyes against the strain that kiss brought to her heart. "You're welcome."

And just like that, ten years of pent-up anxiety fizzled down to nothing, her future uncertain but Blaine's feelings for her far from it. Maybe she, too, could do away with some of her uncertainty.

"Blaine?"

"Yeah?"

"All those years apart. I missed this."

He didn't reply, but she got the sense that maybe she'd stunned him. So, she let loose with her one final secret, one that wouldn't let her close her eyes until she'd spoken it out loud.

"I missed you."

Thirty-Four

"I TOLD you I can get to work on my own."

Despite last night being one heck of a cozy affair, Emilia found herself in a bad mood this morning. Mostly because the reality of her new life was kicking in. And that reality sucked.

"And I told you, you're not going anywhere by yourself until we hear back from LA."

Yep, they'd been at this for hours, and now Blaine marched by her side into Aggie's nursery, his hand hooked around her elbow because he refused to step away until he saw her safely delivered. Seriously, this guy could quit being a carpenter and start up his own courier service.

"What's happening here?" Aggie approached, her hands planted on her hips, a firm glower pointed at Blaine.

He paused his nursery-storming mission for a moment, though the grip on Emilia's arm did not stop. "Let's just say, I have very real concerns for Emilia's safety and am doing something about it."

"*Hmph.*" Aggie's face lit up, and her gaze switched between Emilia and Blaine. "Must be love. Gets some men all territorial."

She shrugged and threw Emilia a cheeky wink.

"Yeah, well." Emilia wriggled, elbowing Blaine in the ribs so he'd let go. "This one takes territorial to a whole other level. You might not want to get too close. He might try to bite, angry lion style."

"Emilia." Her name was a low growl in his throat. It pointed out the truth of this matter, that he'd shown grace in not letting Aggie into the specifics, and Emilia was pushing her luck with her sarcastic jokes.

Well, what did he expect? That she'd be happy to be caught in the middle of operation *"Save Emilia from Anthony"*? Aside from the new rules to her life, there was a real shame that went with having to admit she even needed those rules.

"Okay. Fine. Fine." She shook him off, taking a decent-sized step away. "I'm here now, can you relax?"

He glared toward Aggie. "The only reason I'm letting her come in today is that I know you keep a big old rifle somewhere around here, and you know how to use it."

Aggie rocked on her heels, seeming mighty proud of herself. "You betcha, and that's just the weapon you know about."

This time her wink was directed at Blaine, who jolted a little before his expression lightened some. "Good, then don't let this one out of your sight, not until Ally comes by to pick her up this afternoon."

He pointed at Emilia and shook his head, not saying another word to her before leaving for his truck.

"I know Blaine's bein' heavy handed, but he's right, ya know." Aggie stepped closer and put her arm through Emilia's, patting her sleeve as she coaxed her along. "We can't have you living out in that cottage alone and not knowing how to defend yourself."

"I don't think there's enough time for me to pick up martial arts, Aggie."

The old lady chuckled. "There's also not enough time for me to get you a gun, either, but knives... knives, oh ya, we can do those. Did you follow the instructions in that little package I had delivered to you the other day?"

Emilia felt her eyes pull wide, fully aware Aggie was asking whether she'd hidden that weird bundle of knives around the cottage. "I thought you were joking."

Aggie sighed and shook her head, leading Emilia to the back of the nursery and a wall of stacked hay bales. "You just stay right here, dear. I'll be right back."

***

That afternoon, when Emilia finally made it to Ally's car, Aggie leaned into the passenger side and imparted a few final words.

"Now don't look at me like I fell outta the silly tree or something. You do exactly as I told ya, okay? Put those knives in places you'll reach easy if someone breaks in." Aggie pointed to Ally. "And you be sure to help Miss Emilia too."

Ally turned to Emilia and mouthed the words, "What the heck?"

After the last twenty-four hours, Emilia lacked the energy to explain. Not about the knives, especially not about her overly possessive ex-husband, and certainly not the absurdity that had been Aggie, running her through exercises that involved stabbing and throwing knives at the nursery's hay bales. *Seriously, what a day.*

Granted, the woman's skill level was way above that of a stereotypical feeble old lady, but still, Emilia just wanted to get home and get ready for the soiree. Getting prettied up for a good night out sure beat focusing on just how disastrous her life was.

By the time she and Ally got into her cottage and distributed knives, the two were in near hysterics, which made getting dressed and applying makeup all the harder.

"Fer cute! Blaine's gonna faint when he sees you in your costume." Ally adjusted the strap of Emilia's rose-pink dress, then stepped back to glance over the full-length, sheath-cut gown.

"I hope not." Emilia winked, careful not to disturb the multicolored crystals pressed to her cheeks. "I'd like him to stay conscious."

"That better not be sexual innuendo. I don't care to think of my boss in that way."

Emilia turned to her bathroom mirror, avoiding Ally's probing stare. "No comment."

And once again, the two women burst into laughter.

"*Ish.*" Ally swiped a tear from her eye, sighing as though she needed to catch her breath. "This is gonna be a heck of a fun night."

"You think people will be pissed about seeing me at the soiree with Blaine?" All day, Emilia had imaged a multitude of leers and whispers, all because she, a relative stranger, had nabbed their golden boy away from Sarah… probably Harlow's golden girl.

"*Pfft*, even if they are pissed, they'll have to learn to mind their own business and survive. You've got nothing to worry about, okay?" Ally swatted a hand, just as the crunch of tires over gravel sounded from outside. "Betcha that's Blaine now. We should go."

Emilia double-checked the crisscross of silk ribbons around her waist, her pulse speeding up. For all intents and purposes, she looked every inch the enchanted fairy, but she didn't feel like one. For a self-confessed introvert, as much as she'd looked forward to the soiree's novelty, socializing and being watched left a hot prickling between her shoulder blades.

She followed close behind as Ally raced down the hall, soon swinging the front door wide open just as Blaine held his hand up, ready to knock.

Ally stumbled back. "Geez Louise, watch the face!"

When it appeared she was safe, she landed a hurried kiss on his face, leaving a fuchsia lip print on his left cheek.

She ducked under his arm, laughing and running toward her car, escaping the scene of her lipstick crime. "See you both at Mirabella Falls. Emilia, probably no need to pack any knives in your purse tonight."

She gave a high and excited wave, followed by another cackle before sliding into the driver's seat.

By the time Emilia turned back to Blaine, he held a confused glower. "Knives?"

She shook her head. "Just don't ask."

A beat passed, and his gaze slid over her face and then down her body, a wide, childish grin lighting his expression. "You look incredible."

"The same goes for you." She stepped forward and used the heel of her hand to wipe the lipstick off his cheek, her heart pounding at a break-neck pace because he smelled incredible, all smoky and somehow crisp. The billowy, white shirt he wore pulled wide at the collar, revealing the thin sprinkling of pale brown hair over his sculpted chest.

She whipped her focus up to his face, and the thick waves curled over his brow, his hair styled in a deliberate and delectable mess. The man resembled a steamier version of a Shakespearian hero, minus the tight stockings, feathered cap, or the hard-to-understand *ye old* English…

She laughed at that thought, and a roguish smirk took over his lips. Deciding to end the bone-melting stare-off before she literally melted, she nodded to his costume. "Which character are you meant to be?"

"Lysander." His eyes did another obvious scan of her body, her heart pulsing again in response. "What about you?"

"Hermia."

He quirked a brow. "That's ironic."

He was kind of right. Hermia did make for an ironic choice—a character from *A Midsummer Night's Dream* who'd been adamant she wouldn't marry the man her father chose for her, her heart belonging to someone else—Lysander.

So yeah, there was irony here, though so far, their misadventure hadn't yet resulted in the play's same happily ever after.

One day, maybe, one day…

She took his hand, allowing him to guide her to his truck. "You know, for a carpenter, you have a strong grasp of Shakespeare."

"That'll teach you to make assumptions about a man's profession." He opened the car door for her and waited for her to climb in. "Though I did look up the play's summary online, so maybe your doubts have some basis."

He joined her in the truck's cozy cab, his analytical stare holding while his hand poised over the ignition. "You smell different."

She pointed to the crown of flowery vines on her head. "It's jasmine."

"You look like a dream tonight, you know that?" His gaze lingered for a while longer, before snapping to outside the windscreen as if he'd come to his senses. "Shit! We should go. Otherwise, we won't make it to this party."

She let out a soft chuckle. "We won't?"

The depth of green in his eyes relaxed over his easy smile. "Let's just say, unlike you, who snored for hours last night, I hardly slept a wink."

She gave him a playful slap on the arm. "I *don't* snore."

"Okay, fine, it was more of a cute rattle than a snore." He backed out of her driveway, his grin staying put as he looked over his shoulder. "But my point is, if you were worried that our presence at the soiree might make us stars of this town's rumor mill, you should be. Tonight, I plan to prove every one of those rumors about us true."

Thirty-Five

A THOUSAND FAIRY lights twinkled from the trees above the soiree's large clearing. Blaine stood behind Emilia, his arm warm around her waist, while a crush of people filed past and Mirabelle Falls trickled in the background.

"Wait here." His low whisper sent a ripple through her body, alluring, reassuring. "I'll drop off our food and be right back."

His hand slipped from her arm, and he strolled toward a giant buffet table adorned with berry speckled garlands and various decorated cake stands. She used her alone time to pivot in a full circle, drinking in the dreamlike spectacle—the fancy costumes, the happy faces, the indigo and fire-colored sky descending into night.

The people passing her were dressed in elaborate ancient Greek togas and whimsical fairy outfits decked in yards of frothy tulle. Meanwhile, a quartet of flute, harp, and strings played a sweet rendition of "En Bateau" at another far-off corner. The music brought the fairy theme to life and proved that Harlow had well and truly pulled out all the stops.

"Now, don't you look like perfection?"

Emilia whipped around, coming face-to-face with Maureen Cooper, though Frank was nowhere to be seen. The woman had a silver fairy wand in her hand, her cheeks heavily blushed, her dress overflowing like a purple-chiffon puddle at her feet.

Emilia kept her smile light on her face, though her insides churned a little. Maureen and Frank had acted as surrogate parents to Blaine after he'd been forced from LA. What if they weren't happy to see her with him? What if they preferred Sarah?

Of all encounters, this was the one she'd dreaded most. "I could say the same for you."

Maureen's gray eyes held a sparkle. Maybe she was yet to notice Emilia had arrived with Blaine. "I drove past the cottage the other day. Your garden is so cute. Aggie has unearthed real talent in you, there."

"Thank you, her help made all the difference." Emilia shuffled where she stood, not sure she'd say the same about this morning's impromptu training on how to wield a knife. "And I guess I have you to thank for directing me to her, back when I had that wasp problem."

And with all the upheaval over Anthony's disappearance, she could take comfort in knowing she'd at least survived long enough to see her garden bloom, even if right now her temperature rose and her palms sweated.

"Oh yes, the wasps." Maureen cringed. "I'm still so sorry about that. The cottage had been empty for so long and—"

Blaine sidled up to Emilia and kissed her on the cheek.

Maureen's mouth fell open. "Jesus, Mary, and Joseph, I…"

"Hello, Maureen."

Though Emilia couldn't see him, there was no missing the brightness in his tone. Meanwhile, her face heated and her muscles stiffened as his hand slid to the small of her back, making it undeniable they were more than just friends.

"When did this happen?" Maureen's expression remained slack. "How did I miss this?"

"I'm sorry." Emilia's throat went dry. "We probably should have picked another occasion to reveal our news, but—"

"What did I tell you about apologizing so much?" Blaine held a frown, though his brows raised in a somewhat softer expression.

Maureen reached out a hand to his forearm, letting him know he didn't need to get defensive. Next, she turned to Emilia and engulfed her in an excited hug. "Dear, don't say another word. I was just surprised, that's all. I'm usually the first to know about these things, dontcha know."

Emilia nearly drowned in a cloud of Maureen's strong flowery perfume, and she gasped for her next breath under the crush of the enthusiastic embrace. "You're not angry?"

"Geez, no. No." Maureen pulled away, her eyes holding a happy glitter. "I'm glad he got you to come around in the end."

"Hang on a minute." Emilia turned to Blaine. "You told her about us?"

He shook his head, looking just as confused.

"He didn't need to." Maureen gave Blaine a congratulatory nudge with her elbow. "The whole town has figured something's been happenin' between yous guys. Some even took bets on whether our boy here would win you over or not."

"Wait. What?" Blaine held up a hand, signaling for Maureen to pause. "How did everyone know?"

"Oh, ya"—Maureen patted his cheek half-condescendingly—"You two put on enough public showdowns for folks to put two-and-two together. Anyway, all that matters is we're all so happy for you both."

Emilia's heart rate slowed, and she settled back in her posture, her inner world morphing into a mass of unpredicted elation. Though she figured Maureen didn't know the full history about her being the same girl from Blaine's past, something told her that when he did get around to filling everyone in, this woman would come to terms with that bit of news easy enough.

Harlow had been good to Emilia, and so far tonight, all she had was confirmation that the people here accepted her in a way that had been lacking in all her twenty-eight years alive.

A cotton candy station stood some distance away, and her gaze fell on Aggie handing out sticks of fluffy pink sugar to a group of teenagers.

Emilia patted Blaine's arm. "I'll be back in a moment."

She slipped from his hold.

"On you go, dear." Maureen nodded to Blaine. "I'm sure this one has a lot to tell me while you're gone."

Emilia gave him a sympathetic shrug and turned away. Aggie waved just as the teenagers moved on from her stand. "Nice to see you twice in one day."

Rich crimson velvet embellished Aggie's tiny frame, a plethora of gold costume jewelry hanging from her neck. She was a fairy-tale matriarch if ever there were one.

"I'd say you look somewhat different from how I left you." Aggie's eyes twinkled before she offered a cheeky wink. "And dontcha know, you're doin' a fine job of getting that gorgeous man to follow you around."

Emilia rested her hand over the stand's polished wood counter, the sugary scent emanating from the candy machine, warming her with a sense of childhood wonder. "He puts forward a compelling reason to leave the house."

"Oh, ya got it all wrong, dear." Aggie *tsked*, shaking her head. "If I were fifty years younger, me and that poor man wouldn't be settin' one foot out the front door."

Emilia hacked back a rough giggle, her mind reeling while she waited for the burn in her cheeks to go down. "Lucky for both of us you're not younger, Aggie."

What with all the gun-toting and knife skills… Who was this woman?

Aggie sashayed around the table, a toothy grin in place as she reached out to grip Emilia's forearm. "I'm so proud of you, ya know?" Her voice dropped to a fragile whisper, eyes peering up in an imploring sort of stare. "Not many kids around here pay much mind to what I have to say, but you did. You did. And look at you now."

Emilia's heart seemed to swell at Aggie's acknowledgment. Even with her strange passion for weaponry, she'd been the first person in Harlow to hear Emilia's problems and be the strong female figure she'd needed for so long.

"I'm so glad you were there for me that day on my porch." She gave Aggie a soft smile, hoping her delivery now would convey just how much she appreciated this woman's friendship. "That you pushed me to start a garden, work at the nursery, and to work on myself. You got me out of my head and breathed enough space into my life that I could consider letting Blaine in."

And not just Aggie but Ally, and even Sarah too. All three women had acted so selflessly, and she owed each of them in different ways. Heck, she owed herself for all her leaps of faith.

"Oh, ya sure. I've seen the way he looks at you. That boy's in love." Aggie squeezed Emilia's arm. "Help or not, Blaine would have done anything to get you back. Yous guys oughta give yourselves some credit too."

Tears prickled at Emilia's eyes, but she fought them off. That Blaine's feelings were so obvious to everyone when, for years, she'd yearned for even the tiniest bit of affection anyone around her.

"I love him too." Her heart gripped a little tighter. She hadn't expected to say that out loud. "So much, it's almost terrifying."

Aggie's gaze took on a glossy sheen, and she reached up to press her fingertips to Emilia's cheeks. "It's great, isn't it?"

Emilia's shoulders shook with gentle laughter. Aggie was right. These last few weeks with Blaine had been overwhelming but wonderful, and his conviction held strong through her every doubt.

He'd shocked her out of her comfort zone, challenged her into making plans beyond what she'd intended—plans grander than living out her days alone and on the run. He made her want to lay down roots. To hold strong. For once in her life, to grasp what she wanted and not let go.

And as horrid as her past had been, as ungracefully as she'd handled that past at times, she had someone she could talk to, someone who looked out for her and helped glue the fallen pieces of her shattered life back together.

He'd made her *believe*.

In a future. In a better future.

All while she'd fought him and pushed him away.

She had no doubts now. Blaine was her everything. Her one and only. She'd recognized that the first time she met him—ten years and another lifetime ago.

Because of him, she'd learned that having freedom didn't mean doing everything on her own. And love didn't mean sacrificing integral parts of herself to keep the peace.

She could have love and walk her own path at the same time.

"I know that faraway look." Aggie's sage smile pulled at Emilia's daydream.

"You do?"

Aggie's eyes softened. "You finally know what it's about to let someone else in."

Emilia's vision dropped to the ground, her stomach hard with regret. "I wish it hadn't taken so long to understand. I've been a real idiot."

"No, dear. See it like this…" Aggie's imploring stare pleaded for Emilia to challenge her thinking once more. "You went to hell and back, had a lot workin' against you, and still came out okay. I bet that's why Blaine worked so hard to get you back. You're resilient, and you don't hold on to bitterness. Take this win, it's well deserved."

Whatever tension dragged at Emilia slipped away, a greater sense of pride taking over. True enough, she'd fought her demons and moved on. A life with Blaine lingered on her horizon, and all the other stuff weighing her down would just have to settle into the background.

She looked over her shoulder at Blaine, urgency pushing her before she bobbed down and gave Aggie a hurried kiss. "Thank you, Aggie, you're a real-life fairy godmother."

Aggie chuckled in the background, and Emilia raced back to Blaine.

He tilted his chin toward the candy stand. "What was that about?"

"Never mind." She took his hand and pulled. "Just follow me."

He gave a moment of resistance and then moved from his spot, allowing her to pull him through the crowd, despite the crush of bodies slowing her down.

Sarah's golden hair glinted from across the clearing, the woman sitting alone atop a fallen tree trunk. Emilia paused. Heavy guilt lifted her hand in an apologetic wave at Blaine's ex.

Sarah waved back, though her slouched posture suggested she wasn't in the mood to party. She'd sacrificed her engagement to make room for Emilia in Blaine's life, and it was clear enough that a price had been paid. Emilia owed it to her not to waste this second chance.

Her attention caught on a man some way off to Sarah's left. He was built like a human skyscraper. Tall and solid. He appeared out of place. Emilia's stomach roiled. She'd never seen him in Harlow before, but for some reason, his overly focused scowl seemed familiar.

A high-pitched squeal blasted in her ear. So much happening at this soiree. She spun around to find the gleeful sound came from Ally; a sturdy-looking guy, who looked like he probably played football, lifting her into the air. The younger woman's head flung her head back with a tidal wave of laughter.

Emilia smiled, glad her friend had found her own fun.

"Emilia!" Blaine tugged at her hand, spinning her to face him. She barely missed slamming into his chest. By the time she looked over her shoulder to the man she'd noticed in the clearing, he was gone. "What's happening? Where are you taking me?"

That's right, Blaine had no clue of her plan, and now that his face bore a deep frown, she needed to keep moving.

"For once, be the one who has to trust me, okay?" She fixed him with a determined stare, though her blood pounded wildly in her veins.

The gorgeous man in front of her would learn what her heart had waited ten-hellish-years to reveal. That words would not suffice.

But first, she'd lose this crowd.

The band's violins faded and a thumping Celtic drum took over, a fevered Irish jig adding to the sense of wild abandon. Blaine's brow furrowed, but he squeezed at her hand and nodded for her to lead on.

Before long, they disappeared into a thick line of trees, the dark and lonely woodland offering a buffer against the party lights and sounds.

"What's the problem?" He stared down at her now, deathly serious, his face hard to see under the scattered moonlight.

"What makes you think there's a problem?"

"You nearly ripped my arm out to get me here." The soft glisten of his eyes danced about her face, causing her heart to clench and blood to race.

"I want you to kiss me." She crossed her arms, not used to being so direct.

His posture seized, and he glowered at her, his silence a sign that she'd stunned him.

That silence pulled the muscles at her face, a slow smile taking her over. "I want you to kiss me like the last ten years didn't happen."

Despite her smile, his frown bowed deeper. "What are you talking about?"

She growled, annoyed that he didn't understand. "I don't want you to treat me like I'm breakable anymore. It's time we lightened up, don't you think?" She grabbed his collar, dragging him closer. "I want a whole-hearted kiss. One that will make me go weak all over and turn my body into water."

"I don't think that's physically possible." The outer corner of his lip quirked up, and his eyes flashed their dazzling green. "And is this still you talking, Emilia Bonacci? Or has the ghost of a sex-crazy teenager possessed you? I need to check. I'm not sure I believe my ears."

She pushed herself into him, insistent and frustrated all at once, his toying burning her up from the inside out. "I'm trying to be brave here, and you're making this more difficult than it should be."

"I'm sorry." His voice fell to a comforting whisper, and he slid his hands over her hips, his forehead meeting hers, though the smirk remained. "I'm sorry. And you don't need to try at being brave. You already are."

His lips met hers but all too briefly, though that brevity in itself sparked her desire like a match to dry kindling.

She swallowed hard and lifted her hands to his shoulders. "More. Please."

"Say that again." He shuffled her back, one slow step at a time, until he had her pressed against a tree. "I like this new Emilia. She's very impatient."

His words were a dare, one she wanted to laugh at. But the fire in his eyes and the rock-hard feel of him had heat pooling between her thighs, turning that desire to laugh into a low sigh.

Her mind flashed to the nineteen-year-old boy—now replaced with this all-encompassing man—those memories clashed, past onto present, spurring her to whisper again. "More."

Before she could rise to kiss him, his mouth crashed over hers, his kiss fierce and unbroken, her entire body giving in to him, even though she'd been the one to start this.

He kept her trapped against that tree, his fingers clasped at the silk of her costume, his palm engulfing her ribcage, his thumb caressing the underside of her breast while a satisfied groan fell from her mouth. She surrendered further.

He nipped at her bottom lip before breaking the kiss completely, his molten stare melting her some more. "Is that what you wanted?"

Her hand slid down his stomach, stopping at his waistband, a deeper meaning to his question filtering through.

"Not *what*, Blaine. *Who.*" She held his gaze, no doubt left in her mind. "I want you."

Thirty-Six

BLAINE GROWLED, his last thread of control snapping as he grabbed Emilia's hand and wrenched her away from the tree and out toward the parking lot.

If it were up to him, he would have taken her right there and then, but on soiree nights, the horny teenagers would soon make their way into the woods to make out in semi-privacy. Kind of like he and Emilia already had…

"Where are we going?" She stumbled behind him, and he slowed, vowing not to embarrass her just so they could get their kicks in the woods.

She was still new in town, and he refused to share this moment with anyone, even though his blood heated, and his body screamed for release. "Just get to the car."

Seconds felt like hours, and he scooped her up, pretty much dumping her in the passenger side of his truck before bolting around to the driver's seat. Soon, he had the engine roaring to life, and he gunned it back to his place, occasionally hooking his gaze to his right and catching a glimpse of her startled expression pointed ahead.

He pulled up to his house and yanked the hand brake, a thick cloud of dust lingering in the air. His heart surged. Close. So close. The moment he rounded the vehicle and opened her door, Emilia threw herself into his arms, and their lips meshed together for the journey to his front porch.

He fumbled with his keys, dropping them in a sharp, metallic clang at his feet. She let out a soft chuckle and so did he, but he was mostly absorbed in her kiss. So, damn the keys. At least for a minute.

He pressed her to his front door and ravaged her lips some more, her head falling back with a loud sigh while her hands tangled in his hair, pulling him closer. He wanted her right here. Right now. In the open air and underneath the stars. But then a car zoomed past on the road behind him, and he thought better of that idea.

Got to open the door. Got to get inside. Got to have her.

Yes, his vocabulary had reduced to fragmented sentences, but that was fine because Emilia was the best kind of distraction—her wild curls wilder than usual from this sizzling interlude that could only get hotter.

Her fingertips met his chest through his shirt's gaping collar, her warmth kneading at his body, crawling his desire up another notch. *Holy smokes.* He let her go and scrambled for the keys, managing to shove the door open, only for them to stumble through the threshold.

They landed together on the hardwood floor and burst into a fit of laughter. He pushed her hair from her face, the heat dying a little and giving way to something else. Affection. Genuine affection. The thing that had bonded them together from that very first meeting a decade ago.

The wilderness of his darkened house surrounded her, and still, her chocolate brown eyes glinted with real joy, her wondrous curls fanning out in all directions beneath her.

At that moment, he found himself lost for words—or maybe just altogether lost—his emotions taking over and leaving nothing else but her and him, that beautiful nothingness swallowing his laughter.

Though her eyes still shone, she watched him in the stillness before speaking again. "Don't ever leave me again."

She reached out and stroked the edge of his forehead, and his world stilled. He shook his head, holding her gaze, meaning every bit of his next promise. "Never again."

Because with all the uncertainty swirling around them, for all the Anthonys and Vittorios, and the myriad other unknowns, one thing held true. "You're mine."

He pressed his lips to hers, gentle this time, a silent vow that whatever came next, they'd be in it together. A single tear trailed down the side of her face, and he kissed her through it. She gave a hurried nod against that kiss and then hooked her hand around the back of his neck, holding him to her.

Moonlight poured in through a nearby window, the whites of the jasmine crown on her head glowing like a luminescent halo. Her ethereal beauty jarred against his rougher edges, and still, he wanted her. Had *always* wanted her.

He no longer believed what her father had said about him. That he wasn't good enough. Rich enough. Or refined… None of that mattered because she wanted him too. And *that* was the most important thing here.

So he took the kiss deeper, sweeping his tongue over hers and savoring her soft heat, the kiss turning hard and insistent, teeth scraping and mouths pressing. He allowed his demand for her to consume him, just as her needy groan broke free.

She smelled of pear-scented shampoo and jasmine, and her featherlight touch slid under his shirt. Everything about her teased him, shook him to the core, provoked him to tug away his shirt.

He pushed the thin strap of her dress down next, wanting her naked and exposed too. Her breath hitched, and her eyes pulled wide, the black of her pupils dilating into expansive pools that lit his nerve endings and spurred him to bend and touch his lips to the underside of her breast.

She inhaled again and arched against him, the tip of his tongue brushing her nipple until she lifted her hands and raked her fingers through his hair. Under a whisper, she begged for more, and a blistering sensation undid his restraint.

He slid his callused hands over the delicate skin of her inner thigh, doubling back until he hit the sensitive juncture of her sex—stroking, penetrating, continuing to kiss her until he worked one shudder out of her after another, allowing him to swallow each beautiful sigh and moan.

Her head tilted back in pleasure, eyes pressed shut when he took the moment to bury himself deep inside her. She clenched around him and released a keening cry, making him damn near lose hold right along with her. He didn't want this to end. Not just yet. He wanted more. Wanted to feel her. To impart a piece of himself on her soul forever.

And so he took her, slow, grasping for everything he'd needed and hadn't had in all those years apart; one needy, desperate thrust at a time until her beautiful chocolate eyes flung open again, allowing him to see her surprise.

He got to her like she got to him.

There'd never been any escaping what they shared. No miles. No years. No family interjections. No keeping them apart. Every pain he'd held onto fell away, and he surged within her, losing and finding himself all at once.

Even as lust ebbed, it left him repeating what he now understood on a deeper and undeniable level. "You're mine, Emilia Bonacci. You've always been mine."

Thirty-Seven

"Hey, wake up. I can't feel my arm."

Emilia wriggled her fingers and tried to get some feeling back, her arm trapped in an awkward position while Blaine hugged her in her bed from behind. She pressed her cold foot to his shin and tried to rouse him.

"Ouch." He stirred, his heavy arm draped over her ribcage, his voice low and groggy. "What did I do?"

"Well for one, you're crushing me." She groaned, trying again to slide out from under him. "And two, I drew the line when you stole the blanket."

He rolled onto his back, giving her enough space to turn around and face him, his softened gaze dancing about her face.

"Sorry about that." He gave the sweetest boyish grin, one that made her forgive him. Next, he swept her loose curls from her forehead and pressed a kiss right there. "We'll practice this bed sharing thing and get it down to an art form. I promise."

Her lips trembled at the pull of a smile. "We *didn't* make it to bed last night and did well enough."

He gave a low chuckle. "How long have you been awake?"

"A few minutes. I wanted to watch you sleep for a while before I realized I was stuck and my arm was struggling for circulation."

"I can pretend to be asleep again if you like?"

She laughed, her heart melting a little at his unruly morning hair and the rough stubble along his jaw. Her eyes had a hard time deciding which rugged feature to settle on, while his sleepy expression warmed her body into wanting a replay of last night.

She paused her musing long enough to remember this was the real world, and she couldn't live forever in the dream bubble they'd created. *Unfortunately.* "Don't you have a stall at the town fair to attend to today?"

He rose onto an elbow, a bit too fast, like the haze of last night had made him forget he had a job to do. "Damn it, yes I do. At least, I have to stop in to make sure Wayne and Jacob have done a decent job of setting up, and Ally has actually arrived to work on time."

She raised a brow and gave him a disbelieving look. "Did you see how much fun she was having last night?"

"Yeah, I'm not holding out much hope."

She laughed and sat up. "Right, well I guess that means we're starting our day now."

Blaine grabbed her arm and pulled her down to him again, before rolling on top of her. "Not until I've kissed you about a hundred times first."

Except, she was the one who kissed him, only to break away again the moment an ache of desire awoke in her lower tummy. "Oh, no you don't. Don't start something you can't finish."

He growled. "I'll be back." He rolled away, pointing to her as he stood. "A couple of hours and then…"

He smiled and went about digging around in a chest of drawers while she found her phone on the nightstand, wanting to see the time. "Urgh. My battery is flat, and my charger is still at the cottage."

He turned back to her while tugging on a pair of jeans. "I guess you could come along with me and grab your charger first, then we can drop in on the fair together."

"No, actually I was thinking." She paused to chew on her lower lip for a moment. "Since the plan is to have me here more often, maybe you could leave me at the cottage while you do your work thing, and I can pack some boxes to bring here?"

He stared at her for a while, his face inordinately still, though with a distinct tension. "I don't like that idea."

"You don't have to." She climbed out of bed and searched about for her clothes. Were they in this room or still downstairs? "But I need to pack a few things, either way. How long will you be at the fair?"

"Forty-five minutes if I'm quick, but Em—"

"Perfect." She snatched her dress up from an armchair in the room's corner.

"No. Not perfect." She kept her back to him, but the hard edge to his tone was unmissable. "I don't want you at the cottage by yourself."

She spun around, for once in her life unashamed of her nakedness as she swanned over to him, dress draped over her forearm.

"Please." She pressed against him, and as if by instinct, his hands wrapped around her, the warmth of those big palms at her ribcage once more prodding at her low aching need. "I'll have my phone plugged in while I pack. I'll call you if there are any issues. Once I'm done, I'll be here and all yours forever."

The hard bulge of his excitement nudged against her belly through his clothes. At that moment, he wasn't the only one tempted to draw things out and not leave. She arched up, catching his lips with hers, for the first time in forever using her sensuality.

He pulled his lips away and rested his forehead to hers, though the firm curl of his fingers on her skin suggested she had him at least a little. "Can't it wait until tonight?"

She shook her head. "I know you want to be there to help me, but this is something I want to do on my own. A rite of passage. A goodbye to that place and that part of my life."

His brow pressed down into a hard line. "I still don't like this."

"I know." She kissed him again, stroking the side of his face. "But you'll let me do it because you love me, and you know how important it is to me."

He leaned back, pushing her slightly away in the process. "That sounds like blackmail."

"It *is* blackmail." A new smile plucked at her lips, and she bounced where she stood, willing him to give in a little.

He growled, throwing one last flinty stare before turning for his wardrobe. "Fine, but only as long as it takes me to check on our stand at the fair, and then I'll be right back to pick you up. You plug in your phone, lock the doors, call if there are any problems."

She bit her lower lip and nodded, more excited than rational. A new chapter of her story was about to begin, and she couldn't wait to start. Because despite all obstacles, her future would be with Blaine.

———

Blaine parked in Emilia's driveway, the morning sun picking up a searing edge through his windshield. If not for his extra work at the fair, and Rochelle's visit to peruse his work sometime this weekend, he wouldn't be dropping Emilia off at the cottage right now.

There'd been her naked body pressed to his earlier and her promise to move in with him later in the day. She'd clouded his judgment. She'd done it on purpose. And though he admired her growing confidence, did it have to come at the cost of him being so easily distracted?

He drew the parking brake and turned to her. "If anything happens, you call, okay?"

A cheerful light brightened her eyes, and she leaned in and kissed him quickly. "Sure thing. I can handle an empty cottage and a few boxes."

He hadn't seen her this carefree and confident since her teenage years. And his attention dropped to the crumpled pink dress hanging off her, the same dress from last night. She looked even more beautiful now, the sparkling makeup and perfect hair replaced with a ruffled, loved-up appearance.

His body warmed all over again, and he clutched at the steering wheel to keep from reaching for her again just as she climbed out and onto her driveway.

Too bad he had to watch her walk away.

She took light steps toward the cottage, near prancing, before she stopped and turned to him, her audible laugh cutting through the distance and hitting him square in the chest.

"See you soon." He said it out his window, more a prayer than a glib goodbye.

She waved, eyes squinting against the sun. "I'm counting on it."

Anthony hid against the sun-heated weatherboards, the old cottage creaking at his back. After an entire night waiting for Emilia to return, he shouldn't have been surprised to see her stepping out of another man's car.

And still, he *was* surprised.

Stupid bitch. She'd left behind her high-flying life with him for *this*? To hook up with some small-town hick who lived in the middle of a dust-bowl hell pit.

He hacked back and then spat at the dry, yellow gravel beneath his feet, a rage-filled fire eating up his insides, every muscle in his body coiling like a hungry boa constrictor. A boa constrictor ready to crush its prey.

He hadn't distinguished the other guy's face. The daylight's glare on the car's windshield had stopped him from that. But the truck was unique enough, and it had a logo on the side that said, "Oak Tree Furniture." He'd finish with Emilia, then track down this guy. Put a bullet in his head. Leave town. Move on, richer and happier.

A tight smirk pulled at Anthony's face. Emilia belonged to him. She was *his* wife. No halfwit yokel could change that, and she'd learn her place soon enough, though still all too late.

Maybe it was a good thing his wife was a lying whore. Her absence last night meant he had a huge advantage. She'd gifted him hours to dig through her house and plan an end to this saga. Even though Luciano's man had been tasked with following her through the night and was still a no-show...

Maybe the crony had made good on his threat to ditch the job. Maybe he'd decided to take a poorly timed nap. Who the fuck cared? Anthony preferred it this way. No one to hold him back. No one to share the spoils of what he was about to do. No one to keep him from the joy of watching Emilia Bonacci beg for her life.

Not that begging would save her.

He'd have fun with the deceitful bitch first—the flimsy-as-fuck locks on this piece-of-shit house and the bottle of gasoline in her garden shed would take care of that—then he'd put her out of her misery.

And make no mistake, she *would* be miserable.

Thirty-Eight

INSIDE HER BEDROOM, Emilia slipped out of her fairy costume and pitched it toward her bed. A loose-fitting sundress hung in her wardrobe, and she pulled it out, her phone already charging from an outlet on the nearby wall.

The last twenty-four hours had brought more than she'd bargained for—a surplus of love and acceptance from her new community. A zest for life because of Blaine. The entire night solidified the fact that she now, finally, had somewhere she belonged.

Aside from the uncertainty over Anthony, life was just fine.

She slipped the sundress over her head and decided that letting go of the cottage didn't have to be a sad affair. Maybe, some years, a husband, and a couple of children from now, she'd forget all about the loneliness and upheaval.

And maybe, every morning for the rest of her life, she'd wake next to Blaine. Each day would be spent together, living out their perfectly normal and boring second chance.

Her charging phone began to ring, and she laughed. Blaine was probably not even at the fair yet and already stressing about her being at the cottage alone, like she hadn't done just that for weeks already.

She pressed the phone to her ear, her tone bright because it felt good to have someone calling her out of genuine concern and not merely a need to keep tabs on her movements. "Hey, what's up?"

She waited for his familiar voice but got nothing more than silence. She pulled the phone away. Maybe it was glitching or something. But the scene displayed a call from a private number, so that wasn't it. It wasn't Blaine calling her, either.

"Who is this?"

Maybe a spam caller? Already? This was a new phone and number, and it wasn't like she'd spent her limited time in Harlow signing up for random mailing lists or services. She waited a few moments longer. Her skin taking on a sharp prickle. Still nothing.

She searched the empty room around her, her heartbeat picking up pace, her head aching under the rush of worst-case scenarios playing through her mind.

Maybe she just had a bad connection. Someone who'd misdialed and got her number...

"Okay, I'm hanging up now."

"I like the fear in your voice, Emilia." A low and menacing drawl cracked down the line, and her breath stalled in her lungs. Not Blaine, but still familiar. And for all the wrong reasons. "Come out front, honey, I want to hear that fear in person."

Blaine drove the long road into town, smiling to himself and shaking his head at how Maureen would no doubt chew him out over Emilia closing her lease early.

Of course, he had zero regrets about stealing her from the cottage, a cottage he glanced at through his rearview mirror. A huge part of him wanted to turn back and be with her again, to hang his duties at the fair and stay, despite her insistence that he go.

Last night was all the vindication he needed. He didn't want to wait any longer. He'd waited years. Wasn't that enough? He wanted to start the rest of their lives together. To have her with him. Always. Forever. Sure as hell not alone in that damn, isolated cottage.

The dull pain of her absence made him glance back through his rearview mirror again. For the longest time, he saw nothing, just a cloudless sky telling him not to be paranoid. But something could be said for instinct because, in the next beat, he *did* spot something.

A strange thin, gray smudge muddied the sky—far in the distance, twisting, and curling. His heart lurched, while his hopes turned to literal ash. Literal, because Emilia's house was on fire.

The line went dead, and Emilia ran from her bedroom, her blood cold as she headed for the kitchen. When she got there, a trail of smoke crept from under the back door's sill.

She stopped in her tracks, heat radiating through the timber at her feet, a sickly charred scent filling the air as she pried the door open. A wall of flames leaped up, halting her escape.

Fire licked at her entire back porch, the orange and blue glow engulfing her beloved potted plants along the edge and turning them into cinders. A scream jerked from her mouth, and she tripped backward, slamming onto the hardwood floor. Whatever had happened, happened quickly. This fire was no accident.

Somewhere out there, her monster of a husband waited for her to come out.

Or he waited for her to stay and die.

And her phone. It didn't yet have enough charge for her to call for help while she ran. So, what could she do? Sit in her bedroom, attached to her charging phone, just waiting for someone to pick up while her house burned and her ex hovered somewhere nearby?

The weight of her predicament sank in, and she pressed her hand to her mouth, catching the sob ripping through her throat. She stood, then bolted for the bathroom since Anthony had told her to come out the front of the house, and she definitely wasn't going there.

Tears stung her eyes, and she threw herself onto the cool tile floor, slamming the door shut behind her and setting the lock. She turned around, her gaze catching on the tiny frosted window above the bathtub. Her only chance at escape.

Hard breaths exploded from her lungs, and yet, each breath was an effort to produce. She scrambled forward and used the bath's edge as a step up to the window, all while acknowledging there'd be a fall on the other side.

She cranked the window open and did her best to keep quiet, her heart pained from its racing pace. She hoisted herself over the sill, armpits aching from her weight on the thin ledge. The sky's bright blue freedom a few scrambling movements away.

A loud crack sounded behind her. The sound of splitting wood.

She climbed faster, unable to see behind, but her best guess was that someone had kicked the bathroom door down.

Firm fingers wrapped around her ankle. She screamed, the hard tug of that hand crushing and leaving her to cling to the window sill for literal life. She kicked, trying to get him to let go, already exhausted.

"Stupid, fucking bitch!" Anthony's voice tore into her like the physical blow of a heavy blade.

The tugging got harder, leaving her panicked like he'd tear her in half if she didn't let go. But it didn't come to that. No. He kept the tug of war going until his size and weight won, her arms so fatigued she let go.

She fell from the window, her head smacking into the tile wall on the way down. She'd made the wrong choice. Shouldn't have attempted a quick escape. Maybe she should have stayed in her room and called for help. Her shoulder, the not-so-good one, hit the raised bath's edge, prying a great cry from her. One she'd never known herself capable of making.

But that cry held so much more than the pain of her fall. Pure hatred stared back at her from Anthony's glacial blue eyes, his perfect teeth bared in a sneer, his overly tanned skin, and that too straight and pointed nose… She froze. Wanted to curl up. To give up. To cower and admit defeat.

But fear and defeat alone would not be enough for this man. No. He grabbed her hair and dragged her out of that bath, removing her option to give up.

"I told you to come outside." He shoved her over the broken door and into the hallway, making sure to jerk the hand clutching at her hair as he went, her scalp burning. "You never could listen, could you?"

Cold fear held her hostage, and even then, she wanted to get through this. She wanted to live.

They were in the living room now. Doing as he commanded. Always as he commanded. Like the universe conspired to help only the truly horrible people in this world.

"We had it good, Emilia." His breath stunk of cigarettes, and he shoved her so she fell to the floor, cornered between him and the fireplace. "Now look what you made me do. You should have just stuck to being my sweet, obedient wife, huh?"

For a brief time, this room had held nothing but happy memories. Of her and Blaine. Oh, God. *Blaine.* She'd let him down. And as if to mirror her thoughts, Anthony added, "And then you went and stuffed everything up."

He stood over her and tilted his head to one side, mocking, sneering again. "You know what I'm here for, don't you?"

She shook her head, her stomach roiling at the sick joy backlighting his icy stare. He relished her fear. Would set her up to fail so he could get off on punishing her every wrong move. Just like he always had.

"They've taken all my money, but you're about to help me get it back, aren't you, honey?" He nudged her leg with the pointed tip of his snakeskin shoe, shaking his head. "Look at you, pathetic."

Her chest ached from the strain of her panic and having to force each staggered breath, but her only hope would be to stall until help arrived, or they burned in this house together. "What do you need me to do?"

He crouched down, getting on her level, though a stream of warm blood now dripped from where her head had hit the bathroom wall, down the side of her neck, and onto her dress.

"Well to start, you're going to call the bank and tell them who you are." His gaze dropped to her lips, his mouth already too close to hers, her throat clogging at the thought of him trying to kiss her. "And trust me, honey, that's just the start. You'll get back my money or die trying."

"They'll never believe me." Her voice twisted, hopeless and hollow. Pathetic. Just as he described.

Never had she imagined her life ending at the hands of a man who'd stood before all their family and friends and promised to love her forever. And over something so trivial as money. "Anthony, I don't have the authority to get your money back."

He shrugged way too casually, grabbed the back of her neck, and jerked her forward so their lips almost touched. "You'll figure it out, Em, because you don't have any other choice. You see, I had to get help to find you, and you know how business works. Everyone wants to be paid. So, you're going to return every last fucking penny, do you understand?"

She gave a shaky nod, her breaths staggered, her muscles weak and trembling. She knew enough about Anthony to understand "the help" meant he'd hired some very dangerous people.

But even if she could get his money, she wasn't stupid. He wouldn't make good on his promise to let her be free.

He released her with a shove, his demeanor falling to tense control before he dragged a cell phone from his black-zippered jacket.

"I'm more use to you alive." She spoke while he stabbed at the phone's touch screen.

"Don't overestimate your value," he mumbled, his tone flat and careless as he held the phone to his ear, then shifted it to hers. "Just take the fucking call."

A dial tone left her to wait, but she refused to fall into a fragile mess amidst the uncertainty of this moment. Not just yet, anyway. "If the bank doesn't budge, call my dad, okay?"

"Just shut the fuck up and do what I tell you." He glared at her, genuine disgust directed her way.

Sweat trickled down the side of her forehead, the scent of smoke creeping in from the other side of the house. She wanted to make him feel like she was cooperating, that she wanted to make nice, though to what end beyond not dying, she had no clue. "What do I say when someone picks up?"

"Tell them who you are. Nothing clever, okay?" The tension in his tone eased, like maybe her scheme succeeded in some small way. "Just tell them it's an emergency, it's your money, you're a Bonacci, and you need it."

His instructions made her stomach seize and a harsh prickle rake over her skin. She'd never heard of a more half-baked plan. To go to so much trouble to enlist help in finding her, all under the assumption a bank would just hand over millions upon millions of corporate dollars to a random voice on the other end of a phone. Anthony took entitlement to a whole other stratosphere.

There'd be no telling what he'd do once he learned his plan had tanked. Or maybe there was. Either way, he was forcing her onto this manic joyride right along with him, and the consequences of the grim news to come would be hers to bear.

An automated message picked up and rolled through a list of service options. She ignored each one and set about appealing to Anthony's arrogant side. "How did you find me? I was so careful."

"Like I said. I have friends in low places, and you made it easy when you started contacting people."

Of course, *her dad, Rochelle…*

She peered down and faked disappointment—not that it took much acting—giving him what he wanted yet again. Her misery.

Her chances of breaking free dwindled with every passing second. She'd wanted so much more for herself and Blaine. More than their bleak past and a few chaotic weeks together. He'd counted on her, and she'd failed him. Despite Anthony's ridiculous plan, he'd won again.

The second his plan fell apart, she'd be dead. He wouldn't get the money, but he'd get his revenge.

"You should have known I'd hunt you down." His cold stare bore into her, upper lip tugging higher.

"I've been so scared I forgot to tell you to press two on the keypad." She swallowed hard. Again, appealing to his ego. Again, trying to buy time.

He gave her a sideways glare, then pulled the phone away to press the button. She filled the quiet moment with more words. "There's an easier way to get your money. Please, Anthony, just let me call my dad."

"I'm not an idiot." He half spat the reply, pressing the phone to her ear with one hand, the other disappearing somewhere behind his back. "You think I don't know what you've been doing all this time?"

His hand reemerged, this time holding a gun. She scrambled back against the cold, hard bricks behind her, her mind fuzzy with the sensation of standing outside her body.

"You think I'd believe a lying whore like you?" The words squeezed through his gritted teeth, and he prodded the gun's muzzle to her cheek, pressing, pressing, pressing until pain radiated to other parts of her face. "We're not calling your fucking dad."

Thick, silent tears spilled down her cheeks, and still, she said nothing.

His expression lifted, like he enjoyed what he saw, while his eyes held that same soulless stare.

He shook his head now, slow and mocking. "What chance did we have? My family gave you and your dad the world, and you insisted on being a sour bitch the entire time. You spent the first years of our marriage pining over some other man. What did you think would happen between us?"

A ball of heat ignited in the center of her tummy. An angry heat. One she would have been too afraid to express in the past. But not now.

"You call me a whore?" She panted and spoke through her pain, her head aching and her body tired. "But I was never up for sale. My dad repaid your family ten times over. I was never yours, Anthony. I never chose you. What did *you* think would happen when you bullied and broke your way into my life? You took it as a given that I would be thankful. But how much clearer can I make it? I never wanted you. I *never* wanted you."

She spat the statement out, somehow not regretting those potential last words, even as his stare turned hard, and the muscles over his cheekbones grew taut. He drew his hand back and swung the gun toward her face as if her head hadn't already taken enough punishment.

She reeled back and slammed her eyes closed, anticipating the bite of unforgiving metal.

But no blow came.

A loud thud had her flinging her eyes open. Blaine held Anthony pinned to the floor.

Blaine!

He stared at her. "Get out."

Just as the thunder of a bullet rippled through the air.

Thirty-Nine

EMILIA SCREAMED AGAIN, the slug from Anthony's gun biting into the wood floor mere inches from her knee. A plume of wood chips and dust spilled over her.

"Go," Blaine yelled at her, slamming an elbow into Anthony's face with a dull crack. If his nose wasn't broken before, then it would be now.

In a daze, she pressed her fingers to the warm stream of blood still curling over her collarbone, her stomach heaving at the wet crimson mess. Any moment now she'd vomit, pass out, or both, when she couldn't afford either.

She startled at a loud crash followed by a grunt, the ruckus putting her back on task so that she placed her blood-soaked palms to the ground, beginning to crawl out.

So much about this moment reminded her of ten years ago. *Of leaving Blaine behind.* And even though he'd ordered her to leave, she just couldn't do it.

Another loud shot punched through the air. She jolted back, both men yelling as the gun crashed to the floor mere feet from her hands.

Blaine landed on his back, a growing red stain obscuring the pattern on his blue plaid shirt. Her mouth fell open in a silent scream while Anthony continued to wrestle, and Blaine fought back.

"Emilia, go." His voice choked out and his movements already slowed.

Anthony landed a fist into Blaine's face, and suddenly everything seemed to happen in a vacuum. All sight and sound halted as she eyed the door, followed by the scrunched pain in Blaine's expression. Freedom had been her priority for so long, but now, she didn't want to be free. She only wanted Blaine to live.

She couldn't leave. Just couldn't.

He'd given her so much. Given up so much. All because of her. Now was her time to grow up. To give back.

She scrambled forward, hoping Anthony would remain distracted, her fingers outstretched for the gun. Once again, Anthony clenched the upper hand, but this time she'd stay and fight.

He stood over Blaine, landing a kick to his ribs. Sensing time running out, she moved faster and snatched up the gun.

Anthony's stare froze on her. "You're too chicken shit to try."

She aimed and squeezed the trigger.

He stumbled back, blood quick to pour from the meat just above his collar bone. He peered down, touching his fingers to that blood, his scowl soon landing on her. "You'd be in a gutter somewhere begging for loose change if it weren't for my family."

His cool voice added a chill to the room, but despite the firearm's kickback having already jarred her wrists, she gripped the gun for dear life. "Is that all you've got?"

This time she was the one sneering. "Will you go to your grave moaning about the same tired thing? I know, after ten years, I'm done hearing you sing that same obnoxious song."

He cocked his head to one side and took a step toward her. "How brave are you feeling, Em?"

She'd always hated when he called her Em. He damn well knew it too. "Stay back."

"Give me the gun."

He took another step, his bloodied hand outstretched.

"Anthony. Stop." Her voice wasn't so strong anymore, and the distinct quiver from before returned.

Sweat glistened over his face, a face grimacing in pain from his wound. "If I stop, I'm as good as dead. So you're going to have to shoot me or hand over the gun."

"No." She glanced over to Blaine slumped in a corner, hand clutched over his wounded ribcage, complexion sallow, and eyes fluttering open and closed. She needed to take action. *Shoot Anthony?* Oh God, but something in her nature prevented her from doing that.

"You always thought you were better than me." Anthony's gaze flicked toward Blaine too. "You and him. I worked hard for what I had, and all you did was sit in our apartment crying over that loser."

Her heart hitched. Despite first assumptions, Anthony recognized Blaine.

"And everything you had, including your job, was handed to you by someone else. And as for him." She jutted her chin toward Blaine. "None of us would be here right now if you'd dealt with your jealous bullshit and let us be."

Anthony glowered; she'd never been audacious enough to speak so harshly, or honestly, before. "You think I care what a dumb bitch like you has to—"

He threw himself at her, knocking her off balance, the trigger sinking beneath her finger.

Somehow, he smacked the gun away in time, and a bullet landed in the drywall behind him. Just as quickly, the gun was out of her hands. This time, he did strike her face, with the weapon too.

Her cheek split open like a piece of overripe fruit, pain stealing her breath, while a sheet of blood poured from her new wound. She tried to push away, but his hand caught her throat. Tight enough to control her, but not so much that he cut off her air.

He held the gun loose by the trigger guard, letting it swing off his fingertip before tossing it to the mantle. "I won't need that for now. Your boyfriend's already half-dead, and I have new plans for you before he departs. Since you decided to make this ugly, give me your hands."

He unbuckled his belt, tugging it free of the loops.

Her head spinning from the blow to her cheek, she didn't react fast enough, so his hand around her throat tightened, a reminder of where she was and what was happening to her.

Her heart sank and she lifted her hands slowly, more tears coming. He wound the belt around her wrists, so tight the edges cut into her skin, burning, bruising, then shoved her around so she faced Blaine.

His straining breaths could be heard even from yards away, but despite the constant drifting of his eyelids, he held her gaze, moving his shoulders as though he wanted to get up. "Let her go. Please. Do anything you want to me instead."

"I've already put a bullet through you." Anthony wrenched her back toward him. "No, the only thing I want now is for you to finally see that she's mine."

The wet, warmth of Anthony's mouth met with the lower curve of her neck, and he bit down into her, his teeth sinking deep. She screamed, wrestling away, but he wrenched her back, his mouth now next to her ear. "Perfect, isn't it? A bullet for me. A bite for you. It's only fair."

He swung her around with him and threw her onto the couch. She scrambled to sit, as much as she could with her bound hands. He prowled toward her with a pinched look, one that left no doubt of what he wanted.

What she'd denied him the night before she'd left LA.

"No." She shook her head and shifted back. He just stared at her with that dead gaze of his, his fingers slow to unbutton his pants.

She knew already, her "no" was little more than useless noise. Not just in this but in every scenario. "No" had always meant nothing to him.

"Get your hands above your head." He leaned over her. Again, she didn't move fast enough, so he grabbed her bound wrists and threw them over, her hands landing in the space between the edge of the cushion under her head and the couch's armrest.

He pressed the bulk of his weight down over her. She couldn't move. Could hardly draw a breath. "Now you'll remember who you belong to, won't you, Em?"

That name again. Even with what was happening to her, it stirred new hatred.

He pressed his cheek hard against hers, causing more pain. "Won't you, Em?"

She gave a weak nod, but not enough to appease, because he shoved against her, moving her enough that her fingers connected with something hard and plastic behind her cushion.

His hand moved to her dress's hem, and she fought against him while he kneed her legs apart. She sobbed, manic, kicking wildly to keep him away, but he was stronger, heavier, and she was tethered.

All the movement brought the hard object behind her into her grasp. Another panicked sob broke from her.

She was falling apart. She turned to Blaine, needing some strength. He was still in his slumped position, though his head already dipped. Either he wasn't conscious, or he simply didn't want to watch.

"Don't worry about him." Anthony trained his snappish eyes on her, propping himself up on one elbow. "It's nothing he hasn't already seen before, right, Em?"

Getting ready, she wrapped her fingers tight around the object in her hand. For the first time in her life, she willed Anthony closer—a rage-filled inferno igniting—just as he leaned in and seized her mouth with his. She pulled her tied hands out, fingers locked around each other, and she slammed down as hard as she could in a high arch.

Anthony flung his head back and roared an agonized cry. His sudden movement pulled the knife from her grip.

"I fucking hate the name Em." This time, and maybe for the first time, she was the one to swear. She kicked him off her. He fell to the floor like a sack of potatoes. "And I fucking hate you."

She pried the knife from his back, the action needing considerable effort, and nothing like what she'd experienced with the hay bales Aggie made her practice on. Here, there were hard bones and the draw of muscle. Blood. It spilled from his back and into her rug like an open faucet.

Air hissed from him, and she guessed that maybe she'd pierced his lungs.

All she could do was stare, her own blood rushing loud in her ears.

She took stock of what she'd done, all the while expecting him to spring up and hurt her all over again.

She shuffled back. Stunned. Even now, she recoiled at his closeness, at what he'd tried to do to her, what he'd succeeded in doing to her so many times over so many years.

She'd told him. Told him again and again. To let her be. To leave her alone. It would have been so easy for him to give her that space, and yet, he hadn't. He came back. Time and time again. *He came back*.

And years from now, she wouldn't escape that trapped feeling. She knew that much.

"You're not coming back now." Her voice tore open her frozen state and turned her toward Blaine, her limbs feeling soft like jelly.

She scrambled across the room to his side. Despite his rasping breaths, he was the first to speak. "You're okay?"

She pressed her hand to his cheek, his statement a sign that maybe he wasn't all that cognizant of what happened. "I'm fine. Hang on. Please. I just need you to stay alive, okay?"

His gaze held onto hers, lids heavy, before they slammed shut again. She bit back a cry and ran for her bedroom. Her phone still lay charging on a bedside table. Even as she tried to place a call, her shaking hands were still bound, and her wrists screamed with pain.

She crossed the hallway, waiting for the call to connect, swatting at the smoke burning her lungs with each breath, while she tried to ignore the glow of fire down her hall. Somehow, she'd have to get them both out of here, but how?

"Blaine!"

He'd fallen to one side.

Putting her phone on speaker, she rushed over so she could lay him down properly.

His eyes fluttered open, and his gaze caught hers again. "You're not allowed to blame yourself. Promise me."

"No. I don't need to." She shook him, her voice pitchy and panicked, like she tried to convince herself. "You're going to live. We're going to be together."

His eyes closed again, as if to prove her wrong, just as an

emergency responder spoke through the phone. Emilia rattled off her address and the basic details of the situation.

The dispatcher stated someone had already called in emergency services, and fire and ambulance crew were already en route. That's when Emilia noticed faint sirens wailing in the background.

Another sob broke from her. This was all so overwhelming. In a lifetime of being shunted aside, and in a town that kept her so geographically isolated, someone had still noticed she needed help.

Probably Blaine.

He'd likely called 911 on his way back to her house, all before he'd rushed in to save her.

But would anyone save him now? Or would help arrive far too late?

She stayed on the line as requested and grief rushed at her in the sudden quiet. Her time with Blaine was possibly about to end. Decades too early. And before she'd had a chance to tell him how much she loved him. How he'd transformed her life and given her hope. How he was the only man she'd ever wanted. That for all his attempts to hide his insecurities, he'd never needed to be more for her than the person he already was.

She doubled over and rested her head on his chest, his blood soaking her cheek, her mind focused on the fading rhythm of his heart and the growing crackle of fire beyond. He'd never hear all the plans she'd already begun to make for their future.

Anthony, in all his failures, might have succeeded in one thing. He might have dragged the love of her life down with him into death. After all she'd run from and overcome, a lifetime of loneliness stretched before her.

Hot tears slid down her cheek, and she pressed Blaine's cold hand to her lips, praying he would hear her in what might be their very last moments together. "Please, don't go. It's not supposed to end like this."

Forty

EMILIA SAT in the air ambulance while it rocked through the slow descent to the hospital roof. Blaine was propped upright on a stretcher, soaked in his own blood. She was also soaked in blood. Her own, Anthony's, a great deal of Blaine's… and they both stank of smoke.

Back in Harlow, she'd stood outside the cottage, the fire trucks with their hoses bursting forth with water, extinguishing flames while the paramedics freed her raw and heavily bruised wrists. The situation took another overwhelming turn the moment another set of paramedics pushed a giant needle through the top of Blaine's ribcage

She froze in place, just as a deluge of blood squirted from the needle. Apparently, that meant he was bleeding internally and would need surgery. That's when the air ambulance was phoned in. Meanwhile, he'd been set up with an IV line and a mask to help him breathe; she'd collapsed right there in the dirt before her home, only to wake minutes later, assaulted by the renewed memory of everything that had happened.

The adrenaline only now seeped from her body, and she began to shake, a weak sensation overrunning her body. She felt like she sat outside herself, watching this surreal moment unfold while she begged repeatedly for someone to tell her none of this was real. Blaine would be okay.

In reality, no one gave her a clear answer.

The helicopter now on the ground, she helplessly waited as Blaine was wheeled away from her, her heart sinking, the rest of her numb, save for the constant ache of her wounds. Her face. Her neck. Her hands.

She watched but somehow saw nothing. A woman going through the motions. But the motions of what? Pain and exhaustion, the discomfort of being a smoke-scented shell of herself. Even her hair clumped with blood.

Her entire life consisted of hearing the importance of being "put together." Of playing her part. Well, now she was playing the part of something out of a horror movie.

A sob wrenched from her, jolting her ribcage up and down before hot tears seared her cheeks—no longer a woman going through the motions, but a woman unraveling. A woman who'd held so much in and together for far too long.

But this was no horror movie. This was real life. *Her life.*

She should have cared about what she looked like. Why didn't she care?

She'd just killed a man. *Her husband.* Or her ex-husband.

Hadn't she promised to love him forever too?

But he'd hurt her. Abused her. Degraded and disparaged. He'd stolen her life and coerced her in every way imaginable. He'd broken his vows first. To love and honor. Vows *he'd* insisted on taking.

Her tremors intensified, and her tears grew thicker, her grief no longer silent as a keening cry tore from her chest. The shame. She had so much shame. And now she'd have to tell everyone. Wouldn't she? What he'd done to her. All those years. And then today. Physically attacking her, shooting Blaine, attempting to rape her while her house burned around them.

But there'd been a knife.

How had the knife gotten into her couch cushions?

Ally. Must have been Ally. The day before when they'd laughed at

Aggie's insistence that they hide knives about the place. Only Ally would think to stuff a knife down the side of a couch.

"Come along, darling." A woman with a kindly looking face and russet hair crouched down before her and hooked her hands under Emilia's arms, helping her out of her seat. "Let's get you inside and clean those wounds."

A broken laugh burst past Emilia's lips, and her knees buckled the moment she tried to put any weight on her feet. The woman continued to prop her up, her help filling Emilia with more painful memories. *This time, of her new friends.*

The women of Harlow had saved her too. Aggie with her instant acceptance and those damn knives. Ally with her friendship. And Sarah with her selfless maturity. But would any of those women still love her? Harlow's golden boy was fighting for his life. All because of her. A woman who was now a murderer.

And yes, as the woman helping her from the helicopter had stated, Emilia had wounds. So many wounds and in so many ways. Though some not as easily washed away as others.

She'd overheard the paramedics saying the wound on the back of her head would heal okay. But the one at the side of her face where Anthony had struck her with the gun, that one needed stitches. She'd have a scar where her cheek met her ear. And the bite mark on her neck? Well, she'd have a lighter scar there too. A scar in the same spot where Anthony had left his mark on Blaine all those years ago.

So many wounds and scars. Not all physical. Even if Blaine survived, Anthony had been right. They *would* remember him forever.

The next day, Emilia sat on a chair beside Blaine's bed. She refused to stay in her room, and the hospital staff had given up trying to convince her. Or maybe they'd taken sympathy. Either way, she waited and watched, her hospital gown too loose and cool for her liking.

Blaine slept, something he'd done a lot in the last twenty-four hours. And all she wanted was to have a decent conversation with him. To tell him she loved him. To get some kind of sign he wasn't so bad.

But he is bad. Look at what I did to him… Again.

She pressed a hand to her lips and tried not to cry. She didn't want to risk him waking, only to find her in tears, even if she couldn't shake the feeling that she should never have come to Harlow.

The sting in her eyes continued to nudge at her, so she shot from her seat and hurried out to the hallway. A row of beige chairs sat just outside his room, and she lowered herself down and allowed the tears to flow, a thing she'd become a true natural at lately.

She swiped her fingertips over her eyes, sniffling, while an ache grew roots inside her head. Her injuries, heartbreak, and exhaustion took a toll, but none so bad as when she turned her gaze down the hall. Her sight caught on Vittorio Bonacci striding toward her in his tailored navy suit and his gray-streaked hair.

Any normal person might have run for their dad, sought comfort, but children were masters at knowing what they could rely on from their parents. Emilia was no exception. So she merely sat, her strength too far gone to fight or walk away. After all, there wasn't much her father could say that would add to the hurt she already felt.

He sat beside her, and for the longest time, they just stared at each other. She blinked, internally startled as she began to speak. "Have you come to deliver me to the Stucco's next most eligible bachelor?"

Her father's eyes narrowed. She couldn't tell if he displayed annoyance or a shame-filled wince. Did her dad ever experience shame? Then again, she'd never spoken back to him. So maybe his expression was of surprise.

He shook his head and turned his attention to his polished, black leather shoes. "I probably deserved that."

Everything within her stilled, forcing her to wonder if she'd heard right. Her father conceding to something… anything… ever.

She watched him a while longer, flicking her gaze at his lowered stare. One that, for once, wasn't meeting hers, a deflated energy flowing off him.

"There's no 'probably' about that, Dad." She clamped her lips together, amazed and shocked that she was finally taking him to task.

This time she turned away, staring in the opposite direction toward some nurses swapping papers at a small station up the hall. She refused to look at him for the longest time, even though she wished to see some kind of evidence her words inflicted just a fraction of the hurt she experienced now.

"I know." His low tone crossed the small space between them, just above a whisper, and so unlike the staunch man she'd known her whole life. "I never saw things as you did. I only saw things as a man from the village, and I thought, 'This is the way things are. How they're supposed to be. Who am I to do different?'"

"You're Vittorio Bonacci." She swung her head around, glaring at him, her eyes hot as though her burning home still surrounded her. "Being 'different' was always in your power."

"I know. I know." He slammed his eyes shut. The gray tinge to his skin and the added wrinkles over his forehead made him appear older and frailer. "I let everyone else get in my head. And maybe being *Vittorio Bonacci* meant I didn't want to admit I had gotten it so wrong. And before you say it, all that should have mattered was that my little girl needed me."

He opened his eyes, giving her his direct stare, so much about his words and demeanor making her feel as though he meant what he said. Still, she refused to believe him. "But it didn't, did it? What I needed didn't matter at all."

The strain over his cheekbones dropped, denoting hurt. If she looked close enough, she swore she could see a red and glistening sheen to his eyes. "Who was I before your mother died? Do you remember?"

Something tiny shifted inside her, an inexplicable knowledge.

Happy. He was always happy. And kind. And someone I could talk to.

The memory wasn't enough to forgive her father, but enough to remind her that her mother's death had changed him. *No. Not changed.* It *broke* him.

She'd been too young and immature to think deeply about what her father experienced. Too immersed in her own grief. Had never put two and two together to truly connect her mother's death with her father's sudden bullheadedness and drive to succeed. Yes, she'd figured success had become his coping mechanism, but time and maturity tended to cast a different light on events.

And maybe because of her, he forgot about me.

That idea sent a dull pain winding through her belly. The new perspective explained so much about why he'd become so cold. Now that she stood on the precipice of losing Blaine, maybe she saw a little of how losing love could fracture someone forever.

If Blaine died right now, who would she be? Would she ever find it in her to let others in? Allow them the chance to hurt her?

"With money came more pressure, more people looking at us, Emilia. I wasn't little Vittorio from the village anymore." His expensive watch, the one with the black face and gold details, glinted up at her, but what she noticed most was the powerless curl of his hands on his lap. "Success hasn't been the blessing I expected."

She didn't want to let him off the hook so easily, likely never. Not likely. Probably. *No,* definitely never. "So, you abandoned me to the Stuccos? Every time I came to you for help, you *abandoned* me."

"Let me try to help you now."

She spluttered out a laugh, one loud enough to have the staff, patients, and visitors in the hall turn to her like she'd lost her mind. Well, maybe she had. Or maybe she'd finally found it since she was now capable of telling her father what she really thought.

I have Blaine to thank for that.

Yes, Blaine. But also herself. One good thing to come from her escape had been finding herself. Her hidden courage. Her ability to tell someone how she felt about their horrible behavior.

So, she shook her head and uttered the one truth she could hold on to in all that had happened. "There's not a thing you could do that would make me forgive you, Dad."

His stare paused on her for a while, the lines over her cheekbones ever deeper and his skin pale before he gave a slow understanding nod. "I should expect you not to forgive me but let me explain this. Anthony manipulated me too. All those years ago, he said he saw you in the car with Blaine and that you were trying to fight him off. Anthony said Blaine had been trying to take advantage."

Anthony's lies never seemed to end. They went back so much

SAPPHIRES AND SECRETS   265

further than she anticipated. Perhaps this new information did explain some of her father's actions at the time, but not nearly enough to excuse everything. "The only man to ever take advantage of me was Anthony. And all I want to know is, if you were me, would you forgive you so easily?"

Her father fell silent again, his gaze veering like maybe he was beginning to see how deep the pain of his decisions ran. "You have to understand, at the time, I knew who Anthony was. He was a punk, yes, but I figured he'd mature. I *didn't* know Blaine. To me, he was some outsider kid who came out of nowhere and caused all this trouble in my family. I got defensive. I know that. But Anthony, he played me like a fiddle, told me untrue things, including that Blaine only wanted you for your money. I thought I was protecting you. It's taken me all these years to get over the embarrassment that I wasn't and to admit I got everything so completely wrong."

"I didn't need you to protect me. I needed you to get out of my way. Instead, you sent me to be with family who hated me, only to bring me back to marry the 'punk' you made excuses for." Her face grew tight, and she figured she glared, a growing burn of anger filling up space in her tummy. "All these years, and I couldn't talk to you. You had no idea what I dealt with every day. Alone. And look at what happened."

She flicked a thumb over her shoulder, pointing to Blaine's room, her voice cracking before she could utter another word. Once more, years of holding back exacted their revenge, this time in plain sight of her father.

"Please." He lashed out his hand, catching hers. She wanted to throw him off, moved to do just that, only to stop. "Tell me what I need to do to make it up to you."

"There's no making up for this." She stared down at her dad's hand over hers. Why wasn't she recoiling? "It's something I'll never forgive you for, do you understand?"

His hand gave a gentle squeeze over hers, and it was then she figured why she didn't move. It was the first gentle gesture he'd given her in years. Not since her mother had been ripped from their lives.

"And I'll never forgive myself." He held her stare, a line of moisture balancing along the edge of his lower eyelids.

He looked broken. Truly broken. So much like the day he'd learned his wife had died, but instead, now he'd lost his daughter.

And because of that brokenness, she had the first sign that the feelings she'd assumed were missing actually did exist, and now she knew that this relationship would go one of two ways.

Vittorio Bonacci would leave today, a lonely man, destined to live out his life minus any family. Or his words now, his burgeoning tears, all of which had been missing all those years, were a sign that he was less broken and more "broken open"—that recent events had dragged him from the apathetic fog he'd insisted on living in. That maybe, just maybe, he'd learned and could change.

"But there are things you can do for me." She paused, inspecting his reaction, the quick release of his facial muscles denoting hope. "You can start by accepting that I'm never going back to LA."

He dropped his gaze, seeming defeated. "I already have."

She cleared her throat and sat a bit taller. She'd been strong throughout all those years she'd thought herself weak. Sometimes just surviving one day at a time took immense character. If she'd been strong before, then she could do it again. "And if you love me, if you've *ever* loved me, you'll promise to never again make decisions about my future."

"I don't think I could, even if I wanted—"

She gave him a squinted expression, one that said, *Just promise me.*

"Okay. Yes, I promise."

"Lastly—" She huffed out a breath, deciding to test the waters with her next admission. "I haven't been well for a while and my mental health is in a bad state, but there's a doctor in Harlow, Dr. Richards, I think I can trust him. If I'm allowed to stay in Harlow, if I don't get arrested over what happened last night, then I want to be there for Blaine, and I want to work on myself. I want you to help me get the help I need."

The anxiety running through her since last night was her last straw. She couldn't keep putting off dealing with her years of trauma. She wanted to be able to trust herself. That she wouldn't pass out in fits of panic. That she could make decisions and mistakes, and that everything would be okay. And maybe the person to get her the help she needed *should* be someone who'd contributed to her problems in the first place.

"I'll do whatever you need." The way her father held her gaze, the softened edge to his voice, and his hand over hers… for a moment there, she felt she might be able to trust him one day. It would be years before that trust would be anything she'd truly rely on, but maybe this was a start.

"If you need money, you'll have it." Her father patted her hand now. "But I want to do more than that. If you'll let me, I'll stay in town and help you get back on your feet."

"I don't think—"

"I'll stay as far away and as uninvolved as you need." He shifted his body, a sense of seriousness tightening his features, the tightness infiltrating his voice and adding a level of desperation too. "I won't meddle, I promise. I just want to reconnect with you. I want to help. Please, just let me help. And If I'm getting on your nerves, you can tell me to leave."

Years of distrust made it hard for her to respond, but he'd given her more today than she could remember, and saying no seemed wrong too. Granted, she owed him less than nothing, but another part of her didn't want to send her father away. Perhaps because she still remembered who he'd had been, back when they'd been poor but rich in other ways.

She still hadn't spoken, and he leaned in, his gaze poring over her face in a look of worry. "Honey, have you eaten?"

Her throat clogged, and new tears prickled her eyes but for a whole new reason. To any outsider, his question would seem insignificant, but to her, it was the most heartfelt concern he'd expressed for as long as she could remember. Since when did Vittorio Bonacci look, much less sound, concerned?

She gave a weak shake of her head and a short, wobbling laugh.

He patted her knee and stood, an unsteady smile dragging the corners of his mouth upward. "Okay. Let's start with that."

Epilogue

"What's he looking at?" Emilia spoke to her father from across the timber picnic table, the murky Mirabelle River low after weeks of dry weather.

Her dad's gaze stayed on Blaine, who stood along the river bank several yards away. "I believe he's thinking that on the first day out of the hospital, he has a lot to get used to."

Yes, six weeks since she'd almost lost Blaine, since that night of blood and violence when Anthony forced a final and deadly showdown. And now, her life was irrevocably changed.

If so much could change in mere seconds, then the last six weeks had been no different. The Great Vittorio Bonacci had stayed true to his word. He'd stayed in Harlow and helped her. He'd drawn a line across the things he'd once excused and shown a change in priorities.

He was always around. Always present. Either at her new residence at Blaine's house or helping her visit Blaine at the hospital. If he didn't see her, then he made the effort to call. Even though she'd mostly ignored him at first. Years of anger and hurt were hard to shed, but on rare occasions, relationships could be redefined. This was one of them.

"What are you two talking about?" Blaine abandoned the river and trudged closer, his torso slumping ever so slightly to the left where he'd been shot.

Her heart hurt to see him still struggling, but he'd come a long way since the incident.

"You, of course." She smiled, raising her brow in a tease.

"I'm sure you're not the only ones." He turned to scowl at her dad's wary face, like her father still skated on thin ice.

To be fair, her dad wore the distrust with grace. He'd done wrong and clawing back what he'd lost all those years ago would take considerable time and effort.

Emilia still wished for the return of the loving dad from her childhood. His opening up about his grief over her mother's death was a start, and then there was his unlimited support, both financial and moral.

He'd helped line up regular online appointments with a top therapist in Minneapolis. She also had access to medication for her anxiety and fainting spells. She'd only begun her recovery, but her life was already greatly improved.

And on top of all that, her dad had also sourced a skilled out-of-town carpenter to fill in at Oak Tree Furniture while Blaine recovered. Ally's natural friendliness had won Rochelle over at the Harlow Fair, and the deal for her clients went ahead.

"Any news on the investigation?" Blaine kept his attention on Emilia, the extra creases on his forehead hinting at the stress behind his question.

"I've been meaning to talk to you about that. I spoke to the detective this morning." She peered down at the picnic table's aged wood beneath her hands, Blaine's darkening stare getting too much.

She'd never denied stabbing Anthony, and though Blaine had already been dismissed of any wrongdoing, clearing her name wasn't as straightforward.

"As you know, the paramedics confirmed they found me bound, and neither yours nor my fingerprints were on the belt around my wrists, only Anthony's." She shrugged, her tummy clenching at having to remember that day, much less recounting anything to do with it. "Ally admitted to hiding the knife in the side of the couch but forgetting to tell me it was there, so it's unlikely I planned on using it until it was in my hand. And Dad confirmed Anthony had a long history of jealousy and interference. The detective said there's enough evidence that I tried to escape over causing any harm, and that Anthony insisted on pursuing me. That means my actions were in self-defense, and there's no real case for pressing charges."

The strain over Blaine's face eased, and his shoulders lowered, his eyes taking on a jovial glint. "So, there's a good chance I won't need to visit you behind bars?"

She chuckled and shook her head, only for her dad to cut in.

"If not, my lawyers will have a lot to say about it." Vittorio rose from his seat. "Blaine, sit down, you look tired."

Blaine shook his head. "No, I'm fine. I've spent weeks in bed, and I should work on staying upright, especially for this."

She glanced between the two men, the tense quiet between them and the way Blaine rubbed the back of his neck, gave her the sense they knew something she didn't. "Especially for what? What's happening?"

For weeks now, she'd had nightmares of kneeling in a pool of blood —Blaine's blood—his body limp, and she, with her bound hands, helpless.

So many in Harlow hailed her a hero, but she didn't feel heroic; saving Blaine had been a given. And while the drama of Anthony's death made national news and her face graced screens across the country, she didn't want the attention or speculation. Positive or negative.

She just wanted her quiet life back.

Her life with Blaine.

Though many still wondered how Anthony had come to be in Harlow in the first place, a mystery the police were yet to answer since there'd been no car found at the cottage. He'd mentioned having help during the attack, and so far, his dealings were linked to a crime syndicate in LA, but that's where the track ran cold. Whoever brought him to Harlow seemed long gone.

Blaine tucked a finger under her chin and tilted her gaze up to him. "Don't look at me like that."

"Like what?"

"Like I might suddenly disappear."

Despite his order, she frowned deeper since she couldn't imagine a day where the prospect of losing him wouldn't haunt her. They'd come so close to that reality so many times already.

She peered over at her dad, his lips held in a firm, thin line. "You guys are acting strange, now spill."

Blaine flashed a grin, the new lightness in his expression sending her heart fluttering. He nodded to her father. "It's time we broke the news to her."

She was truly confused since Blaine had been avoiding her dad, and now they seemed to share knowledge of some sort of ominous news.

She turned to her dad, hoping for clarity, only to be hit with the sight of him producing a familiar royal-purple velvet box from his shirt pocket. The Bonacci embossed case passed from her father's hand into Blaine's, and she drew back, her hand finding an instinctive home over her mouth.

Not even fine crystal glittered as much as Blaine's radiant green eyes did at that moment. "She's figured us out."

"Us?" She snapped her attention back to her dad, her mind blurring and her throat muscles growing thick, making it so she had to choke out her next words. "You worked on something together?"

"Not just something." Her father smiled, gesturing to Blaine. "Now let the man speak already."

"You have no idea how much I've struggled to keep this secret over the last weeks, what with all the sadness in your eyes and the worry written all over your face. I wanted so much to give you something to be happy about... At least I hope—" He dropped to one knee before her and took her left hand. "Emilia Rose Bonacci, it's taken ten years to get to this, but will you please marry me?"

Her mouth fell open, and her heart strained. He pried the box open and revealed an elegant rose-gold band with a tiny gold butterfly. The tips of its wings were embellished with delicate pink sapphires, a touch that harked back to their first-ever meeting when she'd sold him a pink butterfly bracelet for his sister.

She turned to her father, eyes misting over. "This is your work?"

"After my foolish attempt to keep you two apart, the least I could do was agree to Blaine's request to design the ring. It was my jewelry that brought you two together, wasn't it?" The wrinkles over his cheekbones creased deeper than usual, and he peered down. "Blaine took a bullet for you. If that doesn't say love, I don't know what does. Now, don't you think we've made this poor guy wait long enough?"

She twisted back to Blaine, still on one knee. *This was actually happening.*

"You're sure?" Her voice reduced to a whisper, everything about this moment surreal, especially since her dad stood by approving of this whole thing.

"I've never had any doubts. Not once in ten years, no matter how much I tried to escape the truth of who held my heart more than any other. I've dreamed of this, Emilia. Of finding you again, even though you're the one who found me." A broken chuckle spilled from her, and Blaine joined her laughter, before speaking again. "It's time for our future together, for having children, and many more decades than the one we missed. I want to grow old with you. I want it all. And if that's what you want too, then all you have to do is say, 'Yes'."

She opened her mouth, her words throttled between gleeful sobs. Every night for the last few weeks, she'd woken to an emptiness in her chest. The direct result of everything that had happened to her. She'd cried so many tears without this beautiful man at her side.

He was everything she'd ever wanted too. No doubt about it. Her light in her darkness, her good karma after years of misfortune.

For so long she'd merely survived while he pushed her toward something more, toward clearing away all that held her back, toward being happy. Truly happy. This moment was a glimpse of that. Of what would come.

As he'd stated, all she needed to do was say, "Yes."

She had that freedom now. To marry the man of her choosing. And she had more than freedom. She had love, community, people who accepted her.

Tears blurred her vision, and she blinked, allowing the pain and joy to spill from her like she'd learned to do. No more holding back or holding in. Though since words were impossible to form right now, she settled for nodding her answer. A definite *yes* to the man she loved.

He leaped to his feet and pulled her hard against him, seizing her lips in a deep and passionate kiss. When he did draw back, he gifted her with an effortless look of joy. "Miss Bonacci, I took a beating for you, then a bullet, and you're the best-worst thing that's ever happened to me."

She laughed, tilting her head down to watch as he slipped the ring onto her finger.

"Mr. Callaghan, you took a beating for me, then a bullet, but the best thing you ever did was never give up." Her breath hitched, and another tear rolled down her cheek. She peered up and kissed him once more. "You make even the most impossible things seem like they could happen. You made me fall in love with you all over again. I love you. I love you from the top of my head down to my feet. I can't wait to spend the rest of my life with you."

He bundled her up in his arms, his tight hold saying he would *never* let her go. Love flowed from the depths of his stare, concluding ten years of hardship and waiting. With Blaine, she would never be alone. He was her morning light at the end of her nightmare, her reward for all the risks she'd taken in her search for true love and freedom. Her time for hiding was over. She could finally be the woman she was always meant to be.

THE END

JOIN TO GET A FREE NOVELLA AND EXCLUSIVE KATERINA SIMMS MATERIAL

Building relationships with my readers is one of the great joys of writing, it keeps me from turning into a robot! My newsletters are filled with information on new releases, cover reveals, sales, giveaways, and news relating to my series.

To claim your copy simply go to the "Free Book" page on my website.

www.katerinasimms.com

Secret Surrender

THE HARLOW SERIES, BOOK 2

One handsome stranger. One dangerous secret.

Jilted bride, Sarah Overton, thought a steamy night with a handsome stranger would heal her broken heart, but now her mystery man won't leave…

Curl up with this small town romance, with a twist!

Learn more: katerinasimms.com/secret-surrender

Or use this QR CODE:

Also by Katerina Simms

The Love at Last Series:

The Last Heartbeat — Love at Last, Book 1

The Last Place You Look — Love at Last, Book 2

The Last in Line — Love at Last, Book 3

For latest releases, go to:

https://katerinasimms.com/books

or QR code:

About the Author

Katerina Simms is a   contemporary romance author and RWA Emerald Award Finalist; originally born on a sunny Mediterranean island, only to move to the weather-challenged suburbs of Melbourne, Australia.

Tea addict, nature lover, and sloppy speaker of Russian, Katerina's novels feature vivid modern settings and heart-stirring characters, punctuated with the occasional good laugh. Her romances skirt the edges of women's fiction, and her favorite troupes are opposites attract, slow burn, and heat with heart.

www.katerinasimms.com

Acknowledgments

Believe it or not, though *Sapphires and Secrets* is the third book I've released, it's the first book I ever wrote back in 2011! I was stuck in bed with the flu, unable to carry out my job as a performer at the time. I was also healing from a crummy breakup, and thus binging a bunch of uplifting romance books. I got bored (not with the books, just with being bedridden), so did the math. If I got a certain number of words into my computer every day, in a few months, I'd have my own precious romance book.

Because writing a book is that simple, right?

Of course, naive me sorely underestimated how much work I'd signed up for, or how much I'd love writing. The original draft of Sapphires still had the heart of Emilia and Blaine's love, but there was still *so* much to learn.

Many drafts, lessons, writers groups, editors, and years of this project being abandoned... it wasn't until 2021, a good ten years later, that my writing style and ability developed enough to finish this story.

I'm so glad I waited. The book is so much more for all those extra years. Even though an early incarnation somehow managed to final in RWA Australia's *Emerald Award*. I'm still scratching my head on that one.

I also wanted to address the theme of marital rape that runs throughout Sapphires, but didn't always. The thing is, as a Southern European myself, I can say that much of the cultural and emotional struggles Emilia encounters throughout this book, are struggles I've personally heard women within this culture recount.

In editing this book, I felt it remiss to merely say Emilia had a bad marriage, without mentioning how culture and community can not only ignore, but outright encourage marital abuse.

Same goes for any violence depicted in Sapphires, which is less about shock or entertainment value, as it is about writing with a sense of honesty and not "prettying up" instances of control or abuse.

Lastly, it's important to note that marital rape is by no means a 'Southern European' thing, and continues to be unrecognized even within so many progressive countries across the world.

With all that said, I want to thank my editor Chris Hall, of The Editing Hall. Her feedback breathed extra life into this story, beyond the nuts and bolts of writing. Thanks also to proofreader Kath Macfarlane, and my cover designer Sarah Paige of Opium House.

To my friend Amanda, as always, for all the story-related medical suggestions. Thanks to another advisor, who I can't name for privacy reasons, who provided advice regarding all things guns and other stuff used in this series.

Thank you to my writing groups, who keep me motivated—the MRWG or Melbourne Romance Writers Guild, RWA Australia, and extra special brunch buddies, The Romantic Elephants.

Last but not least, heartfelt thanks to my readers. To everyone who subscribes to my newsletter and leaves a review. For every book purchased and your comments of support. There would be no me (as an author, anyway), without you.

So, thank you a million times over.

Lots of love. Always.

X Katerina

How About A Review?

Authors love reviews, and good ones help us make a living, and thus write more books! If you've enjoyed this book, please consider leaving a review on Goodreads or your retailer of choice.

Eternally grateful,

Katerina Simms

www.ingramcontent.com/pod-product-compliance
Lightning Source LLC
Chambersburg PA
CBHW020005140726
47904CB00018B/1826